THE CADWAL CHRONICLES:
Araminta Station
Ecce and Old Earth
Throy

Here at last Jack Vance concludes the brilliant science fiction trilogy that he began in *Araminta Station* and continued in *Ecce and Old Earth*. The trilogy is set in the region of space he calls Mircea's Wisp, and encompasses worlds and cultures such as only could be conceived in the mind of science fiction's master stylist.

The Planet Cadwal has an ecosystem unique in the human-explored galaxy; a thousand years past it was established as a natural preserve, protected from normal colonization and exploitation. Official residence was restricted to a precisely limited number of scientists and their immediate families. But over the centuries exceptions were made, as children wished to stay on their home world, and the elite of the planet brought in "temporary" employees—employees who were not, of course, "residents."

The population grew, until the human Conservators faced a conspiracy of humans and aliens to wrest control of their world away, and open it to full commercial use.

D0939425

Tor books by Jack Vance

JACK VANCE

THROY

Book Three of the Cadwal Chronicles

TOR

A TOM DOHERTY ASSOCIATES BOOK
NEW YORK

THROY

Copyright © 1992 by Jack Vance

Cover art by Vincent Di Fate

A Tor Book
Published by Tom Doherty Associates, Inc.
175 Fifth Avenue
New York, N.Y. 10010

Tor® is a registered trademark of Tom Doherty Associates, Inc.

ISBN: 0-812-51140-9
Library of Congress Catalog Card Number: 93-12454

First edition: May 1993
First mass market edition: May 1994

Printed in the United States of America

0 9 8 7 6 5 4 3 2 1

To Cornelis "Pam" Pameijer
Far-ranging genius, visionary and percussionist.
My best respects as well to that merry
band of Black Eagles with which
he is so happily associated.

PRECURSORY

I. THE PURPLE ROSE SYSTEM
(Excerpted from: THE WORLDS OF MAN, 48th edition.)

Halfway along the Perseid Arm, near the edge of the Gaean Reach, a capricious swirl of galactic gravitation has caught up ten thousand stars and sent them streaming off at a veer, with a curl and a flourish at the tip. This strand of stars is Mircea's Wisp.

To the side of the curl, and seeming at risk of wandering away into the void, is the Purple Rose System, comprising three stars: Lorca, Sing, and Syrene. Lorca, a white dwarf and Sing, a red giant, orbit close around each other: a portly pink-faced old gentleman waltzing with a dainty little maiden dressed in white. Syrene, a yellow-white star of ordinary size and luminosity, circles the gallivanting pair at a discreet distance.

Syrene controls three planets, including Cadwal, an Earth-like world seven thousand miles in diameter, with close to Earth-normal gravity.

(A list and analysis of physical indices is here omitted.)

II. THE NATURALIST SOCIETY

Cadwal was first explored by the locator R. J. Neirmann, a member of the Naturalist Society of Earth. His report prompted the Society to dispatch an expedition to Cadwal, which corroborated Neirmann's lyrical descriptions: Cadwal indeed was a magnificent world, of beautiful landscapes, congenial climate and—not the least—a flora and fauna of fascinating diversity. The Society registered Cadwal in its own name, was awarded a grant-in-perpetuity and immediately declared the wonderful new world a Conservancy, protected forever against wanton depredation, vulgarity, and commercial exploitation.

A Great Charter defined the administration of the new Conservancy and specified the tolerable limits of interference in the ecology.

The three continents Ecce, Deucas and Throy, were distinctly different. Araminta Station, the administrative node of the planet, occupied a block of a hundred square miles on the east coast of Deucas, most hospitable of the continents. The Charter additionally authorized a chain of wilderness lodges, disposed at especially scenic or interesting sites, for the convenience of administrative personnel, Naturalist Society members, scientists, and tourists.

III. THE WORLD CADWAL

The three continents Ecce, Deucas and Throy, were separated one from the other by expanses of empty ocean, unbroken by islands, with three trifling exceptions: Lutwen Atoll, Thurben Island and Ocean Island, all volcanic in origin and all in the Eastern Ocean off the coast of Deucas.

Ecce, long and narrow, lay along the equator: a flat tract of swamp and jungle, netted by sluggish rivers. Ecce palpitated with heat, stench, color and ravenous vitality. Ferocious creatures everywhere preyed upon one another, and any human being rash enough to venture within reach.

Three volcanos reared above the flat landscape. Two of these, Rikke and Imfer, were active; Shattorak was dormant.

The early explorers gave Ecce little serious attention; no more did the later scholars, and Ecce, after the first flurry of biological and topographical surveys, remained a land abandoned and unknown.

Deucas, five times as large as Ecce, occupied most of the north temperate zone on the opposite side of the planet, with Cape Journal, the continent's southernmost extremity, at the end of a long triangular peninsula which thrust a thousand miles below the equator.

The fauna of Deucas, while neither as grotesque nor as monstrous as that of Ecce, was yet, in many cases, savage and formidable, and included several semi-intelligent species. The flora tended to resemble that of Old Earth, to such effect that the early agronomists were able to introduce useful terrestrial species at Araminta Station, such as bamboo, coconut palms, wine-grapes and fruit trees without fear of an ecological disaster.* Throy, to the south of Deucas and about equal in area to Ecce, extended from the polar ice well into the south temperate zone. The terrain of Throy was the most dramatic of Cadwal. Crags leaned over chasms; dark forests roared in the wind. When storms blew across the great ocean, waves a hundred feet, or sometimes two hundred feet, from trough to crest struck into the cliffs of Peter Bullis Land, creating awesome sounds and jarring the landscape.

IV. ARAMINTA STATION

At Araminta Station a resident staff of (nominally) two

---

* The biological techniques for introducing new species into alien surroundings without danger to the host environment had long been perfected.

hundred and forty persons monitored the Conservancy and enforced the terms of the Charter. Superficially the administrative structure was simple. A Conservator coordinated the work of six bureaus.*

The original six superintendents were Deamus Wook, Shirry Clattuc, Saul Diffin, Claude Offaw, Marvell Veder, and Condit Laverty. Each had been required to assemble a staff not to exceed forty in number. Nepotism had been the rule rather than the exception; each Bureau Superintendent recruited extensively from his kinship and guild associates. The practice, if nothing else, brought to the early administration a cohesion which otherwise might have been lacking.

After many centuries, much had changed. The original rude encampment had become a settlement dominated by six palatial edifices, where lived the descendants of the Wooks, Offaws, Clattucs, Diffins, Veders and Lavertys. Each House had developed a distinctive personality, which its residents shared, so that the wise Wooks differed from the flippant Diffins, as did the cautious Offaws from the reckless Clattucs.

The station early acquired a hotel to house its visitors; also an airport, a hospital, schools and a theater: the 'Orpheum.'

When subsidies from Society headquarters on Old Earth dwindled and presently stopped altogether, the need for foreign exchange became urgent. Vineyards planted at the back of the enclave began to produce fine wines for export, and tourists were encouraged to visit the wilderness lodges.

---

*   Bureau A: Records and statistics.
              B: Patrols and surveys: police and security services.
              C: Taxonomy, cartography, natural sciences.
              D: Domestic services.
              E: Fiscal affairs: exports and imports.
              F: Visitor's accommodations.

Over the centuries, certain problems became acute. How could so many enterprises be staffed by a complement of only two hundred and forty persons? Elasticity was necessarily the answer. First, collaterals* were allowed to accept middle status positions at the station. By a loose reading of the Charter, children, retired persons, domestic servants and 'temporary labor not in permanent residence' were exempted from the forty-person-per-house limit. The term 'temporary labor' was extended to include farm labor, hotel staff, airport mechanics—indeed, workers of every description—and the Conservator looked the other way so long as the work force was allowed no permanent residence.

A source of plentiful, cheap and docile labor, had always been needed at Araminta Station. What could be more convenient than the folk who inhabited Lutwen Atoll, three hundred miles to the northeast? These were the Yips, descendants of runaway servants, fugitives, illegal immigrants, petty criminals and others, who at first furtively, then brazenly, had taken up residence on Lutwen Atoll.

The Yips fulfilled the need for cheap labor, and so had been allowed at Araminta Station on six-month work permits.

Subsequently this concession had been rescinded, but the Yips were now so numerous as to overflow Lutwen Atoll. They threatened to spill ashore upon Deucas in a great surge and thereby doom the Conservancy.

For all their undistinguished origin, the Yips were by

---

* Only two hundred and forty Wooks, Offaws, Clattucs, Diffins, Lavertys and Veders could be reckoned 'Cadwal Agents.' The excess became 'collaterals' (co-Wooks, co-Lavertys, co-Clattucs, etcetera), and upon their twenty-first birthday were required to leave the house of their birth and seek their fortune elsewhere. The occasion was fraught always with heartbreak; sometimes fury and, not infrequently, suicide. The situation was criticized as 'brutal' and 'heartless,' especially among the LPFers of Stroma, but no remedy or better method could be devised within the intent of the Charter, which defined Araminta Station as an administrative agency, not a residential settlement.

no means unprepossessing. The men were of good stature
and supple of physique, with luminous hazel eyes, well-
shaped features, hair and skin of the same golden color.
The Yip girls were no less comely and known the length of
Mircea's Wisp for their docility and mild dispositions, and
also for their absolute chastity unless they were paid an
appropriate fee.

Yips and ordinary Gaeans were mutually infertile. After
years of speculation, the eminent biologist Daniel Tem-
ianka, studying the Yip diet, pinned down a certain mol-
lusc living in the slime beneath Yipton as the contraceptive
agent. This discovery also pointed up the fact that Yips
indentured to work on other worlds soon regained normal
procreative ability.

For the administrators at Araminta Station the most
urgent priority had become the dispersal of the Yip population to other worlds.

Already as many as a thousand Yips had been so transferred by Namour, a Clattuc collateral and erstwhile labor
coordinator at Araminta Station. His method was legal and
not intrinsically baneful. He sold indentures to off-world
ranchers in need of workers. The indentures paid for transportation and Namour's fee, and so earned him a considerable profit. Namour had become a fugitive from justice and
no longer pursued his business interests. Furthermore, the
market for Yip labor had not expanded, since the Yips seemed
not to comprehend the rationale of the indenture system: why
should they pay off transportation charges when they had
already arrived at their destination? Toil when they gained
nothing seemed sheer folly.

V. THE CONSERVATOR AND THE INHABITANTS OF STROMA

In the first few years of the Conservancy, when Society
members visited Cadwal, they presented themselves, as a
matter of course, to Riverview House, in the expectation of

hospitality. Often the Conservator was forced to entertain as many as two dozen guests at the same time, and some of these extended their stays indefinitely, that they might pursue their researches or simply enjoy the novel environment of Cadwal.

One of the Conservators at last rebelled, and insisted that visiting Naturalists live in tents along the beach, and cook their meals over campfires.

At the Society's annual conclave, a number of plans were put forward to deal with the problem. Most of the programs met the opposition of strict Conservationists, who complained that the Charter was being gnawed to shreds by first one trick, then another. Others replied: "Well and good, but when we visit Cadwal to conduct our legitimate researches, must we then live in squalor? After all, we are members of the Society!"

In the end the conclave adopted a crafty plan put forward by one of the most extreme Conservationists. The plan authorized a small new settlement at a specific location, where it could not impinge in any way upon the environment. The location turned out to be the face of a cliff overlooking Stroma Fjord on Throy: an almost comically unsuitable site for habitation. It seemed an obvious ploy to discourage proponents of the plan from taking action.

The challenge, however, was accepted. Stroma came into being: a town of tall narrow houses, crabbed and gaunt, painted all in somber tones, with doors and window-trim painted white, blue or red. Observed from a vantage across the fjord, the houses of Stroma seemed to cling to the side of the cliff like barnacles.

Many members of the Society, after a temporary stay at Stroma, found the quality of life appealing, and on the pretext of performing lengthy research, became the nucleus of a permanent population which at times numbered as many as twelve hundred persons.

Over the centuries the special conditions of Stroma—isolation, a tradition of scholarship, an etiquette which defined the propriety of every act—created a society in which doctrinaire intellectualism co-existed with a rather quaint old-fashioned simplicity, occasionally enlivened by eccentricity.

Most of Stroma's income derived from off-world investment; the folk of Stroma travelled off-world as much as possible and liked to think of themselves as 'cosmopolitan.'

On Earth the Naturalist Society fell prey to weak leadership, the peculation of a larcenous secretary and a general lack of purpose. Year by year the membership dwindled, usually by way of the grave.

At Riverview House, a mile south of the Agency, lived the Conservator, the Executive Superintendent of Araminta Station. By the terms of the Charter, he must be an active member of the Naturalist Society; however, with the waning of the Society to little more than a memory, the directive necessarily had been interpreted loosely and—at least for this purpose, where no realistic alternative offered itself—the residents of Stroma were officially known as 'Naturalists' and considered equivalent to members of the Society, even though they paid no dues and took no part in Society proceedings.

A faction at Stroma, calling itself the 'Life, Peace and Freedom Party' began to champion the cause of the Yips whose condition they declared to be intolerable and a blot on the collective conscience. The situation, so they declared, could be relieved only by allowing the Yips to settle on the Deucas mainland. Another faction, the 'Chartists' acknowledged the problem, but proposed a solution not in violation of the Charter: namely, a transfer of the entire Yip population off-world. Unrealistic! declared the LPFers, and ever more categorically criticized the Charter. They declared the Conservancy a now-archaic idea, non-humanist and out of step with 'advanced' thinking. The Charter, so they asserted, was in desperate need of revision, if only that the plight of the Yips might be ameliorated.

The Chartists, in refutal, insisted that both Charter and Conservancy were immutable. They voiced a cynical suspi-

cion that much of LPF fervor was hypocritical and self-
serving; that the LPFers wanted to allow Yip settlement of
the Marmion Foreshore in order to set a precedent which
would permit a few deserving Naturalists—no doubt
defined as the most vigorous and ardent LPF activists—to
establish estates for themselves out in the beautiful Deucas
countryside, where they would employ Yip servants and
farm hands and live like lords. The charge provoked such
spasms of outrage that the Chartists' most sardonic suspi-
cions were reinforced. Such vehemence, they stated, only
certified the LPFers covert plans.

At Araminta Station, 'advanced,' ideology was not taken
seriously. The Yip problem was recognized as real and
immediate, but the LPF solution must be rejected, since any
official concessions would formalize the Yip presence on
Cadwal, when all efforts should be exerted in the opposite
direction, i.e.: transfer of the entire Yip population to a world
where their presence would be useful and desirable.

VI. SPANCHETTA AND SIMONETTA

At Clattuc House Spanchetta and Simonetta Clattuc
were sisters, more alike than otherwise, though Spanchetta
was the more earthy and Simonetta—'Smonny,' as she was
known—the more imaginative and restless. As girls both
were boisterous, untidy and overbearing; both grew to be
large, big-breasted young women with profuse heaps of
curling hair; small glinting heavy-lidded eyes; flat pallid
faces between conspicuous cheekbones. Both were passionate, haughty, domineering and vain; both were uninhibited
and possessed of boundless energies. During their youth,
both Spanny and Smonny became obsessively fixated upon
the person of Scharde Clattuc and each shamelessly sought
to seduce him, or marry him, or by any other means to
possess him for their own. Scharde was uncertain as to
which of the two he found the more repulsive, and avoided
the advances as politely as possible.

Scharde was sent off-world to an IPCC* training camp at Sarsanopolis on Alphecca Nine. Here he met Marya Aragone, a dark-haired young woman of charm and dignity with whom he became enamored, and she with him. The two were married at Sarsanopolis and in due course returned to Araminta Station.

Spanchetta and Smonny were outraged. Scharde's conduct represented an insulting personal rejection, and also— at a deeper level—a lack of submissiveness which they found intolerable. They were able to rationalize their fury when Smonny failed to matriculate from the Lyceum and, on becoming a collateral, was forced to move out of Clattuc House, coincidentally at about the same time Marya arrived, so that the blame could easily be transferred to Marya and Scharde.

Heavy with bitterness, Smonny departed Araminta Station. For a time she ranged far and wide across the Reach, engaging in a variety of activities. Eventually she married Titus Zigonie, who owned Shadow Valley Ranch, comprising twenty-two thousand square miles on the world Rosalia, as well as a Clayhacker spaceyacht. For the labor necessary to work his ranch, Titus Zigonie, at Smonny's suggestion, began to employ gangs of indentured Yips, brought to Rosalia by none other than Namour, who shared the proceeds of the business with Calyactus, Oomphaw of Yipton.

At Namour's urging Calyactus paid a visit to the Shadow

---

* IPCC: the Interworld Police Coordination Company, often described as the single most important institution of the Gaean Reach. IPCC power was immense but carefully monitored and controlled by the IPCC Special Branch. On the rare occasions when an IPCC agent was found guilty of corruption or abuse of power, he was neither reprimanded, nor demoted, nor discharged; he was executed. As a result, IPCC prestige was everywhere high.

Bureau B at Araminta Station was an IPCC affiliate, and qualified Bureau B personnel became, in both theory and practice, IPCC agents.

Valley Ranch on Rosalia, where he was murdered by either Smonny or Namour, or perhaps both.

Titus Zigonie, an inoffensive little man, became 'Titus Pompo, the Oomphaw,' though Smonny wielded all authority. Never had she relaxed her hatred of Araminta Station in general and Scharde Clattuc in particular; and her dearest wish was to perform some destructive atrocity upon them both. Meanwhile, Namour, with utmost sang-froid once again took up his duties as paramour to both Spanchetta and Smonny.

Marya meanwhile had borne Scharde a son, Glawen. When Glawen was two years old, Marya drowned in a boating accident under peculiar circumstances. A pair of Yips, Selious and Catterline, were witnesses to the drowning. Scharde questioned Selious and Catterline at length. Each claimed that he could not swim, so how could he save a drowning woman so far from shore: at least a hundred feet. Why had the woman herself not learned to swim before venturing out upon the dangerous water? In any event, the lady's conduct was no concern of theirs; they were talking and paying no attention to her activities. Scharde, unconvinced, pressed his questions until the Yips became sullen and silent, and he had no choice but to desist and send them back to Yipton.

Had the drowning been something other than accident? Someday, Scharde told himself, he would learn the truth.

CHAPTER 1

I.

The terrace of the Utward Inn at Stroma extended thirty feet out from the cliff into a great region of sunny air, with the cold blue-green waters of the fjord eight hundred feet below. At a table beside the outer rail sat a party of four men. Torq Tump and Farganger were off-worlders; they drank ale from stoneware mugs. Sir Denzel Attabus had been served a gill of herbal spirits in a pewter minikin, while Roby Mavil, the other resident of Stroma, drank green Araminta wine from a goblet. Sir Denzel and Roby Mavil wore garments currently in fashion at Stroma: sedate jackets of rich black serge, flouncing at the hips over narrow dark red trousers. Roby Mavil, younger of the two, was somewhat fleshy, with a round face, softly waving black hair, limpid grey eyes, a black brush of a mustache. He sat slouched back in his chair, glowering down at the wine goblet; events were not going to suit him.

Sir Denzel had only recently arrived at the table. He sat stiff and erect: an elderly gentleman with a ruff of gray hair, a notable nose, narrow blue eyes under shaggy eyebrows. He had thrust his drink of herbal spirits to the side.

The off-worlders were men of totally different stripe. They wore the ordinary garments of the Gaean Reach: loose shirts and trousers of dark blue twill, ankleboots with buckles at the instep. Torq Tump was short, barrel-chested, almost bald, with a heavy hard face. Farganger was gaunt, all bone and dry sinew, with a narrow head, a high-bridged broken nose, a gray mouth like a downward slash across flat cheeks. Both sat impassively but for flickers of contemptuous amusement at the interchanges between Sir Denzel and Roby Mavil.

After a single glance toward the two off-worlders, Sir Denzel dismissed them from his attention, and turned to Roby Mavil. "I am not only dissatisfied, I am shocked and disheartened!"

Roby Mavil attempted a smile of hope and good cheer. "Surely, sir, the picture is not all so grim! In fact, I can only believe —"

Sir Denzel's gesture cut him short. "Can you not grasp an elemental principle? Our covenant was solemn, and certified by the entire directorate."

"Exactly so! Nothing has changed except now we are able to support our cause more decisively."

"Then why was I not consulted?"

Roby Mavil shrugged and looked off across the gulf of air. "I really can't say."

"But I can! This is a deviation from the Source Dogma, which is not just a verbalization, but a pattern for day-to-day, minute-by-minute conduct!"

Roby Mavil turned back from his contemplation of the void. "May I ask where you obtained your information? Was it Rufo Kathcar?"

"That is irrelevant."

"Not altogether. Kathcar, excellent fellow though he may be, is something of a weathervane and is not above malicious exaggeration."

"How can he exaggerate what I see with my own eyes?"

"That is not all there is to it!"

"There is more?"

Roby Mavil spoke with a flushed face. "I mean that, when the need was recognized, the executive council acted with appropriate flexibility."

"Ha! And you apply the word 'weathervane' to Kathcar, when it is he who remained loyal and who lifted the veil upon this astonishing development." Sir Denzel took notice of his drink. He lifted the pewter pot and swallowed the contents at a gulp. "The words 'integrity' and 'faith' are unknown to the fellows of your cabal."

For a moment Roby Mavil sat in gloomy silence. Then, after a cautious side glance, he said: "It is imperative that this misunderstanding be mended. I will arrange talks and no doubt we shall have an official apology; then, with good faith renewed, our team will continue its work, each to his scope and ability, as before."

Sir Denzel gave another bark of laughter. "Allow me to quote you a passage from Navarth's 'Happenings': 'A virgin is raped four times in a thicket. The perpetrator is called to account and tries to make amends. He provides a costly salve to soothe the scratches on her buttocks, but his apologies fail to restore her maidenhead.'"

Roby Mavil heaved a deep sigh, and spoke in a voice of sweet reason. "Perhaps we should back away and use a wider perspective."

"What?" Sir Denzel's voice trembled. "I have reached the Ninth Sign of the Noble Way, and you suggest that I broaden my perspectives? Unbelievable!"

Roby Mavil went on doggedly. "As I see it, we are engaged in a struggle of the Ultimates: Good against Evil, a fact which generates its own imperatives. Our opponents are desperate; when they strike out we are duty bound to ward off their blows. In short, we must swim in the river of reality, or sink and drown, along with all our dreams of glory."

"Come now!" snapped Sir Denzel. "I have lived long in

this world; I know that faith and truth are good: they enhance life. Deceit, coercion, blood and pain are bad, also the betrayal of trust."

Roby Mavil said bravely: "It is not good to let a petty spasm of hurt feelings deter you from our great undertaking!"

Sir Denzel chuckled. "Yes, I am vain and peevish; I want everyone to approach me with reverence and kiss my foot. Is that your thinking? Quite so. Your goals are even more stark. You want me to pay over another large sum of money: a hundred thousand sols is what you expect."

Roby Mavil managed a painful grin. "Dame Clytie said that you had agreed to one hundred and fifty thousand sols."

"The figure was mentioned," said Sir Denzel. "That phase has come and gone. We have entered the time when we recover funds wrongfully spent, down to the last dinket. I am determined on this; you shall not cheat me of my money and spend it upon horrid goods."

Roby Mavil blinked and shifted his gaze. Tump and Farganger looked on imperturbably. Sir Denzel seemed to become aware of them. "I did not catch your names?"

"I am Torq Tump."

"And you, sir?"

"I am Farganger."

"'Farganger'? Is that all?"

"It is enough."

Sir Denzel inspected them thoughtfully, then spoke to Tump. "I wish to ask you some questions. I hope you will not take them amiss."

"Ask away," said Tump indifferently. "However, I expect that Mavil, yonder, would prefer to give you the answers."

"So it may be. Still one way or another I intend to learn facts."

Roby Mavil straightened in his seat, then scowled in new annoyance at the approach of Rufo Kathcar: a man tall, gaunt and pallid, with concave cheeks, burning black eyes under black eyebrows, with violet shadows surrounding.

Black wisps of hair fell to the side of his white forehead; an untidy short beard fringed his bony jaw. His arms and legs were long and lank; with hands and feet so large as to seem ungainly. Kathcar greeted Roby Mavil with a cool nod, glanced sharply at Tump and Farganger, then spoke to Sir Denzel. "You seem a bit disconsolate, sir." He drew up a chair and seated himself.

" 'Disconsolate' is not the word," said Sir Denzel. "You know the circumstances."

Roby Mavil started to speak, but Sir Denzel silenced him with a gesture.

"It is the old story. I laugh and I cry to think of it, that such things could happen to me!"

Roby Mavil glanced nervously to right and left. "Please, Sir Denzel! Your dramatics are entertaining the entire terrace!"

"Then let them listen; perhaps they will profit from my experiences. These are the facts. I was approached with fulsome courtesy; everyone was anxious to hear my opinions—a novelty at which I could not help but wonder. Still, I expressed myself in clear, detailed terms; I left no room for misunderstanding."

Sir Denzel gave his head an ironic shake. "The response surprised me. I was asked as to the source of my philosophy; I replied that I had done no more than provide a glimpse down the Noble Way, and everyone was impressed. They told me that at last a source dogma for the LPF party had been defined, and that everyone was charged with crusading fervor. I could not turn aside now; I was urged to implement my views with all means at my disposal, including financial support: after all, what better use could be found for a hoard of passive wealth? I agreed to fund a relatively large account at the Bank of Soumjiana. This account would be accessible only to three members of the Executive Council. These three were nominated on the spot: Roby Mavil, Julian Bohost and, at my insistence, Rufo Kathcar as the third. I stipulated that no money might be spent in conflict with the precepts of the Noble Way; was this clear to all? Absolutely! The endorsement was unanimous, and Roby Mavil's voice rang out loud and brave.

"So it was agreed in an atmosphere of emotion and bonhomie.

"This morning came the denouement. I learned that my trust had been abused, the Source Dogma cast aside like a piece of rotting meat, and my money given to ignoble uses. 'Betrayal' is a word which fits the case, and I face a new reality, which first of all must include the return of my money."

Roby Mavil cried out in passion: "That is impossible! The money has been withdrawn from the account and used!"

Kathcar asked harshly: "To what exact amount?"

Roby Mavil turned him a glance of utter loathing. "I have tried to observe the amenities of polite discourse, but now I must allude to a situation which had better gone ignored, at least for the moment. The facts are these: Rufo Kathcar's connection with the LPF Executive Council has lapsed. In blunt terms, he is no longer regarded as a good LPFer."

"Good Peefer, bad Peefer: that is sheer tosh!" snapped Sir Denzel. "Rufo Kathcar is my second cousin and a man of excellent connections! He is also my aide and I rely upon him."

"No doubt," said Mavil. "Nevertheless, Kathcar's views are often impractical, or even startling. In the interests of procedural harmony, he has been excised from the directorate."

Kathcar pushed back his chair. "Mavil, be good enough to hold your tongue while I state the facts. They are crude and ugly. The LPF is controlled by a pair of headstrong women, each more obstinate than the other. I need mention no names. In a gaggle of nincompoops and popinjays, among whom Roby Mavil is conspicuous, I was the last bulwark of good judgment against which the folly of these women beat in vain. They have pushed me aside, and the LPF is now an engine without a flywheel." Kathcar rose to his feet. He addressed Sir Denzel. "Your decision is correct! You must deny this cabal all further credits and recover the funds you have already advanced!". Kathcar turned and stalked from the terrace. Sir Denzel also started to rise. Roby Mavil cried out: "Wait! You must listen to me! Second cousin or not, Kathcar has given you a false impression!"

"Indeed? His remarks sounded reasonable to me."

"You have not heard the whole truth! Kathcar was expelled from the directorate, but more than clashing personalities was involved. There was a naked struggle for power! Kathcar declared himself better qualified to lead the campaign than either Dame Clytie or Simonetta, and assigned secondary roles to each of them. Both were outraged, and felt that Kathcar had displayed intolerable excesses of masculine vanity. Kathcar was not only thwarted; he was captured and severely punished, to such an extent that he is now motivated by hatred and spite."

"Well, what of that?" demanded Sir Denzel. "He has mentioned his experiences on Shattorak to me, and in his place I too might be perturbed."

Roby Mavil heaved a sigh of resignation. "Kathcar, however, has learned nothing. He is as reckless and as arrogant as before. He ignores correct LPF doctrine, and may well face new discipline. In the meantime, his advice is worth nothing—in fact, less than nothing, and might even tend to associate you with Kathcar when it comes time to reckon with his misdeeds."

Sir Denzel transfixed Roby Mavil with a cold blue stare. "Can it be possible that you are threatening me with violence?"

Roby Mavil gave a prim cough. "Of course not! Still, realities are what they are, and should not be ignored, even by Sir Denzel Attabus."

"You speak of 'realities.' It was certainly not Kathcar who deceived me and cheated me of my money. I will most definitely carry this affair to its ultimate conclusion." He bowed curtly to Tump and Farganger, then marched off across the terrace.

Roby Mavil sank back into his chair, drained and apathetic. Tump watched him without expression. Farganger contemplated the vast distances south down the great cleft of Stroma Fjord and the blue-green water a thousand feet below.

At last Roby Mavil roused himself. "Nothing persists forever. It seems that at last the time for changes has come."

Tump pondered a moment. "No man can fly."

Roby Mavil nodded somberly. "This is a lesson many men have learned. I know of none who have profited from the knowledge."

Neither Tump's expression nor that of Farganger changed, and no one watching might have guessed the nature of their thoughts.

II.

Two days before his visit to Stroma, Egon Tamm communicated with Warden Ballinder. He announced his plans and asked that the council hall be made available for the occasion. Warden Ballinder agreed to do as requested.

On the day specified, during the middle afternoon, Egon Tamm arrived at the Stroma air terminal: a dark-haired man of compact physique, with features of such regularity and manners so easy that his presence was often overlooked. He came with Bodwyn Wook, Scharde Clattuc, Scharde's son Glawen—all these Bureau B personnel—Hilva Offaw, High Justice of the Araminta Judiciary, and his daughter Wayness.

Up from Stroma had come a number of folk, including three Wardens, several other notables, a few students, and a miscellany of persons with nothing better to do. They waited beside the road which led along the brink of the cliff, hooded black cloaks flapping in the wind. As Egon Tamm approached, a gaunt young man with a red beard, ran out to confront him. Egon Tamm paused courteously and the young man cried out: "Egon Tamm, why have you come here?"

"To speak to the folk of Stroma."

"In that case you must tell us facts!" Truth was a rock to which a man could set his back, but there was none to be found at Stroma, where life had gone weird. If the Conservator had brought a message of hope, could he reveal something of what he was about to say, if only a hint?

Egon Tamm laughed. Very shortly his message would be made known to all; in the meantime he could only recommend patience.

The young man cried out, raising his voice to be heard against the wind: "But is it good news or bad?"

"It is neither," said Egon Tamm. "It is reality."

"Ah!" came the disconsolate cry. "That may be the worst of all!" He stood back; Egon Tamm and his party went to the lift and descended to Stroma.

With half an hour to spare, the party converged upon the Spaceman's Rest, Stroma's second tavern. Bodwyn Wook, Scharde and Glawen went out upon the terrace; Egon Tamm and Hilva Offaw remained in the taproom. Wayness found a group of acquaintances and arranged that all should meet at the old family residence. She went to announce her plans to Egon Tamm, who made a half-hearted objection. "I'll be speaking in about twenty minutes or thereabouts," he reminded her.

"No problem! We will listen to you on the screen."

"As you like."

Wayness left the taproom, climbed to the second level and set off at a brisk half trot to the east. Before long she saw ahead the tall green serpentine-faced house where she had spent the years of her childhood. Then she had considered it unique: the nicest house of all Stroma, by reason of details and color which at the time had seemed of great significance. For a fact the houses of Stroma were much alike, tall, narrow, built one against the other, with the same clusters of tall narrow windows and high-peaked roofs, differing only in their somber colors, which might be dark blue, maroon, umber, ash gray, black, green, with the architectural detail picked out in white, blue or red.

The house where Wayness had lived was dark green, with white and blue trim, and was situated toward the eastern end of the second level: a prestigious area in status-conscious Stroma,

Wayness had been a thin little girl, pensive and self-contained. Her dark curls and olive-pale skin had been inherited from one of her great-grandmothers, a Cantabrian from Old Earth; her features were so regular as to seem unexceptional until the delicate modelling of the short straight nose, the jaw and chin, and the wide sweet mouth were noticed. She had been a warm-hearted friendly child, but neither gregarious nor aggressive. Her brain roiled with wonder and intelligence; more often than not she preferred her own company to that of her peers, and she was not as widely popular as some of her more conventional acquaintances. From time to time she felt a trifle lonely and a bit forlorn, yearning for something far away and unattainable, something she could not quite define, but presently the boys began to notice that Wayness Tamm was remarkably pretty, and the odd moods dissolved.

During those days there had been little dissension or factional dispute at Stroma, and even then it had been almost entirely confined to light-hearted argument and philosophical debate when friends gathered in each other's parlours. Almost everyone considered existence to be settled, static and for the most part benign; only a few persons seemed to take their iconoclastic social theories seriously, and these became the nucleus of the Life, Peace and Freedom Party: the LPF.

As a child, Wayness had been indifferent to the disputes; the doctrine of Conservancy was after all a basic fact of life; was this not the planet Cadwal, totally subject to the regulation of the Great Charter? Egon Tamm, her father, was a staunch if soft-spoken Conservationist; he disliked polemics and kept well clear of the fist-pounding disputes which had started to trouble the atmosphere of Stroma and turn friend against friend. When the time came to appoint a new Conservator, Egon Tamm who was modest and reasonable and showed no signs of activism was the compromise choice.

When Wayness was fifteen the family moved to Riverview House near Araminta Station, and the dark green house on the second level at Stroma was relinquished to an elderly aunt and uncle.

The house would now be empty; the aunt and uncle were traveling off-world. Wayness climbed two steps to the porch, pushed the door open; it was unlocked, like most doors of Stroma. She entered an octagonal foyer, paneled with slabs cut from baulks of driftwood. High shelves displayed a collection of ancient pewter plates and a set of six grotesque masks, representing whom or what no one had ever known.

Nothing had changed. To the left an archway opened upon the dining room; at the back spiral stairs and a lift provided access to the upper floors. To the right another archway opened upon the parlor. She looked into the dining room, and saw the same round table of polished wood around which she had sat so many times with her family. And now, Milo was gone. Her eyes misted; she blinked. Too much sentimentality was not wise.

Wayness turned away. She crossed the foyer and went into the parlor, moving on soft feet so as not to disturb the ghosts which everyone believed haunted each of the old houses. The ghosts at this house had always been cool indifferent beings, showing no interest in the lives of the occupants and Wayness had never feared them.

Nothing had changed; all was as she remembered it, but smaller, as if seen through the wrong end of a telescope. At the front, three bay windows overlooked air, sky, and two miles to the south, the sheer face of the opposite cliff. By standing close to the window and looking down, the water of the fjord below could be glimpsed. The sun Syrene hung low over the cliff and sent dark yellow rays slanting through the windows. The second sun Sing, rubicund and portly, along with its glistening white companion Lorca, had already settled from sight.

Wayness shivered; the room was cold. She kindled a fire in the fireplace, piling up a careful mound of sea-coal and driftwood. Wayness looked about the room. After the expansiveness of Riverview House, it seemed cramped, though the

high ceiling compensated somewhat for the constriction elsewhere. Odd! thought Wayness. She had never noticed this
effect before. She wondered whether an entire life spent in
such conditions might affect the quality of a person's thinking. Probably not, she decided; more likely the brain simply
ignored the whole situation and did as it saw best. She turned
to stand with her back to the fire. To her right a stand
supported an Earth-globe; to her left, a similar stand held a
globe of Cadwal. During her childhood she had studied these
globes for hours on end. When she and Glawen were married,
they must have a pair of such globes in their home—perhaps
these same two. She coveted none of the other furniture. The
pieces, upholstered in dark red and mottled green, were stolid
and conventional, each stationed immutably in its ordained
place; where it must remain until the end of time, since at
Stroma nothing ever changed.

Wayness corrected herself. Changes had already come to
Stroma; others even more decisive, were on the way. Wayness
sighed, saddened by what was about to happen.

Looking from the window she noticed the approach of
her friends along the narrow cliff-hugging way. There were
four girls and two young men, all close to Wayness' own age.
She opened the door; they trooped into the foyer, laughing,
chattering, and calling out gay greetings. All marvelled at the
changes which had come over Wayness. Tradence said: "You
were always so sober and absorbed in your own thoughts. I
often wondered what went on in those reveries."

"They were quite innocent," said Wayness.

"Too much thinking is a bad habit," said Sunje Ballinder.
"It tends to make one timid."

Everyone looked at Wayness, who said: "These are valuable insights; I must take stock of myself one of these days."

So the talk went: gossip and reminiscences, but always
the six seemed set apart from Wayness by a guarded formality, as if to emphasize that Wayness was no longer one
of their own.

The entire group, Wayness included, seemed infected by

an uneasy alertness, which caused all eyes to stray frequently to the wall clock. The reason was simple: in a few minutes the Conservator was to issue a statement which, so it had been hinted, would affect the lives of everyone now resident at Stroma.

Wayness served hot rum punch to her friends and fostered the fire with nodules of sea-coal. She spoke little, but was content to listen to the conversation, which had fixed upon the forthcoming announcement. The political orientation of her friends became clear. Alyx-Marie and Tancred were Chartist; Tradence, Lanice and Ivar were even more resolutely LPF, and spoke of their creed as 'Dynamic Humanism.' Sunje Ballinder, daughter of the redoubtable Warden Ballinder, tall, supple, coolly outrageous in her unconventional attitudes, showed no interest in the discussion. She seemed to feel that commitment in either direction was gauche, and simply too ridiculous to be taken seriously. Tradence could not comprehend Sunje's detachment. "Have you no sense of responsibility?"

Sunje gave a languid shrug. "One muddle is more or less equivalent to another muddle. It takes a keener brain than mine to puzzle out the differences."

Tradence said primly: "But if society organizes itself into groups like the LPF, and everyone sorts out just a small piece of the muddle, and sets it right, then when it's all assembled, the confusion is mended, and civilization wins another victory!"

"Lovely!" said Tancred. "Except the LPF has busied itself with the wrong muddle, and when the pieces that needed fixing were distributed, the person in charge forgot to number them and so when it came time to fit things together, there was more confusion than ever, and even some pieces left over."

"That is sheer nonsense," sniffed Tradence, "and it has nothing to do with Sunje's lack of dedication."

Tancred said: "I suspect that her guiding principle is simple modesty. She will not assert her views since she knows at any instant some sudden insight might force her to change her entire philosophy. Am I correct, Sunje?"

"Absolutely. I am modest, but not dogmatically so."

"Bravo, Sunje!"

Ivar said: "The mad poet Navarth, like Sunje, was noted for his humility. He thought himself to be one with Nature and conceived his poetry to be a natural force."

"I feel much the same," said Sunje.

"Navarth was very intense and passionate and—in some respects—curiously innocent. When he wished to compose a great masterpiece, he often climbed a mountain and worked his genius upon the sky, using clouds for his calligraphic medium. When the clouds flew away, Navarth would only say that the glory of his art lay in its creation, not in its durability."

"I don't understand this at all," said Tradence, rather crossly. "How could such a silly old fool control the clouds?"

"That is unknown," said Tancred, who deeply admired the mad poet, in all his phases and aspects. "Some of his best work dates from this period, so his methods are irrelevant, don't you think?"

"I think that you are as mad as Navarth."

Wayness said: "As I recall, he fell off a cliff while chasing a goat and barely survived."

"Silly old thing," said Alyx-Marie. "What would he want with a goat?"

"Who knows?" said Tancred carelessly. "It's just another of the many Navarth mysteries."

Ivar looked at the clock. "Still another ten minutes. Wayness knows what is going on, but she won't tell."

Alyx-Marie asked Wayness: "Don't you ever get homesick for Stroma?"

"Not really. I've been drawn into the work of the Conservancy, and there hasn't been much time for anything else."

Ivar uttered a condescending laugh. "You embrace Conservancy as if it were a religion!"

"No," said Wayness. "Not religion. What I feel is love.

Cadwal is wild and open and beautiful, and I couldn't bear to see it disfigured."

"There is more to life than Conservancy," stated Lanice, somewhat sententiously.

"I've never bothered to conserve anything," said Sunje in her most indolent drawl. "And after it went I never missed it."

"I'll say this much," declared Ivar grandly, "there's nothing wrong with Cadwal that a little civilization couldn't fix. Two or three big cities with some decent restaurants, a casino or two, and—for me personally—a twenty room mansion on Lake Eljian with hot and cold running maidens surrounded by about two thousand acres of gardens and orchards and fences to keep out the banjees and yarlaps, not to mention the tourists."

"Ivar!" cried Alyx-Marie. "Your remarks are really repugnant!"

"I don't see why. They're at least candid."

"If you say so. The truth is, I'm a staunch Conservationist, so long as the word is applied to other folk and keeping the damned vulgarians off my property."

Wayness asked innocently: "Is that now official LPF policy?"

"Of course not," said Tradence angrily. "Ivar is just being naughty."

"Ha ha!" cried Tancred. "The Peefers, if they lost their fine feathers, would be just another row of plucked owls, shivering in the wind!"

"That is most unkind of you," said Ivar. He turned to Wayness. "Tancred is a fearful cynic. He doubts the existence of Truth! And speaking of which, what is your father about to tell us? Or do you insist upon being mysterious?"

"I insist. In a few minutes you shall hear for yourself."

"But you know?"

"Of course I know!"

"It will come to naught," declared Ivar. "We are quick, keen and resolute; he'll argue in vain."

"You will hear no arguments," said Wayness. "None whatever."

Ivar paid no heed. "Right or left, east or west, up or down, no matter! He can't cope with 'Dynamic Humanism.'"

"He won't even try until he finds out what it is."

"Dynamic humanism is the engine which drives the LPF philosophy! It is far more democratic than Chartic Conservancy, and cannot be denied!"

Tancred cried: "Bravo, Ivar! That would be a grand speech, if it had not been sheer piffle. I must instruct you seriously, once and for all. No matter how much the Peefers yearn for manor houses beside Lake Eljian or Lake Amanthe, with beautiful Yip maidens padding here and there, some fully dressed, others serving rum punches, these wonderful dreams will never become real, and why? Because Cadwal is a Conservancy. Is the idea truly so perplexing?"

"Bah!" muttered Ivar. "That is not the humanist point of view, nor is it mine. Something must be done."

Wayness said: "Something is—though I don't think you will like it." She touched the controls to the wall screen; it glowed with color and detail, to show the interior of the Council Hall.

III.

At the Spaceman's Rest, after Wayness had departed, Egon Tamm attempted to join his comrades on the terrace, but he was waylaid by a group of earnest young intelligentsia who plied him with questions. The Conservator would only repeat his explanation that all would soon be made clear and that it seemed pointless to go over the same ground twice.

His chief inquisitor was a burly pink-faced young man wearing a medal which bore the slogan 'POWER TO THE YIPS!' He asked: "Tell us at least this: are you agreeing to a reasonable accommodation or not?"

"As to that, you will soon be in a position to judge for yourself."

"And meanwhile we must hang by our fingernails," grumbled the young LPFer.

"Why not release your grip?" asked a saucy young woman. She wore a shirt which displayed the image of a sad-faced cat, who was saying: "Grandpa was a Peefer until he gave up catnip."

The burly young man told Egon Tamm: "You must realize, sir, that Cadwal cannot remain in the Stone Age forever!"

Warden Ballinder, a massive man with black hair and a black beard surrounding a round ferocious face, spoke with heavy jocularity. "If the Conservator does not have you deported for sedition and criminal foolishness, consider it good news." He looked to the side. "Here comes another one I'd like to see pulling an oar on a slave ship."

"Bah!" snapped Dame Clytie Vergence, who, as she advanced upon them, had overheard the remark. "That is arrant nonsense! Still, it is what we have come to expect from the notorious Warden. We can only hope that he conducts the business of his office with more decorum."

"I do my pitiful best," said the Warden.

Dame Clytie turned to Egon Tamm. She was almost as tall as Warden Ballinder, with large bones, meaty shoulders, strong legs and haunches. Her coarse brown hair was cut short, and straggled unflatteringly down around her square face. Beyond doubt Dame Clytie was a forceful person, though perhaps deficient in frivolity. "I too confess to curiosity. What is the emergency which brings you so dramatically to Stroma?"

Egon Tamm responded that all would soon be clarified; further, he hoped that she would find his statements interesting.

Dame Clytie gave a disdainful grunt, started to turn away, stopped short and pointed to the clock. "Are you not due at the Council Hall? The emergency would not seem to be so urgent if you are able to loiter here in the Spaceman's Rest tippling with your cronies."

Egon Tamm looked at the clock. "Quite right! I am grateful for the advice!" With Warden Ballinder, Bodwyn Wook, Glawen and the others, Egon Tamm repaired to the Council Hall, at the eastern end of the third level. He paused in the ante-chamber and looked into the hall, where the notables of Stroma stood in small groups, conferring with each other. All wore the garments of conventional formality: long full-skirted black jackets, tight black trousers, long pointed black shoes. He turned to Warden Ballinder. "I see no sign of Julian Bohost."

"Julian is still off on his travels. No one misses him overmuch, save possibly Dame Clytie."

The two men continued into the hall. Egon Tamm showed a bleak smile. "My daughter Wayness saw something of Julian on Earth. His conduct was not the best, and she has nothing good to say of him."

"I am not surprised, and I very much hope that he stays on Earth, since I prefer his absence to his company."

Dame Clytie, who had just entered the hall, searched out Egon Tamm and marched across the room to stop directly in front of the two men. "If you are indulging in casual pleasantries, I will contribute my share and express my pleasure at seeing the Conservator in such robust health, though unaccountably absent from his post of duty. If, however, you are exchanging information pertaining to public matters, I wish to be included in the conversation."

Egon Tamm said politely: "Our talk so far has dealt only with trifles; in fact, I had just inquired after your nephew Julian."

"Julian is hardly a trifle. In any case, the question more properly should have been put to me."

Egon Tamm laughed. "Surely I may speak to Warden Ballinder without your prior permission?"

"Let us not bandy words, if you please. Why are you here?"

"I have come to make an announcement."

"I suggest, then, that you discuss this announcement with

me and the other wardens, so that it may be modified, if necessary, by our wise input."

"We have gone over this ground before," said Egon Tamm. "You are not a Warden and you have no official standing of any kind."

"Not so!" thundered Dame Clytie. "I was elected by a substantial vote, and I represent a definite constituency."

"You were elected by folk who had no franchise. The most that you can say is that you were voted an official of the LPF social club. If you think otherwise, you are embracing an illusion."

Dame Clytie showed a small grin. "The LPF is not utterly toothless."

"I will not argue the case," said Egon Tamm, "since it is now moot."

"That is utter bosh!" declared Dame Clytie. "I have it on good authority that both the original Grant and the Charter are lost, so that you have not so much as a wisp of legitimacy."

"You are misinformed," said Egon Tamm.

"Am I so?" Dame Clytie chuckled. "Inform me, then."

"Certainly. My daughter Wayness has just returned from Earth. She tells me that Julian had gained possession of the original grant and the original Charter."

Dame Clytie stared incredulously. "Is this a fact?"

"It is indeed!"

"Then that is very good news!"

"I thought that you would take it as such," said Egon Tamm. "But there is more to the story. He was allowed these only after they had been superseded by a new grant and a new Charter, which are currently in force. Julian's documents are stamped 'VOID' in large purple letters, and have value only as curios." He looked at the clock. "Excuse me; I must now explain these facts to the folk of Stroma."

Leaving Dame Clytie standing speechless, Egon Tamm crossed the hall and stepped up to the podium. The hall became silent.

Egon Tamm said: "I will speak with as much brevity as

possible—although this may well be the most important news you have ever heard. The gist is this: a new Charter now governs the Cadwal Conservancy. It is based upon the old Charter, but is much less ambiguous and more specific than the original. Copies of the new document have been placed on the table in the anteroom.

"How and why did this come about? The story is complicated and I will not tell it now.

"The new Charter specifies a number of changes. Araminta Station is enlarged to approximately five hundred square miles. The permanent population will be increased somewhat, but still limited to members of the New Conservancy, which replaces the old Naturalist Society. The administrative apparatus will be enlarged and reorganized, but the six bureaus will serve essentially their old functions.

"Present inhabitants of Stroma and Araminta Station are eligible to join the New Conservancy provided that they undertake certain obligations. First, they must abide by the provisions of the new Charter. Second, they must move to Araminta Station. There will be initial confusion, but in the end every family will be assured a private dwelling upon an allotment of land. The Charter stipulates that there shall be no permanent human habitation on Cadwal other than Araminta Station. Despite the initial dislocation, Stroma will be abandoned."

For a period Egon Tamm answered questions. From the pink-faced young man who had questioned him previously came a passionate outcry: "What of the Yips? I suppose that you will drive them into the sea, the better to end their miserable lives?"

"The Yips lead miserable lives, agreed," said Egon Tamm. "We shall help them but we will not sacrifice the Conservancy in the process."

"You would ship them away from their homes, higgledy-piggledy, like cattle?"

"We will transfer them to new homes, with as much dignity as possible."

"Another question: Suppose some of us choose to bide at Stroma: will you then force us to leave?"

"Probably not," said Egon Tamm. "It is a question we have not yet faced up to. It would be better if Stroma were evacuated within a year, but I suspect that it may die by attrition, in a set of ever more dreary phases."

IV.

In the parlor of the old house, Wayness and her six friends listened to Egon Tamm's remarks. When he had finished, the screen went blank and there was a numb silence in the room.

Ivar said at last: "I am confused and I don't know where to start thinking." He rose to his feet. "I had better be on my way."

Ivar departed. Others of the group followed close on his heels. Wayness was left alone. She stood a moment looking down into the fire, then left the house and ran to the Council Hall. She found Glawen listening to the expostulations of the aged Dame Cabb, who did not wish to leave the familiar old home with the dark blue front where she had lived all the years of her life. In his responses Glawen tried to combine sympathy and reassurance with an explanation why processes so definite were necessary. It was clear, however, that Dame Cabb cared little for the dynamics of history and wanted only to end her life in peace and tranquility. "But now it seems that willy-nilly I shall be bundled off, like a sack of old rags, and all my best things cast into the fjord!"

"Surely it won't be like that!" Glawen protested. "You will probably prefer your new home to the old."

Dame Cabb sighed. "So it may be. For a fact Stroma has grown dreary of late, and the wind seems to blow so very cold." She turned away. Glawen watched her join a group of her friends. "Of course she resists moving! Why should she believe me?"

"I believe you," said Wayness. "If other ladies are skeptical, I don't mind at all. Do you plan to stay here? If not, I'll serve you sherry and nutcakes and show you where I spent my childhood."

"I thought you had gone off with your friends."

"They deserted and left me with only the fire for company. I think that they were upset by the news."

Glawen hesitated only a moment. "Dame Clytie is having a go at Bodwyn Wook, which looks interesting, but I've heard most of it before. I'll tell my father where to find me."

Glawen and Wayness left the Council Hall. Syrene had dropped behind the southern cliff; twilight softened the texture of the great spaces. The view, thought Glawen, was hauntingly beautiful.

They climbed a flight of narrow steps to the next level. "I have climbed up and down those steps a thousand times, or more," said Wayness. "You can see our old house yonder: the dark green front with the white window trim. This is the most select area of Stroma; our family, you must know, was definitely upper class."

"Amazing!" declared Glawen.

"How so?"

"At Araminta Station such matters are taken seriously, and we Clattucs must constantly suppress the pretensions of the Offaws and the Wooks, but I had thought that at Stroma everyone was too cold and too hungry to worry about status."

"Ha ha! Do you not recall Baron Bodissey's remarks? 'To create a society based on caste distinction, a minimum of two individuals is both necessary and sufficient.'"

The two walked around the precarious way. Glawen presently said: "Perhaps I should have mentioned this before, but I think that someone is following us. I can't make out his caste through the dusk."

Wayness went to the rail and pretended to scan the vast panorama. From the corner of her eye she looked back along the way. "I don't see anyone."

"He's slipped into the shadows beside the dark brown house."

"It's a man then?"

"Yes. He seems to be tall and very thin. He wears a black cape and is as quick on his feet as an insect."

"I don't know anyone like that."

The two arrived at the Tamm family house. Glawen appraised the dark green facade, picked out with white decorations and window trim. The architecture, while a trifle crabbed and pedantic, after so many centuries of fortitude, seemed only quaint and picturesque.

Wayness pushed open the front door; the two entered, passed through the foyer into the parlor, where the sea-coal fire still glowed in the grate.

Wayness said: "I expect that you will find the room a bit cramped; I do now, myself, but when I was little it seemed quite normal and very cozy—especially when storms blew down the fjord." She turned toward the kitchen. "Shall I make a pot of tea? Or would you prefer sherry?"

"Tea would be very nice."

Wayness went into the kitchen, to return with a black cast-iron kettle which she hung on the hob. "This is how we make tea." She stirred up the fire, threw on new chunks of driftwood and sea-coal, causing flames of green, blue and lavender to lick up at the pot. "Here is the proper way to boil water," said Wayness. "You will spoil it if you do otherwise."

"This is valuable information," said Glawen.

Wayness prodded at the fire with a poker. "I promised myself that I would not become sentimental if I came here, but I can't help remembering things. There is a beach down below which is littered with chunks of sea-coal and driftwood after a storm. The sea-coal is actually the roots of a water-plant, which form nodules. As soon as the storm lets up, we would go down to the beach for a daylong family picnic, load up a scow and float it back under the town to a lift."

At the door sounded the rap-rap of the bronze knocker. Wayness looked at Glawen in startlement. "Who could that be?" They went to the window and looking out saw a tall thin man, his face half concealed by the hood of his cloak.

"I know him," said Glawen. "It is Rufo Kathcar, I brought

him back from Shattorak along with my father and Chilke.[*]
Shall I let him in?"

"I don't see why not."

Glawen opened the door; Kathcar, with a furtive look over
his shoulder, sidled into the house. "You may consider my
conduct theatrical," he said in a fretful voice, "but it would be
as much as my life is worth if I were seen consorting with you."

"Hmm," said Wayness. "Things have changed since I was
little. Murder was strictly forbidden; in fact, if you so much as
sniffed at someone, you were reprimanded."

Kathcar showed a wolfish grin. "Stroma is not as it used
to be. Shortcuts are now taken. Some very passionate people
walk these high windy ways. The water is far below, so that
when a man is flung over the railing, he has time to think a
few last thoughts before striking the surface."

Glawen asked: "And your present visit would be considered a mistake?"

"Definitely so. But as you know, I am a man of steel. When
I have a story to tell, and once I decide upon a denunciation,
I never falter until all is made known."

"And so?"

"We must come to an arrangement. I will tell you what I
know; in return, you must provide me safe-conduct to such a
place as I shall designate and pay me twenty thousand sols."

Glawen laughed. "You are talking to the wrong people. I
will go fetch Bodwyn Wook."

Kathcar threw his arms high in distaste. "Bodwyn Wook?
Never! He bites from both sides of his mouth at once, like a
weasel."

"You can tell me anything you like," said Glawen. "But I
can make no commitments."

Wayness said: "While you argue, I will make tea. Rufo, will
you join us?"

---

[*]   Chilke: pronounced with two syllables, accent on the first, to
rhyme with 'silky.'

"With pleasure."

There was a pause while Wayness served tea in tall fluted cups of amber glass. "Do not break the cup," Wayness told Kathcar. "Otherwise you will be telling your story to my grandmother free of charge."

Kathcar grunted. "I cannot avoid a sense of deep disillusionment. I see now that the LPF never had anything to offer me, whether of a philosophical nature or otherwise. They have cynically betrayed my ideals! So: where am I to go? What am I to do? I have two options. I can flee to the far side of the Gaean Reach, or I can cast my lot with the Chartists, who are at least moderate and consistent in their theories."

Wayness asked innocently: "You have decided to sell your information and depart?"

"Why not? My information is cheap at double the price!"

"All this should best be explained to my superiors," said Glawen. "Still, if you wish, we will listen and act as intermediaries."

Wayness added: "And also advise as to whether your information is worth twenty thousand sols or nothing whatever."

V.

Kathcar's information derived partly from direct knowledge, partly from suspicion, partly from inference, partly from a mix of malice, and wounded self-esteem. Not all was novel or surprising, but the cumulative effect was most disturbing: especially the sensation that events had moved farther and faster and more ominously than expected.

Kathcar spoke first of Dame Clytie's cooperation with Smonny, who was, in effect, Titus Pompo, Oomphaw of the Yips.

"I have previously mentioned the relationship which obtains between Dame Clytie and Simonetta," said Kathcar. "Dame Clytie and the LPF are ashamed of this connection and try to keep it secret from the folk at Stroma, where it would be considered disreputable. Smonny was of course born Simonetta Clattuc. She married Titus Zigonie, who became Titus Pompo, Oomphaw of the Yips, though Smonny wields all control. Smonny cares not a fig for Conservancy. Dame Clytie still gives lip service to the idea, so long as all the unpleasant creatures have been led away to fenced preserves, or kept on leashes, while the worst sort, the kind that jump at you from the dark, might well be sent away.

"In the beginning both the LPF and Smonny were agreed that they wanted to transport all Yips from Lutwen Atoll to the Marmion Foreshore of Deucas, but their motives were different. Smonny wanted to revenge herself against Araminta Station which had treated her so unfairly and hurt her feelings. The LPF envisioned an Arcadian society of happy villagers, with folk-dancing every night on the commons, ruled by a committee of elders under the kindly tutelage of the LPF.

"Now," said Kathcar, "the LPF has shifted its position. It wishes to divide the lands of Deucas into a large number of counties, each centered upon a fine manor house, with a limited number of Yips to act as retainers. About a third of the Yips might be absorbed by this scheme. The remaining Yips would be indentured out to landholders on other worlds. The proceeds would be used to finance the new system. Smonny would become one of the new territorial grandees. For the post of supreme administrative imperator, Dame Clytie nobly volunteered her own talents, but Smonny showed little interest in the scheme, and became a bit haughty. Her own formula, so she declared, was the more rational, since it was looser and more flexible and could be expected to assume an optimum organizational configuration in a very short time. It was in this arena, Smonny suggested, that social experiments must be tested. In any case, the evolutionary process would present an absorbing and instructive exercise.

"Dame Clytie reacted, so I am told, with heavy-handed humor. She stated that she did not wish to serve as a white rat in a cosmic social experiment, which must surely be tempestuous and not at all conducive to cultivation of the Arts, such as poetry declamation, expressionistic dancing and free-association music—some of the genres in which she herself had become interested. Smonny merely shrugged and said that such things had a way of taking care of themselves.

"They now have the new Charter to cope with, but I suspect they will simply ignore it as a meaningless and unenforceable abstraction and proceed as before. Meanwhile," continued Kathcar, "basic conditions have not changed. Neither party commands sufficient air-transport to convey Yips to the mainland quickly enough and in great enough numbers to prevent Araminta Station patrols from halting the operation.

"The same case prevails at Araminta Station. There are no transports to convey the Yips off-world, even if there were a destination which would accept them and provide tolerable living conditions.

"The three parties to the contest are therefore at a temporary stalemate."

Kathcar paused and looked back and forth between Glawen and Wayness. "The intrigues of course do not stop at this point."

"So far your information has been interesting but not startling," said Glawen.

Kathcar was nettled. "I am providing intricate psychological insights which cannot help but be important."

"Possibly so, but Bodwyn Wook would consider me impertinent if I made any commitments to you."

"Very well," growled Kathcar, "call in these boffins, if you must! But warn them that I insist upon courtesy and will not tolerate a single blink of disrespect."

"I will do my best," said Glawen.

Wayness said thoughtfully: "Still, you must realize that Bodwyn Wook's mannerisms are occasionally exaggerated, and are not easily controlled."

VI.

Glawen came upon Scharde, Egon Tamm and Bodwyn Wook as they were leaving the Council Hall. After some small difficulty he turned them away from the Spaceman's Rest and led them to the Tamm's old residence. Here, so he explained, he had come upon what might be a source of important information. He avoided mentioning the name 'Kathcar,' since Bodwyn Wook had taken a strong aversion to the erstwhile LPF official.

At the front door, Glawen paused and issued a cautious warning. "We may be at the brink of a delicate situation. Everyone must use tact, and there should be no suggestion of doubt or suspicion." Noticing Bodwyn Wook's frown he went on hurriedly: "These hints are no doubt unnecessary, since all of you are notably self-controlled, especially Bodwyn Wook, whose aplomb is notorious."

Bodwyn Wook demanded: "What in the world are you trying to tell us? Do you have Julian Bohost in there with his feet to the fire?"

"No such luck." Glawen led the group into the octagonal foyer. "This way, and remember: the word is 'nonchalance'!"

The group entered the parlor. Wayness sat on one of the heavy maroon chairs. Kathcar stood with his back to the fire. Bodwyn Wook jerked to a halt. He cried out sharply: "For what sorry purpose—"

Glawen spoke in a loud voice: "I think you all know this gentleman, Rufo Kathcar. He has kindly agreed to supply us information, and I assured him that we would listen with polite attention."

Bodwyn Wook sputtered: "The last time we listened to that lying—"

Glawen spoke even louder. "Kathcar hopes that we will find his information of high value. I told him that the officials at Araminta Station, and especially Bodwyn Wook, were notably generous —" "Ha!" cried Bodwyn Wook. "That is a canard!" "—and would pay him adequately for his information."

Egon Tamm said: "If Kathcar provides us valuable information, he shall not suffer for it."

In the end Kathcar was induced to repeat his remarks in regard to Dame Clytie. Bodwyn Wook listened in stony silence.

Kathcar at last gave a flourish of his big white hand. "So far, you have heard what I shall call 'background information.' It reflects my intimate knowledge of what has been going on, and what I have been forced to endure. I confess to a great bitterness. My ideals have been betrayed; my leadership ignored."

"Tragic! Quite sad!" declared Bodwyn Wook.

"I am now a philosophical orphan," declared Kathcar. "Or—perhaps better to say—an intellectual soldier of fortune. I am rootless; I have no home; I —"

Egon Tamm held up his hand: "Our need is for facts. For instance, when Dame Clytie was last at Riverview House, she came with a certain Lewyn Barduys and his associate, who called herself 'Flitz.' Do you know anything of these folk?"

"Yes," said Kathcar. "And no."

Bodwyn Wook roared: "And what, pray, do you mean by that?"

Kathcar inspected Bodwyn Wook with austere dignity. "I know a number of interesting bits and pieces, which conceal as much as they reveal. For instance, Lewyn Barduys is an important magnate both in the transportation and construction industries. This information by itself lacks significance, until fitted into a context with other facts, whereupon patterns emerge. In this way I am able to justify the fee which I am compelled to charge."

Bodwyn Wook turned a peevish side-glance toward Scharde. "You seem to be amused. I cannot imagine why."

"Kathcar is like a fisherman chumming the water," said Scharde.

Kathcar nodded graciously. "The analogy is apt."

"Yes, yes," growled Bodwyn Wook. "We are the poor credulous fish."

Egon Tamm said hastily: "Let us hear some of these bits and pieces, so that we may appraise their value before committing ourselves to a specific fee."

Kathcar smilingly shook his head. "That approach lacks spontaneity! The value of my information is high, and far exceeds the fee I have in mind."

Bodwyn Wook gave a hoot of raucous laughter. Egon Tamm said ruefully: "We cannot risk so reckless a commitment! You might ask for ten thousand sols, or even more!"

Kathcar raised his black eyebrows in reproach. "I speak in all sincerity! My hope is to establish trust between us, and a true camaraderie, where each gives his all and accepts to the measure of his needs. Under these conditions a few thousand sols become a trivial, or even contemptible, side issue."

There was silence. After a moment Egon Tamm suggested: "Perhaps you will release a few more facts while we weigh your proposition."

"Gladly," declared Kathcar, "if only to establish my bona fides. I find Barduys and Flitz an interesting pair. Their relationship is curiously formal, though they travel in contiguity. The ultimate nature of this relationship? Who can guess? Flitz demonstrates an unusual facade; she is taciturn, cool, barely polite, and is not an instantly likeable person despite her superb physical attributes. At one of Dame Clytie's dinner parties, Julian turned the conversation to the fine arts, and insisted that, except for Stroma, Cadwal was a cultural desert.

"Barduys asked: 'What of Araminta Station?'

"'A curious survival of the archaic ages,' said Julian. 'Art? The word is unknown.'

"Julian turned away to answer a question. When he looked back Flitz had gone off to the far end of the room, where she sat staring into the fire.

"Julian was puzzled. He asked Barduys if he had said

something to offend Flitz. Barduys said: 'I think not. Flitz simply cannot tolerate boredom.'

"Dame Clytie was astounded. 'We were discussing Art! Does this topic exceed her scope of interest?'

"Barduys replied that Flitz' ideas were unorthodox. For instance, she admired the wilderness lodges of Deucas, which were created by the folk of Araminta Station. 'These isolated inns are true art-forms,' said Barduys, and went on to describe how the visitor is provided a unique sensation of place.

"Julian's jaw dropped. He could only scoff. 'Wilderness lodge? We are talking about Art.'

"'So we are,' said Barduys, and changed the subject." Kathcar looked around the room. "It was a most interesting event. I pass this intelligence on to you freely, in the interests of cooperation and trust."

Bodwyn Wook only grunted. "What else can you tell us about these two?"

"Very little. Barduys is a practical man, as impenetrable as steel. Flitz tends to enter a state of moody introspection, and becomes remote, or even surly. One day I spent an hour exerting my most dependable gallantries, but she paid no heed, and in the end I felt as if I had suffered a rebuff."

"A dismal episode," said Egon Tamm. "Did you learn their business at Stroma?"

Kathcar weighed his reply, and answered carefully. "That is an expensive question, and I will reserve my response." He stared into the fire. "I recall that Julian jocularly suggested that Barduys hire Yips for construction labor. Barduys replied that he had already made the experiment, and his tone suggested that he had not been happy with the results. Julian asked if he had dealt with Namour, and Barduys replied: 'Just once—and once was enough.'"

Scharde asked: "Where is Namour now?"

"I can't say. I do not enjoy Namour's confidence." Kathcar's voice was becoming sharp, and he was making restless movements. "I strongly suggest that you —"

Bodwyn Wook interrupted. "Is that all you can tell us?"

"Of course not! Do you take me for a fool?"

"That is not germane. Pray continue, then."

Kathcar shook his head. "We have come to the transition. What remains must be considered valuable merchandise. I have already mentioned my terms; now I must have assurances that you agree to them."

Bodwyn Wook growled: "I do not recall hearing your exact demands, nor have you indicated what information you are still withholding."

"As for my fee, I want twenty thousand sols, passage to an off-world destination of my choice, and protection until I depart. As for the information, it is not overvalued."

Bodwyn Wook cleared his throat. "Let us stipulate that Kathcar's fee shall be exactly metered to the value of his information, as calculated by an impartial committee when all the facts are known. So then: speak freely, Kathcar! You are now assured of justice."

"That is absurd!" cried Kathcar. "It is now that I need funds and security!"

"So it may be, but your demands are lavish."

"Have you no regard for your own reputation?" stormed Kathcar. "Already your name is synonymous with cheese-paring parsimony! Now is your chance at redemption! I urge that you seize upon it, for my benefit and your own!"

"Ah! But the fee is much too high!"

"Twenty thousand sols is cheap for what I can tell you."

"Twenty thousand sols is unthinkable!"

"Not by me! I think it very easily!"

"Arbitration still is the best plan," said Bodwyn Wook.

"And who will be the arbiter?"

Bodwyn Wook spoke in measured tones: "He must be a person of high moral quality and keen intelligence."

"I agree!" declared Kathcar with sudden unexpected verve. "I nominate Wayness Tamm!"

"Hmmf," said Bodwyn Wook. "I had myself in mind."

Egon Tamm said wearily: "We will take counsel on your proposal and give you our answer later in the evening."

"As you like," said Kathcar. "You may also wish to ruminate upon some other matters, such as Smonny and her wanderings. Sometimes she is to be found at Yipton; at other times she will conduct her business elsewhere—from Soum, or Rosalia, or Traven, or as far afield as Old Earth. How does she arrive and how does she depart undetected?"

"I don't know," said Egon Tamm. "Scharde, do you know?"

"No, for a fact."

"Nor I," said Bodwyn Wook. "I assume that Titus Zigonie's Clayhacker spaceyacht drops down, scoops her up and disappears."

"Then why is this event never registered on your monitors?"

"I can't say."

Kathcar laughed. "It is indeed a mystery."

"Which you can clarify?" demanded Bodwyn Wook.

Kathcar pursed his mouth. "I have made no such claims. Perhaps you should consult your friend Lewyn Barduys; he also might be able to speculate. I have said enough. Your so-called investigative agency, Bureau B, seems strangely inept; still, you should not expect me to shoulder the full load of its deficiencies."

Egon Tamm said coldly. "In any case, you are subject to Gaean law and you must report illegal activity or face charges of criminal conspiracy."

"Ha ha!" sneered Kathcar. "First you must prove that I know the answers to questions you don't know how to ask."

Egon Tamm said: "If you are in earnest about leaving Stroma, be on hand tomorrow when we depart, and you may accompany us."

"Then you will not guarantee my fee?"

"We will discuss the matter tonight," said Egon Tamm.

Kathcar reflected a moment. "That is not good enough. I

want my answer, one way or the other, within the hour."
Kathcar went to the door, where he paused and looked back.
"You are returning to the inn?"

"That is correct," said Bodwyn Wook. "I am hungry
despite all, and I intend to dine like a gentleman."

Kathcar showed him a wolfish grin. "I recommend the
baked rock-rack and greenfish, and the soup is always worth-
while. I will meet you at the inn within the hour."

Kathcar opened the door, peered right, then left along the
way, which was now indistinct in the starlight. Reassured, he
stepped out into the gloom and was gone.

Bodwyn Wook rose to his feet. "The brain works best
when it is not distracted by hunger. Let us return to the inn;
there, with our noses over the soup, we can settle this matter,
one way or another."

VII.

The group took seats at a table in the dining room of
the inn. A few moments later the massive form of Warden
Ballinder loomed in the doorway. His heavy round face,
never gladsome, by reason of coarse black hair, black beard
and unruly black eyebrows, now seemed actively morose.
He crossed the room, seated himself at the table and
addressed Egon Tamm: "If your announcement was
intended to resolve all doubts, it has failed. There are more
worries now than ever. Everyone wants to know how soon
they must leave Stroma, whether a fine mansion awaits
them or a tent out among the wild animals. Everyone won-
ders how they are expected to transport themselves and
their possessions so far and so soon."

"Our plans are not yet exact," said Egon Tamm. "All
householders should place their names on a list; they will
then be moved in order, first into temporary quarters, then
into permanent dwellings, which they may choose for themselves. It will be a simple uncomplicated change, unless the
LPFers drag their heels, which will make the transfer more
troublesome."

Warden Ballinder scowled dubiously. "It might go fast—or it might go slow. I estimate a hundred to a hundred and fifty households, five or six hundred people on the first list. These represent the Chartists. There are about as many devout LPFers and a like number of fence-straddlers who will wait until they have no other choice, and we shall have to deal with them separately."

Kathcar entered the room. Looking neither right nor left he went on long loping strides to a table beside the wall. Here he sat, summoned a waiter and ordered a bowl of fish soup. When he was served, he took up a spoon, hunched over the bowl and ate with avidity.

"Kathcar is now present," said Scharde. "Perhaps it is time to begin our deliberations."

"Bah," muttered Bodwyn Wook. "Does the lily need so much gilt?"

Egon Tamm said: "When the question is reduced to its essentials, it becomes: can we afford to take such critical chances? The money seems of secondary concern."

Warden Ballinder asked: "Am I supposed to understand what is happening, or not?"

Egon Tamm said: "You must keep this confidential. Kathcar wants to sell important information for twenty thousand sols. He is also a very frightened man."

"Hm." Warden Ballinder reflected. "One thing to remember is that Kathcar is secretary, or aide, to Sir Denzel Attabus, from whom the Peefers have been extracting large sums of money, if my information can be believed."

Scharde said slowly: "The idea that Kathcar knows something we don't know is beginning to seem ominous—especially when he values the information at twenty thousand sols."

Bodwyn Wook scowled, but said nothing.

Across the room a young man stocky and plump, almost squat, with a fleshy round face, thick black hair, a stern black mustache and fine clear grey eyes, had joined Kathcar at his table. Kathcar, staring up from his soup, was clearly displeased by the intrusion. The young man, however, spoke with earnest emphasis, and presently Kathcar's eyebrows rose. He put down his spoon and sat back, his black eyes glittering.

Scharde inquired of Warden Ballinder the identity of Kathcar's companion. "That is Roby Mavil, one of the career Peefers," said the warden. "He is an official and sits on what they call their directorate. Julian Bohost outranks him, but not by much."

"He doesn't seem a fanatic."

Ballinder grunted. "Mavil is a conniver. He likes plotting and intrigue for their own sake. He's not at all to be trusted. He'll be over here next, to make himself charming."

But Warden Ballinder was wrong and Roby Mavil, jumping up from Kathcar's table left the room.

Glawen spoke to Bodwyn Wook. "What about Kathcar? Do you intend to meet his terms?"

Bodwyn Wook had been put out of sorts by Kathcar's epithets and by the nagging sense of opportunities slipping irretrievably from his grasp. He growled: "If Kathcar freely and at no charge told me of Holy Jasmial's Third Coming, I'd still find the news too dear, even if it were true."

Glawen said nothing. Bodwyn Wook studied his expression for a moment. "You would pay the money?"

"He is not stupid. He knows the value of what he can tell us."

"You'd let him be the sole judge of this value?"

"We have no choice. I would guarantee his terms, I would listen to him and pay over the money. Then, if the material was trivial or if I felt cheated, I would find some way to get the money back."

"Hmm." Bodwyn Wook nodded. "That is a concept which does both you and Bureau B, and the Bureau B Superintendent credit. Egon Tamm, what is your opinion?"

"I vote yes."

"Scharde?"

"Yes."

Bodwyn Wook turned to Glawen. "You may apprise him of our decision."

Glawen rose to his feet, then halted in his tracks. "He is gone!"

"That is unacceptable conduct!" stormed Bodwyn Wook. "He makes us a proposal, then attempts insolent tricks! I consider him a man without honor!" He made an angry gesture. "Find this man; explain that we cannot allow him to void his contract! Hurry; catch him up! He will not have gone far!"

Glawen went out into the road and looked to right and left. The cliff loomed high to one side; to the other opened dark space, sighing to far currents of air.

Glawen walked a hundred yards up the way, but came upon no one. Above and below dim yellow lights spangled the sides of the cliff.

The quest for Kathcar was clearly hopeless. Glawen turned and went back to the inn. In the taproom he noticed Warden Ballinder in earnest conference with a red-bearded young man—the same who had confronted them earlier along the edge of the cliff. The young man was speaking with passionate vehemence; Warden Ballinder stood with head bent forward.

Glawen turned away and went into the dining room, to resume his place at the table.

Bodwyn Wook asked sharply: "What of Kathcar?"

"I saw no sign of him, or anyone else."

Bodwyn Wook grunted. "He will be back in a few moments, cringing and grinning, his price considerably lower. You'll see that I was right! I never submit to extortion!"

Glawen had nothing to say. Wayness jumped to her feet. "I will telephone his home."

A moment later she returned. "No one answers. I left an urgent message."

Warden Ballinder returned from the taproom, accompanied by the young man with the red beard. Warden Ballinder said: "This is Yigal Fitch. He is a legal practitioner. An hour

ago Sir Denzel summoned him, apparently to institute some
sort of legal action. Fitch approached Sir Denzel's house and
arrived in time to see Sir Denzel falling from his deck and
tumbling out into space. Fitch was horrified. He tried to look
up, to see who had launched Sir Denzel. He saw no one, but
he was afraid to investigate and ran back here. I telephoned
Sir Denzel's house. The maid knew nothing, except that Sir
Denzel was no longer on the premises. Unless Sir Denzel 'has
learned to fly,' as the saying goes, he is dead."

CHAPTER 2

I.

In the morning, shortly before his return to Araminta Station, Egon Tamm spoke a second time to the folk of Stroma. In this decision he had been influenced by the comments of his daughter Wayness. She had told him: "Your statements were clear and distinct, but you were too formal and not at all friendly."

"What?" Egon Tamm was surprised and a bit nettled. "I spoke as Conservator, of whom dignity is expected. Should I tell jokes and dance a jig?"

"Of course not! Still, you need not have looked so menacing. Some of the old ladies think you are planning to march them off to a penal camp."

"That is absurd! I was dealing with a serious subject; I tried to approach it in a suitably serious manner."

Wayness shrugged. "I'm sure that you know best. Still, it might be nice if you were to talk to everyone again and explain that Araminta Station is far more comfortable and pleasant than Stroma."

Egon Tamm reflected. "It's not altogether a bad idea—especially since there are one or two points I would like to bring up again."

For this second address to the folk of Stroma, Egon Tamm tried to convey the impression that his ordinary temperament was genial and tolerant—as indeed it was. He wore casual clothes and spoke from Warden Ballinder's untidy office, half-leaning half-sitting on the table in a manner he hoped would seem informal and even jaunty. His features, which were regular, austere and somewhat saturnine, were more of a problem, but as best he could he assumed a kindly and cordial expression and began his address.

"Last night I spoke to you without advance indication as to what I was about to say. Perhaps I was too emphatic, so that my message came to you as a shock. Still, I believe that you deserve to have the clear uncompromising facts at your disposal. Now everyone understands the force of the Charter and continuity of the Conservancy. There must be no mistake or misunderstanding or self-deception.

"We do not minimize the inconvenience which you must suffer, but the compensations are significant. Each family or household will be allowed a residence situated in one of four communities, or a tract of arable land in the back country, if this is preferred. The first community will parallel the beach south of Riverview House. The second will be situated in the hills west of the station. The third will surround a chain of four circular lakes west and north of Riverview House. The fourth will be adjacent to Araminta Station itself, just south of Wansey Way, on the other side of the River Wann. Each house will be situated on at least two acres. The family may design the house to suit their own needs, within reasonable limits. We are anxious to avoid uniformity. If anyone wants a more elaborate establishment, he must pay for the construction himself, with our blessings. We have no ambition to stratify our society along levels of prestige, wealth or intellectual attainment, but we will not enforce egalitarianism upon persons whose instincts prompt them in a different direction.

"Sign your name to the list as soon as possible—if only because the information helps us with our planning. "Remember, Araminta Station will not function as an interplanetary retirement community. Everyone who is able works for the Conservancy, one way or another.

"In general, this is what you can expect. The first to put their names on the list will have the first selection of site— though I think that everyone, early and late alike, will be pleased with their new circumstances."

Egon Tamm slid off the desk, faced the camera and smiled. "I hope that I have relieved some of the anxiety you might have felt after hearing me last night. Remember only that you must obey the law, which is to say, the Charter. If you choose otherwise, you will incur the usual penalties for illegal behavior. This cannot come as a surprise to anyone."

From the office, Egon Tamm and his party ascended to the air terminal, accompanied by a miscellaneity of town's folk. Rufo Kathcar was not present, nor did he appear before the group departed for Araminta Station.

II.

Three days later, Glawen was summoned to Bureau B headquarters, on the second floor of the New Agency, at the end of Wansey Way. He reported to Hilda, the crusty old virago who for uncounted years had guarded Bodwyn Wook against visitors and other intruders. She grudgingly acknowledged Glawen's presence and indicated the bench where he would wait a proper forty minutes or so, "—to let some gas out of his bloated Clattuc ego."

Glawen said politely: "I think the Supervisor wants to see me at once; that is my impression."

Hilda gave her head a stubborn shake. "Your name is not on the list and he is very busy at the moment. He may be able to spare you a few minutes later in the day. While you are waiting, prepare your material so that you can be logical and succinct. Bodwyn Wook gives short shrift to juniors who stammer and burble and waste his time."

"All else to the side, you had better let him know that I am here. Otherwise—"

"Whatever, whatever! 'Patience' was never a word in the Clattuc speech!" Hilda touched a button. "Glawen Clattuc is here, stamping back and forth in an outrage. Do you want to see him when he is acting so wild?"

Bodwyn Wook's responsive remarks rattled the speaker. Hilda listened a moment, raised her eyebrows, then turned to Glawen. "You are to go in at once. He is annoyed by the lethargic way in which you have responded to his summons."

This had been a relatively easy encounter. Glawen slipped past Hilda and pushed through the door into the inner office.

Bodwyn Wook swiveled around in his tall-backed leather chair, which emphasized his lack of stature.[*] He greeted Glawen with a brisk wave of the hand and indicated a chair. "Sit."

Glawen silently took a seat.

Bodwyn Wook, leaning back, clasped his fingers across his small round belly. So far there had been no sign that he harbored any lingering traces of resentment in connection with Glawen's recalcitrance in the inn at Stroma. Still, Bodwyn Wook was devious and his memory was notoriously long. For a moment or two he surveyed Glawen through heavy-lidded yellow eyes. Glawen waited passively. Bodwyn Wook, so he knew, liked to surprise his subordinates, on the theory that such small startlements kept them on the alert. Nonetheless Bodwyn Wook's initial remark caught Glawen off guard.

---

[*]   An unkind detractor had described Bodwyn Wook sitting in his great chair as 'an old yellow monkey peeking out of a barrel.' Still, his orders were seldom disobeyed, and no one ever boasted of having outwitted Bodwyn Wook. There had been another remark to the effect that: "When Bodwyn Wook is conniving and fooling you, his eyelids droop and a dreamy look comes over his face, like a Mongoloid baby sucking a sugar-tit."

"I understand that you are contemplating matrimony."

"That is the plan," said Glawen.

Bodwyn Wook gave a prim nod. "No doubt you have taken all necessary advice on the subject?"

Glawen looked suspiciously toward the bland face. "All that was necessary—which was not very much."

"Just so." Bodwyn Wook leaned back in the chair and gazed toward the ceiling. His voice took on pedantic overtones. "The subject of matrimony is rife with a thousand myths. It is not at all a trivial subject. As an institution, it probably antecedes the history of the Gaean race. Much time and effort have been devoted to the topic, both in theoretical study and in the practical research of several quadrillion human beings. The consensus seems to be that the institution is not inherently logical and that many of its aspects are needlessly arbitrary. Still, the system persists. Unspiek, Baron Bodissey, has pointed out that, were it not for the institution of marriage, evolution need not have differentiated the sexes with quite such loving care."

Glawen wondered where the conversation might be leading. At Bureau B, when an operative was summoned to the inner office, the level of Bodwyn Wook's discursiveness was considered a gauge as to the difficulty of the task he was about to assign. Glawen felt a twinge of uneasiness. Never before, in his experience, had Bodwyn Wook rambled on so capriciously.

Nor had he come to an end. Frowning toward the ceiling he mused: "As I recall, Wayness was born in Stroma."

"That is correct."

"Our problems at Stroma, along with those at Lutwen Atoll, are now serious. Wayness must feel a degree of personal involvement."

"Mainly, she wants the affair settled quickly and painlessly in accordance with the Charter."

"So do we all," declared Bodwyn Wook piously. "We can allow no more shirking; each of us must put his shoulder to the wheel."

Aha, thought Glawen. At last we are coming down to cases. "And you have found a wheel for my shoulder?"

"In a manner of speaking, yes." He rearranged the papers on his desk. "Our colloquy with Rufo Kathcar was not a success. No one was sympathetic. You were as dreary as a dead fish, Scharde was caustic, Egon Tamm made no secret of his doubts, while I was somewhat too noncommittal. All in all, we were not at our best, and an opportunity went flitting."

Glawen looked out the window and along the flow of the Wann River. Bodwyn Wook watched him keenly, but Glawen allowed not so much as a twitch to disturb the serenity of his expression.

Apparently satisfied, Bodwyn Wook relaxed in his chair. Events had now been rearranged in what would henceforth be the official version. "This morning I decided to renew contact with Kathcar. To this end I called Warden Ballinder. He informed me that Kathcar had not been seen for several days. Apparently he has gone into seclusion."

"There may be another explanation."

Bodwyn Wook gave a curt nod. "Warden Ballinder is looking into the matter."

Glawen had no wish to return to Stroma, to find Kathcar or for any other reason. He and Wayness were currently preoccupied with plans for the house they would build after their marriage; it was a most interesting process.

Bodwyn Wook continued. "Now we must use what crumbs fall our way. Kathcar hinted at much but told us little. He mentioned the names 'Lewyn Barduys' and 'Flitz.' It seems that Barduys is active in the transportation industry. Smonny and the LPF want transport to ferry the Yips ashore. Barduys can provide this transport: hence he is a popular man, as well as hard to find, which evidently is the way he likes it."

"Has the IPCC any information?"

"He has no criminal record, so there is no file on him. The current Gaean Industrial Directory lists him as principal stockholder in several companies: L-B Construction, Span

Transit, Rhombus Cargo Transport, perhaps others. He is an extremely wealthy man, but he keeps himself out of sight."

"He is not invisible. Someone must know something about him."

Bodwyn Wook nodded. "This brings us to the subject of Namour, who supplied Barduys with a gang of Yip laborers."

"It seems a complicated business," said Glawen in a subdued voice. Whoever ultimately took this case in hand would find little time for private activities, such as discovering the exactly right site for a new home, and making all kinds of other interesting decisions.

"So it does. Namour took most of his indentured Yips to Rosalia. Barduys is not included in the Handbook's list of Rosalia ranchers—which may mean much or nothing."

"You should ask Chilke," said Glawen. "He spent quite some time on Rosalia."

"That is a good idea," said Bodwyn Wook. "Now then: to business! You seem particularly adept with these off-world cases—"

"Not really! It only seems that way! A dozen times I have escaped death by a hair's breadth! It is a wonder—"

Bodwyn Wook held up his hand. "Modesty is rare in a Clattuc, and it becomes you. However, I am almost inclined to look for an ulterior motive!"

Glawen had nothing to say. Bodwyn Wook went on: "Bureau B manpower is stretched to the limit, what with our continual patrols and inspections, so low-rank operatives like yourself must be sent to deal with important affairs."

Glawen pondered a moment, then said: "If you promoted me to a higher rank it would ease half your problem."

"All in good time. Hasty advancement makes for a poor officer; that is tried and true doctrine, valid across the ages. Proper seasoning, over eight or, better, ten years will be to your ultimate benefit."

Glawen made no comment. Bodwyn Wook went on briskly: "Despite all, I am entrusting this investigation to you. It will, of course, take you off-world—where I cannot predict. Keep in mind that you are looking for both Barduys and Namour, although Barduys is your primary concern. No doubt he will easily be found through his business connections. I mention Namour because Barduys and the Yip labor gangs may provide a clue as to Namour's whereabouts. It is natural to think of the world Rosalia and Shadow Valley Ranch in this connection. You must deal cautiously with Namour; he is a callous and resourceful murderer. We have much unfinished business with him back here at the Station, and he will make no mild submission. Indeed, according to rumor, he runs with a gang of bloody-minded thugs. Still, you will deal with him relentlessly and make a standard Bureau B arrest."

"Alone?"

"Certainly! Never forget that in your person resides the full force and consequence of Bureau B!"

"Very good, sir! I will remember this point. Still, my death will not solve your personnel problems."

Bodwyn Wook, leaning back in his chair, surveyed Glawen dispassionately. "You have some valuable qualities, patience and persistence among them, which help make you a competent operative. But I suspect that your most valuable adjunct is luck. For this reason I doubt if you will be killed or even maimed. Your marriage will still be viable when you return—provided that you do not stay away too long."

"I almost feel sorry for Namour, once I lay my hands on him," Glawen muttered.

Bodwyn Wook ignored the remark. "Report here tomorrow at noon for your final instructions. In the afternoon you will board the *Mircea Wanderling* which will take you down the Wisp to the junction at Soumjiana."

III.

On the following day, five minutes before noon, Glawen arrived at the Bureau B offices. He checked in with Hilda, who languidly glanced at a list. She shook her head. "He is in conference at the moment; you'll have to wait until he is free."

"Please tell him that I am waiting," said Glawen. "He asked me to report at noon precisely."

Hilda grudgingly spoke into the communicator, and sniffed disapprovingly to hear Bodwyn Wook's emphatic response. She jerked her head toward the door. "He says for you to go on in."

Glawen entered the office. Bodwyn Wook was not alone. In a chair to the side sat Eustace Chilke. Glawen stopped short and stared, momentarily taken aback. Chilke gave him a casual wave of the hand, along with a rather sheepish grin, as if he too recognized the incongruity of his presence here in Bodwyn Wook's office.

Chilke had been born at Idola, on the Big Prairie of Old Earth. At an early age, the lure of far places had become irresistible, and he had gone off to explore the worlds of the Gaean Reach. The years went by, and Chilke wandered here and there. He visited strange landscapes and exotic cities, where he dined on odd concoctions and slept in strange beds, sometimes in company with mysterious companions. He worked at many employments, acquiring a variety of unusual skills. Arriving at Araminta Station, he found a congenial environment and came to rest. He now worked at the air terminal, where an important title 'Director of Air Operations' augmented his relatively modest stipend.

Chilke, a few years past the first flush of youth, was of middle stature and sturdy physique, with innocent blue eyes and short dusty-blond curls. His features were blunt and somewhat askew, which gave him an air of droll perplexity, mixed with muted reproach for the tribulations which had been his lot in life. Sitting now to the side of Bodwyn Wook's office, Chilke seemed quite at ease, his manner unconcerned.

Glawen seated himself and tried to appraise the condition of Bodwyn Wook's disposition. The signs were not reassuring. Bodwyn Wook sat bolt upright at the edge of his chair, squinting as he arranged the papers on his desk. He darted a sharp yellow glance toward Glawen and finally spoke. "I have conferred at length with Commander Chilke. It has been a useful exercise."

Glawen acknowledged the remark with a nod. He might have pointed out that Chilke's title was more correctly 'Director,' but Bodwyn Wook would not thank him for the correction.

"I have ascertained that Eustace Chilke is a man of many competencies and wide experience. I believe that this is your opinion?"

"Yes, sir."

"Yesterday you expressed timidity at the prospect of conducting an off-world mission alone."

"What!" cried Glawen, jarred from his passivity. "No such thing!"

Bodwyn Wook appraised him under hooded eyelids. "You did not express such diffidence?"

"I said that I doubted whether I could capture Namour and a gang of thugs single-handed!"

"It is all the same, one way or the other. You have convinced me that for the proper prosecution of this mission, two agents are required." Leaning back in his chair, he put the tips of his fingers together. "Eustace Chilke, along with his other qualifications, is also acquainted with the world Rosalia, which may well figure in the investigation. Therefore I am pleased to announce that he has agreed to participate in this mission. You will not be alone, as you feared."

"I will be happy to work with Chilke," said Glawen.

Bodwyn Wook continued. "It is important that you both be equipped with official authority. Therefore I have appointed Chilke to the full status of a Bureau B agent, and consequent Accreditation with the IPCC."

Glawen began to feel bewildered. "Isn't Chilke too old to start agency routine? Did you explain the four years of junior training and all the development programs?"

"Chilke's unique capabilities allowed us to bypass the standard regimen. He cannot be expected to take a cut in salary; therefore he has been appointed to a rank of appropriate salary-level. The rank which Chilke has earned for himself is 'Sub-Commander': a grade between 'Captain' and full 'Commander.'

Glawen's jaw dropped. He turned to stare at Chilke, who shrugged and grinned. Glawen turned back to Bodwyn Wook. "If Chilke becomes a 'Sub-Commander,' he outranks a 'Captain,' such as me."

"True, of course."

"And if we go out together on a mission, Sub-Commander Chilke will be the officer in authority."

"That is inherent in the concept of 'rank.'"

"Do you recall that yesterday I suggested a promotion, and you told me that I needed another ten years of seasoning?"

"Of course I remember!" snapped Bodwyn Wook. "Do you consider me senile?"

"And today, instead of ten years, ten minutes is enough seasoning for Eustace Chilke?"

"Such are the exigencies of the moment," said Bodwyn Wook.

"Here is another exigency," said Glawen. He rose to his feet, brought out his warrant card, tossed it upon Bodwyn Wook's desk. "There you have it: my resignation. I am no longer associated with Bureau B." He turned to go.

"Just a moment!" cried Bodwyn Wook. "This is an irresponsible act, in view of our personnel problems!"

"Not at all! I have learned my lesson. The last two times you sent me out in this style I barely escaped with my life."

"Bah," muttered Bodwyn Wook. "It was your mad Clattuc rashness which prompted you to play the cock-a-hoop bravo at all costs. You must blame only the flaw in your own personality."

Glawen, halfway to the door, stopped short. "Tell me this: how can I be at once timid and diffident, and sweating with fear, while still indulging in these escapades you describe."

"Clattucs are all mad," said Bodwyn Wook. "That is well

known. This is how the disease affects you, and it is truly pitiful that you should blame me, a tired old man, for your trouble."

Chilke spoke in a gentle voice: "Let me make a suggestion. If you promote Glawen to 'Commander', as he probably deserves, everyone would be happy."

Bodwyn Wook sank back aghast into his seat. "He would be the youngest man ever to use such a rank! It is unthinkable!"

"I thought it," said Chilke modestly. "What about you, Glawen? Can you think it?"

"Just barely, after what I have been through. But I can think it."

"Very well," said Bodwyn Wook hollowly. "So be it!" He leaned forward and spoke into the communicator. "Hilda! Bring in a bottle of the best Averly Sergence, along with three glasses! Commander Clattuc, Sub-commander Chilke and I wish to celebrate a happy occasion."

"Sir?" asked Hilda. "Did I hear you rightly?"

"You did indeed! Make sure of the vintage; we drink no paltry stuff today!"

Hilda brought in the wine and the goblets. She listened frozen-faced as Bodwyn Wook notified her of the promotions. Wordlessly she poured wine into the goblets, then turned away and marched toward the door. As she passed Glawen she spoke a single word in a clenched and sibilant mutter: "Madness!"

Hilda left the room and shut the door. Bodwyn Wook gave his head a wry shake. "I suspect that the news took her by surprise, but after she rests a few minutes, she too will rejoice, in her own quiet way."

IV.

Goblets had been emptied, not once but several times, and a number of congratulations had been exchanged. Bodwyn Wook was especially gratified to hear Glawen's salute: "—to Bodwyn Wook, undoubtedly the keenest and most competent supervisor to sit in this office for many, many years!"

"Thank you, Glawen!" said Bodwyn Wook. "This is good to hear, even though it has been many many years since anyone else has sat here."

"I had a more extended period in mind."

"Just so." Bodwyn Wook leaned forward, pushed bottle and goblets aside, took up a sheet of yellow paper. "Now then: to business! Before issuing specific orders, I will indicate our general strategy in connection with the LPF and Lutwen Atoll. It includes a 'North Phase' and a 'South Phase.' Since we cannot cope with both phases together, we intend to hold the Yips static in the north while we deal with the LPF in the south. The program is already underway; in fact it started three days ago when the Conservator issued his ultimatum: obey the law or depart the planet. As of now, the LPFers are no doubt taking stock, conniving and conspiring and wondering what to do next." Bodwyn Wook hitched himself forward in his chair. "Their only hope is to procure a force of armed flyers strong enough to counteract our own deterrent force—and enough transport capacity to move the Yips. So far they seem to have made no progress. However, we should not disregard rumor, no matter how unreliable its source. I refer of course to remarks recently made by Rufo Kathcar."

Glawen held his tongue. Bodwyn Wook continued. "The name 'Lewyn Barduys' was mentioned, and compels our attention, since he is a magnate involved in both construction and transport. He visited Cadwal some months ago with the stated purpose of studying the wilderness lodges. This may be true. He and his companion, a certain 'Flitz,' visited a number of these lodges. They were also guests of Dame Clytie at Stroma. We do not know what business, if any, was transacted, but it is only prudent that we should suspect the worst. This concept dictates the broad scope of your mission. You are to locate Lewyn Barduys and investigate his activities. Specifically, we want to know what arrangements, if any, he has made with the LPF. Thereafter, your procedures must be

guided by circumstance. 'Flexibility, first, last and always!' will
be your slogan. For instance, if commitments with the LPF
have been made, you must circumvent them as best you can.
Am I clear so far?"

Chilke and Glawen agreed that Bodwyn Wook had
expressed himself lucidly. Glawen started to make an additional comment, then remembered his new promotion and
remained silent.

"Good. There are also secondary considerations. You will
keep in mind our own need for transport, when it comes time
to move Yips off-world. During your dealings with Barduys
you might explore this subject with him, though financial
terms must be validated at Araminta Station." Bodwyn Wook
again glanced back and forth between his two commanders.
"There are still no questions?"

"None whatever!" said Chilke. "Our mission is simple. We
locate Barduys, look into his affairs, disrupt all his dealings
with Dame Clytie. Then, if he is still in a good humor, we
arrange for two or more transports on our own account. So
far it is a handshake deal. The final terms will be arranged
later, the next time he visits Araminta Station. There was also
some talk about Namour. I think you said you wanted him
captured and brought back to Cadwal. That's the lot of it, or
so I believe."

Bodwyn Wook blew out his cheeks. "Ha ahem. Your
statement is accurate, in every detail. It is a pleasure to work
with you, Commander Chilke!"

Glawen said in a pained voice: "I am embarrassed to
admit that I have a question or two."

"No matter," said Bodwyn Wook in kindly tones. "Let us
hear your question."

"What is officially known of Lewyn Barduys?"

"Next to nothing. The IPCC has no file on him. He is quiet
and unobtrusive, and travels without display, though in one
respect he cannot avoid attracting attention. I refer to his
companion and business associate Flitz. She is supremely
eye-catching, though her personality is less than effusive. I

have this on the authority of both Egon Tamm and Warden Ballinder." Bodwyn Wook picked up the yellow paper and studied it for a moment. "Barduys seems to have no permanent address, though he is often to be found at one of his construction sites.

"Now then: the question arises. Where did Lewyn Barduys first learn of Yip labor? Did Namour approach him at a construction site? Or did Barduys learn of the Yips on Rosalia where he is unlisted in the Rosalia Directory as a rancher? Our own first meeting with Barduys and Flitz is at Riverview House, where they were in company with Dame Clytie and Julian.

"As to the sequence of events on Rosalia, we have no clues. I theorize that Namour first met Barduys and supplied him with Yip labor, then introduced him to Smonny—perhaps at Smonny's insistence, when she found that Barduys controlled transport equipment. Smonny in turn introduced him to Dame Clytie. This is a reasonable sequence of events. In short, Rosalia becomes a primary area of investigation. Chilke, did you speak?"

"Not really. I made a sick sound."

Bodwyn Wook leaned back in his chair. "The memory of your employment on Rosalia still disturbs you?"

"Yes and no," said Chilke frankly. "During the day I am never troubled. It is only at night that I wake up in a cold sweat. I cannot deny that the events made their impression. Do you care to hear the particulars?"

"Yes, within limits imposed by brevity and pertinence."

Chilke nodded. "I won't go too deeply into philosophical analysis, except to mention that I was never quite sure what was going on. It was as if the real and the unreal had somehow been mixed together, so that I was continually baffled."

"Ha hum," said Bodwyn Wook. "Quite so. Your mental state was confused; we accept this. Please proceed."

"When Madame Zigonie hired me to supervise Shadow Valley Ranch, I thought that I had secured a high-class position, even though I did not care much for Madame Zigonie. I expected a good salary, prestige, a nice house with a staff of Yip maidens. I intended to spend a lot of time on the front porch, drinking rum punch and giving the staff orders about dinner and how I wanted my bed made. Disillusion came fast. I was assigned an old shack without hot water and no Yips whatever. The scenery was strange and wild, but I had no time to notice, since almost at once I became a nervous wreck. I had two principal concerns: how to get paid my salary and how not to marry Madame Zigonie. These were both real challenges and I had little time left for anything else. As for the rum punch, Madame Zigonie allowed me neither gin nor rum for fear I'd use them to bait the maidens."

"Your work was the supervision of indentured Yips?"

"That is correct, as far as it goes. By and large I got along quite well with the help, although it took a week or so before we sorted out our priorities. After that, I had no complaints. I understood them; they understood me. While I was watching they would pretend to work. As soon as I went off for a nap, they did the same. Occasionally Namour showed up with new gangs from Yipton. By and large, the Yips seemed to like the change. They got along well among themselves, since there was nothing to steal and they were too lazy to fight. The big problem was runaways. Once I asked Namour how he could tolerate so many defectors, but he just laughed. After he got his commission, what the Yips were up to next meant nothing to him."

Bodwyn Wook again referred to the yellow paper. "As I mentioned, Barduys is not a registered landholder, though he might be in the process of buying a parcel."

"Perhaps that parcel known as Shadow Valley Ranch?" suggested Glawen.

Bodwyn Wook blinked. "No evidence points in this direction. Commander Chilke is our Rosalia expert; perhaps he has better information on the subject."

Chilke shook his head. "I don't think that either Zigonie or Smonny wanted to sell. The ranch certified them as aristocrats, even though it was relatively small—about seventy thousand square miles, as I recall, which included mountains, lakes and forests. On Rosalia the trees grow big: six or seven hundred feet tall. I measured a featherwood at Shadow Valley which topped off at over eight hundred feet, with tree-waifs living on three different levels. Featherwoods are gray, with lacy white and black foliage. Pinkums are black and yellow, with pink strings dangling from the branches. The tree-waifs use these strings to make rope. Blue mahogany is blue; black chulka is black. Lantern trees are thin and yellow and shine at night; for some reason the tree-waifs won't go near them, which is good news, if you are strolling through the forest, since you are out of range of the stink-balls."

Bodwyn Wook raised high his sparse eyebrows. "What are 'stink-balls'?"

"I won't even guess. Some old friends of Titus from off-world came to visit. One of the ladies, who belonged to the Botanical Society, went out to look for wild flowers. She came back a mess, and Smonny refused to let her in the house. It was a sorry situation; the lady left at once. She said she would never return if that was the way they were going to treat her."

Bodwyn Wook grunted. "These 'tree-waifs,' I take it are some sort of arboreal animal, like a sylvester, or a slayvink?"

"I don't know much about the creatures," said chilke. "I lived on the ground; they lived in the trees, which was quite close enough. Sometimes you could hear them singing but when you went to look, they seemed to flicker away and out of sight. If you were quick, you might catch a glimpse of freakish beings with long black arms and legs. I never could figure out which part of them was a head, if any, although they were ugly enough. If you stood peering up through the leaves, they dropped a stink-ball on your head."

Bodwyn Wook frowned and touched the top of his bald pate. "These habits suggest a degree of mischievous intelligence."

"So it may be. I remember a rather strange story about some biologists who drifted a camp module out over the forest and lowered it into the top of a big yonupa tree.

Working from inside the module they observed the tree-waifs and the intimate details of life in the treetops. Every day for a month and a half they reported back to the base by communicator; then suddenly the reports stopped coming. On the third day a flyer went out to investigate. They found the module in good order, with all the staff dead, but they had been dead for three weeks."

"So what was the upshot?" demanded Bodwyn Wook.

"They took the module away and never went back. That was the end of it."

"Bah!" growled Bodwyn Wook. "Such tales are rife at every back-alley saloon of the Reach. Now then—as to specifics: Hilda will provide you funds and all needful documents. You will proceed aboard the *Mircea Wanderling* to Soumjiana on Soum. The L-B District Offices are situated on Hralfus Place; you may make your inquiries there."

Glawen and Chilke rose to their feet and prepared to leave the office.

"One final word," said Bodwyn Wook. "Your Bureau B status confers an equivalent IPCC rank upon you; however, in the present case, since you are prosecuting Conservancy business, you will operate as officers of the Cadwal Constabulary and use IPCC authority only if it becomes absolutely necessary. That is proper protocol. Am I clear on this?"

"Quite clear, sir."

"Clear in every detail."

"Good. Be on your way, then."

V.

Glawen and Wayness took mournful leave of each other; then, returning to Clattuc House, Glawen made final preparations for departure.

Scharde watched him pack his travel case. Several times he seemed on the verge of speaking, only to stop short.

Glawen finally took notice of his father's odd behavior. "You are worried about something."

Scharde smiled. "Am I that transparent?"

"It's clear that something is troubling you."

"You are right, of course. I want you to do something for me. My worry is that you will think me weak-minded, or foolish, or obsessive."

Glawen threw his arm around Scharde's spare shoulders and hugged him. "Whatever you want done, I will do it, weak-minded or not."

"It's something I've been living with for a long time. I can't get it out of my mind."

"Tell me."

"As you know, your mother was drowned in the lagoon. Two Yips claim they watched from the shore. They did not know how to swim so could do nothing to help, they explained later; and besides, it was none of their affair."

"All Yips know how to swim."

Scharde nodded. "I think they turned over the boat and held her underwater. Boats don't capsize by themselves. On the other hand, the Yips would have done nothing on their own initiative. Someone gave them orders. Before I could investigate, Namour had shipped them back to Yipton. Their names were Catterline and Selious. Every time I speak with a Yip I ask for news of them, but I have learned nothing, and it is possible that Namour has sent them off-world. Therefore, if you meet any Yips, I would like you to inquire for Catterline and Selious."

"Namour must have given the orders. This is yet another reason for finding Namour. I will do what I can."

Glawen joined Chilke at the space terminal. Passage aboard the *Mircea Wanderling* had been arranged for them. As they waited at the ticket counter, Glawen chanced to notice a remarkably tall gaunt woman huddled alone in the far corner of the room. She wore a voluminous black gown and the peculiar black bonnet of a Mascarene Evangel. A ribbon of black gauze across her nose and mouth filtered micro-organisms from the air she breathed, thus succoring countless small lives from destruction.

Many odd folk in extraordinary costumes passed through

the spaceports of the Gaean Reach, but here, thought Glawen, was surely one of the more grotesque. The woman was of indeterminate age with a keen beak of a nose, raddled red cheeks, eyebrows painted across the central forehead, so as to join above the root of the nose.

Chilke nudged Glawen's elbow. "See yonder, the lady in black? She's a Mascarene! A long time ago one of them tried to convert me. Partly out of curiosity, and partly because—from what little I could see of her—I sensed youth, a comely exterior and an eager personality. I asked what was involved, and she said it was quite simple: first I must undergo the Seven Degradations, then the Seven Humiliations, then the Seven Penances, then the Seven Outrages, then the Seven Mortifications, and a few more activities which I've forgotten. At this time the acolyte was supposed to be in the proper frame of mind to become a good Mascarene, and go out to convert other like-minded souls and collect their money. I asked if she and I would undergo these rites in a close association, consulting during each degradation, but she said no, her grandmother would make this sacrifice. I told her that I would think things over, and there the matter rested."

The public address system announced embarkation for passengers to Soumjiana. The Mascarene Evangel rose and, hunched crookedly forward, hobbled to the exit. Glawen and Chilke followed—across the field to the spaceship, up an entry ramp into a small saloon, where the purser directed them to their compartments. As the Evangel departed the saloon, her glittering black eyes chanced to fall upon Glawen and Chilke, both of whom were regarding her somberly at the time. She seemed to jerk and blink, then, lowering her head and hunching forward, she marched at best pace from the saloon.

"Most peculiar," said Glawen.

Chilke agreed. "I never gave Kathcar credit for so much flair."

"It is truly impressive," said Glawen.

CHAPTER 3

I.

Glawen halted in the corridor outside the compartment numbered 3-22. He rapped softly against the door panel.

A minute passed without response. Glawen tapped again and waited, head cocked, ear to the door. He felt, rather than heard, a stir of cautious movement. The door opened a crack and a heavy half-muffled voice spoke. "What is it?"

"Open up. I want to talk with you."

"This is Madame Furman's cabin. You have made a mistake; go away."

"I am Glawen Clattuc. Ask Kathcar if he can speak with me."

There was another pause. The voice inquired: "You are alone?"

"Quite alone."

The door opened another few inches. A bright black eye surveyed Glawen from head to foot. The door slid back a few more inches, sufficient for Glawen to sidle through. Kathcar, lips drawn back in a humorless grin, closed the door. He wore ordinary garments: a loose black shirt, grey trousers, open-work sandals which dramatized the dimensions of his long limp white feet. On a rack to the side hung his disguise: gown, bonnet and narrow high-buttoned boots with hobheels, which must have caused him considerable discomfort.

Kathcar asked in a sharp voice: "Why do you follow me? What do you want? Or is it sheer persecution?"

"We were aboard the ship first," said Glawen. "Who is following whom?"

Kathcar grunted. "I follow no one and I precede no one. At last I am my own man and all I ask is that you ignore my existence."

"That is easier said than done."

"Bosh!" snapped Kathcar. He fixed Glawen with a glittering black gaze. "My commitments are absolute! I have renounced the past, and you must take me at my word. Henceforth, we are strangers, and you may purge all thought of Rufo Kathcar from your memory. Leave at once."

"It is not so easy as all that. We have much to discuss."

"Wrong!" declared Kathcar. "The time for discussion has come and gone! And now —"

"Not so fast. Do you remember your last evening at Stroma? You sat at a table with your friend Roby Mavil. Why did you leave so abruptly?"

Kathcar's eyes glittered. "Roby Mavil is not my friend. He is a dung beetle in human form. You ask, why did I leave him? Because he told me that Sir Denzel wanted to see me at once. I knew he was lying, since I had only just parted from Sir Denzel, after receiving his definite instructions. When I looked into Roby Mavil's face and listened to his soft voice, I knew that evil was waiting for me. A lesser man might have panicked, but I merely left the inn hastily and flew to Araminta Station in Sir Denzel's flitter. There is no more to tell and no more to know. Now you may leave."

Glawen ignored the suggestion. "You are aware that Sir Denzel is dead?"

"The news reached me at the hotel. It is a great loss for Cadwal; he was a patrician of full degree, noble in every respect. We had much in common, and I mourn his passing." Kathcar made an abrupt gesture. "I have said enough. Words are insipid; emotion spends its force against nothing. The truth is simple, yet terrible and sweet. It can never be known to you, since you have never studied wisdom."

Glawen considered the remark, but for a fact could resolve little of its meaning. "In any case, why the disguise?"

Kathcar curled his lip. "My conduct has been motivated by logic: a human process unknown at Araminta Station. In short, I am hoping to prolong my life, miserable, deprived and thwarted though it may seem to you. Still, it is my single and only chance among the infinite possibilities of the Gaean worlds, and I cherish my personal little spark of sentience, since after it is gone, I don't know what will happen to me."

"Probably what happens to everyone else."

"Aha! But I am not like all the others! I am cast in a stronger mold! Consider the Titans of old, who defied the Norns and their ruthless edicts; they were indomitable! I keep these heroes constantly at the forefront of my mind!"

"And hence the disguise?"

"The disguise served me well; It brought me aboard the ship in safety, and I must not fault it, despite the rat-catcher boots." He darted Glawen a quick glance. "What of you? Why are you here? Is it another of Bodwyn Wook's hare-brained schemes?"

"Not altogether. You yourself told us of Lewyn Barduys and his dealings with Dame Clytie."

Kathcar gave a sour nod. "So I did."

"That is why we are here. We can't allow off-world support for either the LPF or the Yips."

"And you hope to interdict such support?"

"Reasonable persons will cooperate with us."

"You will find many others who are both unreasonable and vicious."

"Was Sir Denzel acquainted with Barduys?"

"The two met at Dame Clytie's house. They did not take to one another. Before the evening was over, Sir Denzel had called Barduys a 'psychic cannibal, a soul-eater.' Barduys called Sir Denzel a 'silly old pussycat.' Neither took the interchanges to heart and parted on relatively good terms. Now: I have no more to tell; you may go."

"Since I am unwelcome, I will leave," said Glawen. "You should have told me sooner."

Glawen returned to the aft saloon. Chilke sat by a window watching the stars slide by. Beside him was a tray of salt fish and a globular stoneware jug of Blue Ruin. Chilke asked: "How is our friend Rufo?"

Glawen settled into a chair beside Chilke. "He lives a very intense life, in which you and I figure only as minor irritants." He took up the stoneware jug and poured pale blue liquid into a squat goblet. "Kathcar was not communicative. He talked a great deal, but told me nothing I wanted to hear. He explained that both he and Sir Denzel were aristocrats of high degree. He said he was sorry Sir Denzel was dead, but saw no reason to say so, because I wouldn't understand emotions of such refinement. He explained that he preferred life to death, which was why he fled Stroma and boarded the *Wanderling* in disguise."

"That seems straightforward enough," said Chilke, "but a mystery remains. He might have taken passage aboard the *Leucania* for Diogenes Junction in Pegasus, and lost himself; instead he waited an extra day for the *Wanderling* and took passage to Soum."

"An interesting point! I wonder what it means!"

"It means that he has business which takes him to Soum in spite of his fear. Business means money. So: whose money? LPF money? Sir Denzel's money?"

Glawen looked off across space. He said pensively: "Our orders make no reference to Kathcar. On the other hand, we are told that flexibility is an important virtue."

"It is more than a virtue," said Chilke. "It is the difference between up and down."

"There is another point to be considered: Kathcar is withholding information which may well be important. He values this information at twenty thousand sols. If for no other reason, I feel that we should take an interest in his affairs. What is your opinion?"

"I agree. Bodwyn Wook would agree. Kathcar might not agree, but he will certainly take our interest for granted."

"For poor Kathcar we are bad news. In addition to his other worries, now he must deal with these callow Bureau B lollopers, when all he wanted was a relaxing voyage. Kathcar is now pacing his cabin, cursing in all religions at once, and sorting through his options."

Chilke drank from his goblet and considered the flowing stars of Mircea's Wisp.

"Kathcar must bite the bullet," said Chilke. "He has no other choice. In a few moments he will come out and try to ingratiate himself, with a show of candor and good fellowship, meanwhile bamboozling us from right to left."

"That seems a reasonable program. Still, Kathcar's mind works in peculiar ways. For instance, out of a thousand disguises, Kathcar chose to confront the world as a Mascarene Evangel."

"I will be curious to observe his strategy."

"Here is Kathcar now," said Glawen. "He is not even wearing his disguise."

Kathcar approached and, at Glawen's invitation, seated himself. Chilke poured Blue Ruin into a goblet and pushed it across the table. "This will bring the roses back to your cheeks."

"Thank you," said Kathcar. "I seldom take ardent spirits or balms; I cannot believe that they contribute to good internal hygiene. Still—" he lifted the goblet and tasted the effervescent liquid "—this is not offensive."

"Two or three jugs a day will shorten the voyage. Time will go like a flash."

Kathcar gave Chilke a glance of austere disapproval. "That is an experiment I am not prepared to make."

"Out of curiosity, where are you bound for?"

"I believe that Soum is the first port of call. I may stop over for a period and visit the rural areas; in fact, I would like to make at least a brief study of the 'Gnosis,'* which is based upon a graduated system of 'Ameliorations.' Sir Denzel knew the system well."

"That sounds interesting," said Chilke. "And where will you go from Soum?"

"I have no firm plans." Kathcar showed his wolfish gap-toothed grin. "My enemies, therefore, will be equally uncertain, which pleases me."

"You lead an interesting life," said Chilke. "What have you done to deserve such revenge?"

"It is not what I have done but what I am about to do."

"And what is that?"

Kathcar frowned. In a spirit of bravado he had over-spoken himself. He drank from the goblet of Blue Ruin and set the vessel down with a thump. "That is a pleasing beverage. It stimulates the oral cavity and cleanses the sinuses with its invigorating activity. The flavor is mild yet pungent, without rancidity or after-burn. I will take a bit more, with your permission."

Chilke refilled the goblets and signaled to the steward.

"Yes sir?"

"Another jug of Blue Ruin. We are about to get serious so throw away the cork." Chilke leaned back in his chair. "What were we talking about?"

"Kathcar was telling us that he wanted to visit the back country of Soum."

"In disguise?" asked Chilke.

Kathcar frowned. "I think not. Of course I will be cautious."

"But first you will fulfil Sir Denzel's final instructions?"

Kathcar's manner became austere. "This is confidential business which I cannot discuss."

---

* Gnosis: see Glossary A

"You still fear your enemies, even on Soum?"

"Certainly! There were three days during which they might have hired a spaceyacht and preceded me to Soumjiana."

"You expect them to do so?"

"I expect nothing. I will take precautions against everything."

"You would seem to be most vulnerable on your way to the bank."

Kathcar's black eyebrows lofted high. "I said nothing about the bank! How did you know?"

"No matter. But you may rest easy since we will accompany you and guard your safety."

Kathcar said coldly: "You may dismiss this plan. I neither want nor need your interference!"

"You must think of it as an official investigation," said Glawen.

"I still want none of it. If you molest me, I will report you to the authorities. I am protected by Basic Gaean law which supersedes Bureau B pettifoggery!"

"We can make a case by Gaean law, by Charter law and by ordinary Station statute. We need only demonstrate that you have been engaged in illegal acts."

"That will be hard for you to demonstrate, since I have performed nothing of the sort!"

"If Sir Denzel financed or abetted LPF misdeeds, he is guilty of sedition, criminal conspiracy, and who knows what else—no matter how idealistic his motives. As his accomplice, you yourself are in a most precarious position and may well encounter criminal charges—especially since you withheld important information from Bodwyn Wook, who is vengeful beyond belief in such matters. Do you believe me?"

"I believe what you say about Bodwyn Wook. He is a wizened old termagant."

"When we arrive at Soumjiana, if you still doubt my statements, we shall go to the IPCC office, where they will advise you and perhaps make inquiries of their own. I remind you that IPCC justice, though fair, is brisk and impersonal."

Kathcar spoke in a subdued voice: "That will not be necessary. Sir Denzel and I perhaps have been overly influenced by altruistic arguments. Now I see that our trust was abused."

"What of the information you tried to sell us at Stroma?"

Kathcar made a gesture to indicate that the matter was of no significance. "The event is past; circumstances have changed."

"Why not explain the matter in full, and let us adjudge the situation?"

Kathcar shook his head. "The matter must rest here, while I consider my position."

"As you like."

II.

Halfway along Mircea's Wisp, the yellow star Mazda tended a family of four planets: three hulks of rock and ice tumbling along outer orbits and the single inner planet Soum, the financial and commercial node of Mircea's Wisp.

Like its mother-sun Mazda, Soum had entered the senescent phase of its existence. Soum's physiography lacked drama. Tectonic activity was not even a memory; the weather was placid and predictable. A world ocean surrounded four near-identical continents, each a gently rolling peneplain, spattered with innumerable lakes and ponds, beside which the Soumi maintained their rustic vacation chalets. The countryside, diligently tended by the Soumi gentlemen farmers, produced enormous quantities of delectable products, which were consumed with reverent gusto by the entire Soumi population.

Many adjectives had been used across the years to describe the Soumi: bland, industrious, boring, bumptious, shrewd, generous, thrifty, priggish, paternalistic, maternalistic, infantilistic, each term an inkling or a quarter-truth, usually contradicted by another in the sequence. A clear consensus, however, declared the Soumi to be quintessentially middle class; decorous, prone to small vanities and submissive to the conventions of society. Everyone endorsed the 'Ameliorations,' as specified in the 'Gnosis.'

The *Mircea Wanderling* approached Soum from space and settled upon the Soumjiana spaceport. Glawen and Chilke, standing on the lower observation deck, were afforded a view across the landscape. To west and north, spread the far-flung textures of the city: tawny yellow, mustard ocher or amber in the honey-pale light of Mazda, each segment guarding a dense black shadow at its back.

The ship landed; the passengers disembarked into the transit terminal. Glawen and Chilke looked everywhere for Kathcar, and at last noticed an inordinately tall Mascarene Evangel, hunched into a tortured posture, almost as if deformed, hobbling from the ship. A black bonnet and lank black hair concealed the face, save for beraddled cheeks, a rapacious nose flanked by bright black eyes. Voluminous black robes swathed the zealot's body, revealing only two large white hands and a pair of narrow black button-boots.

Glawen and Chilke followed the black-robed figure across the terminal and out upon the avenue. Kathcar hobbled away, glancing malevolently back over his shoulder. Glawen and Chilke strolled behind, heedless of Kathcar's annoyance.

After a painful hundred yards, Kathcar made a furious gesture and limped to a bench in the shadow of a newsagent's kiosk. Here he halted and sank down upon the bench as if to rest. Glawen ignored his sidelong glare and approached, while Chilke went off toward a nearby cab rank.

Kathcar hissed: "Do you lack all discretion? You are blasting my plans! Leave me at once!"

"What are these plans?"

"I am on my way to the bank, and time is of the essence! Also, I wish to avoid death!"

Glawen looked up and down the avenue, but saw only a few Soumi gentlemen strolling about their business at that placid gait which impatient off-worlders often found maddening. "Is it possible that you exaggerate your danger?"

"It is possible," hissed Kathcar, "but why not put this question to Sir Denzel?"

Glawen's lips twitched, and he looked along the street a second time, more carefully than before. He turned back to Kathcar. "Chilke has gone to hire a cab; we will ride to the bank, taking all precautions. Once inside the bank, you will be safe."

Kathcar made a contemptuous sound. "How can you be so sure?"

"When we reach the bank the game is finished, and the reason for killing you is gone."

"Bah!" sneered Kathcar. "What does that mean to Torq Tump, or Farganger? They are hobgoblins, and will kill me if only to set matters straight. But I am prepared; I carry a gun in my reticule and I will shoot them on sight."

Glawen managed a nervous laugh. "Just be sure of your target before you pull the trigger! If you make a mistake no one will listen to your apologies."

Kathcar snorted, but became less truculent. "I am not such a fool as to shoot at random."

"Yonder comes the cab. Once we are underway, you can remove your disguise; otherwise the bank officials will think you eccentric."

Kathcar gave a croak of raucous mirth. "So long as they smell money they will welcome me with delight! However, all else aside, these sacerdotal boots torment my feet; the disguise has served its purpose."

"That is my opinion, as well. Here is the cab. The plan is this: at the bank we shall pull up to the side entrance. Chilke and I will escort you into the bank; then, once we take care of our business, we can confer upon our primary goal: which is to locate Barduys."

Kathcar scowled. "All very well, but the plan must be modified. I will deal with the bank officials in private; it is the most expeditious way to handle this affair."

"Not so," said Glawen, smiling. "You will be surprised how well we work together."

The cab arrived; for a moment Kathcar held back, then with a muffled curse he thrust himself into the passenger compartment. The cab set off along the orderly avenues of Soumjiana: through the semi-industrial suburb Urcedes, past the Gastronomical Institute and the adjacent lake, then along the wide Boulevard of Acclaimanders, with its rows of monumental black iron statues to either side, each representing a grandee of substance and reputation; past the Tydor Baunt University, and its complex of ancillary structures, all built of taffy-colored rock foam in a ponderous, almost over-elaborate mode derived from the ancient 'Spano-Barsile' sequence. Students from everywhere across Soum and from up and down the Wisp sauntered along the malls or sat on the benches.

The cab entered the Pars Pancrator Plaza and halted beside the Bank of Soumjiana. Kathcar had doffed his disguise and now wore narrow black trousers, sandals, a casual white jacket and a loose-brimmed white hat of the sort worn by sportsmen, pulled low over his lank black locks.

Glawen and Chilke alighted. They looked up and down the street, finding nothing to excite their apprehension. Kathcar jumped from the cab and in three quick strides had gained the relative security of the bank. Glawen and Chilke followed with less haste. Once again Kathcar declared that he must deal privately with the bank officials, since Sir Denzel's affairs were all highly confidential. Glawen refused to hear his arguments. "Naturally you want to do well for yourself, but this, at the basis, is Conservancy business, and I cannot allow you to take charge of Sir Denzel's accounts."

"That is a tendentious assertion!" stormed Kathcar. "You impugn my integrity!"

"Chilke and I are Bureau B officials; we are skeptics by profession."

"Even so, I must protect my interests, which are legitimate!"

"We shall see," said Glawen. "Who is the official in authority?"

"So far as I know, it is still Lothar Vambold."

Glawen summoned an usher. "We must see Mr. Lothar Vambold at once. Our business is urgent and cannot wait."

The usher glanced at Kathcar, raised his eyebrows and moved half a step backward, then acknowledged Glawen's wishes with a stiff nod. "Sir, it is our policy to regard everyone's business as urgent. Therefore —"

"Ours, however, cannot wait. Take us to Mr. Vambold."

The usher drew back another half step. He spoke in a rich and deliberate accent: "The officer to whom you allude is a Senior Account Administrator; he never grants interviews without references and a preliminary discussion with junior officers, who are usually able to assist with your needs. I suggest you step over to the wicket yonder, and in due course someone will speak to you."

"Mr. Vambold will speak to me. Announce Commander Glawen Clattuc and Commander Eustace Chilke, of the Cadwal Constabulary. Make haste, or I will arrest you for impeding justice!"

The usher said haughtily: "This is Soum, not Cadwal, wherever that is. Have you not wandered past the limits of your jurisdiction?"

"We hold equivalent rank in the IPCC."

The usher bowed stiffly. "Just a moment, sir. I will convey your message, and perhaps Overman Vambold will agree to make an appointment."

"An appointment for now," said Glawen. "We are here on a matter of immediate concern."

The usher performed the most perfunctory bow permitted him by bank protocol and departed. Kathcar immediately turned to frown down upon Glawen. "I must point out that your manner is incorrect, and close upon arrogance. The Soumi put a premium upon gentility, which they consider high among the virtues."

"What?" cried Chilke. "Not twenty minutes ago you

wanted to rush in here wearing black robes and a bonnet with earflaps. You said it made no difference what anyone thought!"

"So I did. But I am a man of inherent high caste which the underling would have recognized instantly."

"He seemed hardly to notice you."

"Conditions were different."

"We will consider your interests when we confer with Overman Vambold."

"It is always the way," grieved Kathcar. "Never have I found the frank and loyal trust which is my due."

"A great pity," said Glawen.

Kathcar drew a deep breath and squared his thin shoulders. "I am not one to complain; I face always forward. When we meet with Overman Vambold, I will lead the discussion, since I am adept with the requisite niceties."

"As you like. But I suggest that you say nothing of Sir Denzel's death. The news might limit our freedom of action."

"This is my own opinion," said Kathcar coldly. "It is best to keep all options open."

"One more point: remember that you are speaking not for yourself but for the Conservancy."

"These are artificial distinctions," growled Kathcar.

The usher returned. "Overman Vambold has a moment or two to spare. Come with me, please."

The three visitors were conducted along a corridor to a door carved from a single slab of rosewood, which slid open to the usher's touch.

"Sirs, Overman Vambold awaits you."

Glawen, Chilke and Kathcar entered a high-ceilinged chamber of remarkable opulence. A soft black carpet cushioned the floor. At the far end of the room windows overlooked Pars Pancrator Plaza. To the left pilasters of fluted marble delineated bays inlaid with patterned malachite. To the right the bays were faced with white marble; in front of each a marble pedestal supported a black iron bust, honoring a notable who had contributed to the success of the bank.

An odd and unusual room! thought Glawen. There was neither desk, nor work area, nor chairs of any sort, nor couch, sofa, or divan. The single article of furniture was a small kidney-shaped table, with spindly legs and a top surface inlaid with waxen white nephrite. Beside this table stood a man of middle age and middle stature, delicate of bone structure but modestly plump, with cool amber eyes, a long austere nose, a skin as pale and smooth as the nephrite of the tabletop. A crop of tight brown curls clasped his head in a style crisp and artificial. The curls seemed to glisten, as if held in place by varnish, suggesting the decadence of an era long past.

Overman Vambold's manner was neutral. "Gentlemen, I am told that your business is urgent and requires my instant attention."

"True, to the iota!" declared Kathcar. He took a step forward. "I see that you do not remember me. I am Rufo Kathcar, aide to Sir Denzel of Stroma. He maintains an account here at the bank."

Overman Vambold appraised Kathcar with the detachment of a scientist studying an unfamiliar insect. Then, though not a muscle of his face shifted, his manner underwent a significant change. "Ah yes! I now recall our meeting. Sir Denzel is a gentleman of distinction. I trust that his health is good?"

"As good as can be expected, when all is taken with all," said Kathcar.

"I am pleased to hear this. And these gentlemen?"

"They are my associates, Commander Clattuc and Commander Chilke, of the Cadwal Constabulary. With all respect, I must reiterate that our business demands instant action, before irreversible damage is done."

"Just so. In which direction must we exert our speed?"

"It is in connection with Sir Denzel's accounts."

"Ah yes! I have had notice of your imminent arrival."

With an effort Kathcar controlled his surprise. "Who gave you this information?"

Overman Vambold evaded a direct response. "Let us move to where we may confer in comfort." He went to the wall and tapped a silver escutcheon; the malachite panel slid aside. "This way, if you please."

The group filed through the opening into a conventional office, furnished with the usual worktable, chairs, and implements. Glawen now understood the function of the elegant chamber they had just vacated: it was a waystation where importunate persons could be extended a few moments' solicitude, then referred to a sub-official and eased back into the corridor. In the absence of appropriate furniture, the interlopers need not be asked to sit: a tactic which would expedite their departure.

Overman Vambold indicated chairs and settled himself at his desk. He spoke, choosing his words with precision. "Am I correct in assuming that you are here to refresh Sir Denzel's account?"

Kathcar exclaimed in astonishment. "Eh then! Where did you hear this bit of news?"

Overman Vambold smiled politely. "We hear many rumors. This one is not unreasonable, in view of recent rather frantic activity."

Kathcar's apprehensions were now fully aroused. He cried out: "Exactly what has been going on? Inform me at once!"

"Yes, of course," said Overman Vambold. "But tell me this: have you in fact brought new funds to Sir Denzel's account?"

"Absolutely not! To the contrary!"

"That is interesting news," said Overman Vambold. If anything, he seemed relieved, rather than otherwise, by the emphatic statements.

Kathcar, however, had become exasperated by Overman Vambold's evasiveness. "Please explain what is going on, and with clarity! I am bored with your musings and vague hints!"

Overman Vambold responded with impeccable courtesy. "The circumstances, in themselves, are not limpidly clear, and this is the difficulty. But I will do my best."

"Never mind the difficulties! Just present the facts!"

"The account is in a curious condition. There are physical assets, but the cash balance has been reduced—in a certain sense—to twenty-nine thousand sols."

Kathcar cried out in consternation, "What do you mean: 'in a certain sense'? Your ambiguities leave me in the dark!"

Glawen interjected a remark. "Take care of the urgent concerns," he told Kathcar. "Then sort out the curiosities!"

Kathcar gave a grunt of annoyance. "Yes, yes; quite so." He addressed himself to Overman Vambold. "Sir Denzel has had reason to distrust the judgment and even the fidelity of his associates. As of this instant he wishes to place his account under stringent control—what there is left of it." Kathcar produced a document and with an emphatic flourish placed it on the desk. "You may regard this as a formal notification."

Overman Vambold lifted the document with fastidious fingers and scrutinized it carefully. "Ah, hmm. Yes. Most interesting." For a moment he sat motionless, preoccupied with his thoughts. They seemed to amuse him. "I am pleased to receive Sir Denzel's definite instructions. They have arrived at a timely juncture. I was on the point of paying over sixty-five thousand sols into a special fund."

Glawen was astounded. "Sixty-five thousand sols from an account of twenty-nine thousand? That is a financial miracle!"

Chilke was not impressed and explained the mystery. "It is a special way of moving decimal points. Some bankers back home tried it, but they did not understand the system, so they were caught and sent to jail."

Overman Vambold said primly: "We work no miracles, and our decimal points are immutable. At times, however, as in the present case, adroit timing allows us to create some truly remarkable effects."

"Explain, if you please!" said Glawen.

Kathcar cried out: "First—make sure that the account is secure, and that your clerks are not paying out Sir Denzel's last few sols with both hands!"

"That is simple enough." Overman Vambold turned to his

work area and touched buttons. A voice spoke: "Account of Sir Denzel Attabus—now isolated."

"The deed is done," said Overman Vambold. "The account is secure."

"Now then," said Kathcar. "What of this draught for sixty-five thousand sols—who issued it, to pay for what and to whom?"

Overman Vambold hesitated. "These transactions are confidential. I cannot discuss them in the course of casual conversation."

"This is not a casual conversation!" thundered Rufo Kathcar. "As Sir Denzel's agent I am entitled to all knowledge pertinent to his interests! If you withhold information to Sir Denzel's detriment, you, personally, and the bank, institutionally, will be liable to legal redress. I make this statement before witnesses of good reputation."

Overman Vambold smiled a wintry smile. "Your remarks are persuasive—the more so in that they are accurate. As Sir Denzel's designated representative, you have a right to ask these questions. What of these other gentlemen? Can you guarantee their absolute discretion?"

"In every respect! They hold commissions in the IPCC, which speaks as to their character. This present affair is of local concern, so for the occasion they are wearing the hats of the Cadwal Constabulary."

Overman Vambold nodded, without any great interest. "Across the years I have learned something of Sir Denzel's moral principles, and clearly they have not been advanced by either Roby Mavil or by Julian Bohost. You demand information, and rightly so, in view of the rather unconventional manipulations which Julian Bohost has attempted."

"What, then, are the facts?"

Overman Vambold leaned back in his chair, and seemed to ponder the shelves at the far end of his office. When he spoke, his voice was relaxed and his manner less brittle. "It is a complex story, and—in a certain sense—amusing, as you will see." From a slot to the side of his desk he took a sheet of

yellow paper, and for a moment studied the material printed
on its surface. "Two months ago Sir Denzel's account stood
at one hundred and thirty thousand sols. Then the T. J.
Weidler Space Yards presented a draught for one hundred
and one thousand sols in payment for two Straidor-Ferox
gunships. The draught had been issued by Roby Mavil and
seemed no more than routine business. However, knowing Sir
Denzel's opinions in regard to killing and violence, I was not
a little startled by this purchase. In the end I approved the
disbursement, since Roby Mavil was one of the three persons
authorized to draw on the account—the others being Julian
Bohost and Rufo Kathcar. The new balance stood at twenty-
nine thousand sols."

Glawen jerked forward. "One moment! You are telling
us that Roby Mavil used Sir Denzel's money to buy two
gunships?"

"That is correct."

Glawen turned to stare at Kathcar. "You knew this?"

Kathcar's shoulders sagged. "The circumstances were not
easy. I discovered the gunships in a secret hangar and
immediately notified Sir Denzel, who was outraged."

"But you failed to notify Bureau B?"

"It was a complicated situation. I owed three duties: to
Bureau B, to Sir Denzel, and to myself. I therefore resolved to
report the gunships to Bureau B as soon as I had finished my
work at the bank, thus fulfilling all three duties in the most
expeditious manner possible."

Glawen said nothing. Kathcar found the silence unnerv-
ing and turned to Overman Vambold. "Please proceed."

Overman Vambold, who had been watching with cool
amusement, continued. "Two weeks ago I was tendered
another draught, this time to the amount of ten thousand sols,
payable to the T. J. Weidler Spaceyards and authorized by
Julian Bohost. The sum represented partial payment for a
reconditioned Fratzengale passenger transport, leaving a
residual balance of sixty-five thousand sols to be paid in thirty
days. The draught was in order, but I did not approve it for

payment. Instead, I telephoned Dorcas Fallinch, the sales executive at T. J. Weidler, with whom I have good relations; in fact, we are fellow Syndics at the Murmelian Institute. He told me what I had half-expected: the Fratzengale was an antiquated hulk, not worth serious reconditioning. It had been available for two years but Julian had been the first to show any interest. The thirty-day deadline was meaningless, since no one was about to snatch up the Fratzengale from under Julian's nose.

"I remarked that seventy-five thousand sols seemed a viciously inflated price for such a vessel. Fallinch agreed. He would have accepted almost any offer, if only to get the hulk off the premises. The price was unreasonable; he would take the matter up with Hippolyte Bruny, the yard salesman and call me back. There the matter rested. Needless to say, I did not disburse the ten thousand sols deposit on the Fratzengale.

"Two days later Dorcas Fallinch called me back. The price on the Fratzengale had been fixed by Julian and Hippolyte Bruny, working together. Julian would buy two vessels: the Fratzengale for a premium price and a Fortunatus spaceyacht at a very modest figure. It was a ploy by which Julian could charge both ships to what he called 'a fat account' and take over the Fortunatus for his personal use, while Bruny would enjoy an inflated commission. The beauty of the scheme was that everyone profited and no one would be the wiser.

"I found this all very interesting and disturbing as well, since the bank, within certain limits, tries to protect its clients from misuse of their funds. Dorcas Fallinch was about to discharge Hippolyte Bruny with prejudice, but I dissuaded him, since I wanted to find how the scheme played itself out.

"Two days later Julian called upon me. It was the first time I had met him in person. I discovered a tall stylish young man, blond, with fresh and wholesome good looks, though somewhat airy in his mannerisms, as if he wished to be considered both charming and high caste at the same time. He wanted to know why I had not released the ten thousand sols for the

Fratzengale deposit. I said that I had not yet taken time to study the transaction. The remark annoyed Julian. He told me that all the study necessary had been performed by himself. The price was not out of line for a vessel of such large capacity and range. He frankly admitted that the vessel lacked cosmetic refinement, but he declared it to be basically solid and sound—in short, a reliable old craft, by no means deluxe, but adequate to the uses for which it would be needed.

"I said, all very well, but how did he propose to pay for it? His response took me by surprise. That problem was the least of his worries, said Julian, since additional funds from Sir Denzel, in the amount of one hundred or even one hundred and fifty thousand sols, was due at any moment."

Kathcar gave a caw of laughter. "I remember the situation very well. Dame Clytie had taken Sir Denzel aside and bullied him unmercifully, and insisted on the need for funds, and Sir Denzel, thinking only to escape, agreed to anything and everything. This was before I took him to see the gunships, of course. Dame Clytie thereupon sent Julian the glad news. Julian had good reason to believe that a transfer of funds was on its way."

"That explains his sense of financial amplitude," said Overman Vambold.

"Meanwhile, T. J. Weidler had not received the ten thousand-sol binder and time was in short supply, so Julian informed me; indeed, he had been able to secure only a thirty-day option upon the Fratzengale. He confided that he was also looking into another transaction of almost equal importance.

"I asked, what kind of transaction? He told me that it was not yet firm, but it seemed most attractive. I asked how he would finance these transactions if Sir Denzel's account remained without sufficient money? Julian said that a short-term loan from the bank might be the most practical solution.

"And what security would he be offering on this rather substantial loan?

"Julian became a trifle haughty, and stated that he had access to other resources, if need arose. I asked him to identify these resources, but he said the information was not presently germane, and went off in a huff.

"I considered what he had told me and made certain investigations among the bank records, and learned a great deal which I thought germane. I discovered an LPF account almost twenty years old, which had been built up by slow increments to a present total of ninety-six thousand sols, also Dame Clytie Vergence had a personal account of thirty-one thousand sols, and an account in Julian's name totaled eleven thousand sols. Julian was authorized to use any of the accounts. I began to toy with an idea which I was forced to discard as being blatantly unethical.

"Three days ago Julian returned. His manner was confident and affable. For a few moments Julian spoke of the LPF, the movement in which both he and Sir Denzel were active, and of the difficulties his aunt Clytie Vergence was having with the Conservationists at Araminta Station, but I was certain this was not the reason for his visit. Indeed, there was something else on his mind. Along with the Fratzengale transport, he told me, the LPF urgently needed a small courier ship. At the Weidler yards, he had discovered a vessel exactly suited to their requirements, at a very fair price. It was a prime Fortunatus Nine spaceyacht priced at forty-three thousand sols, so that the Fratzengale and Fortunatus together could be had for only one hundred and eighteen thousand sols. It was a phenomenal bargain, and he could not let such an opportunity escape.

"Julian's enthusiasm was intense. The Fortunatus was a charmer! A jewel! Like new, at a most favorable price!

"All very well, I told him, but, once again, how did he propose to pay for the vessels? Only nineteen thousand sols would remain to Sir Denzel's account, after the down payment on the Fratzengale. He insisted that Sir Denzel's transfer of funds was imminent; he had been assured of this by a notification from Dame Clytie Vergence herself!

"Nevertheless, if the money failed to materialize, the ten thousand sols would be lost.

"Julian waved this idea aside as preposterous. What he wanted was a short-term loan from the bank which should enable him to buy the two vessels.

"I told him that yes, the bank could properly make such a loan, on the understanding that both title and physical possession must reside with the bank until the loan had been amortized, and also that, for the bank's protection, I would require a very substantial collateral.

"Julian found these formalities irksome and tried to circumvent them. The two ships themselves should serve as adequate collateral, he argued. I pointed out that the Gaean Reach was broad, long and deep. For this reason spaceships were considered chancy collateral for bank loans."

Again Overman Vambold smiled his cool smile. "Julian drew himself up and became severe. He asked if I thought him the type of person to default on a debt. Yes indeed, I told him. I was a bank officer and trained to suspect everyone.

"Julian went away, but returned the next day, in a state of anxiety. Dorcas Fallinch, at my suggestion, had advised him that other interests were preparing an offer for the Fortunatus. Julian told me that we must act quickly, and that it might not be wise to wait for Sir Denzel's money.

"That decision was his to make, I told him, but had he considered proper collateral?

"Julian explained, rather glumly, that, if necessary, he could use the assets in other accounts for collateral.

"In that case, I told him, he should consider using these assets to buy the ships. The idea had merit, said Julian, but he preferred to channel the funds through Sir Denzel's account, for a number of reasons. I knew that the most important reason was that this was the only way he could use Sir Denzel's money to buy his precious Fortunatus. I told him, the other accounts might well be nominated as collateral, though the process sometimes meant weeks of waiting for approval by a board of review. It was a system of deliberate intricacy intended to discourage speculators, financial high-wire artists and those who contrived inverted pyramid schemes. Julian became indignant. This was foolishly over-protective; after all, he could transfer the money from these accounts into Sir Denzel's account in a matter of minutes. I told him that the decision was his to make; he needed only to issue instructions. Perhaps he might wish to take a few days or a week to think things over. No, said Julian; time was of the essence and he would act immediately. He would transfer money from the other accounts into Sir Denzel's account, and move the money back again as soon as the new funds arrived. Just as he liked, I told him; at this very moment I would prepare the documents and he could transfer the entire accounts if he so chose.

"Julian hesitated. He asked how much money would be needed?

"I said that the money residual in Sir Denzel's account must be used as a reserve against draughts which might be outstanding. Therefore, to the seventy-five thousand sols for the Fratzengale must be added forty-three thousand for the Fortunatus, which amounted to one hundred and eighteen thousand sols. Bank charges might bring the total higher, but one hundred and twenty thousand sols would probably be adequate.

"Julian looked grim, but made no comment. He trans-ferred ninety thousand sols from the LPF fund, twenty thousand from Dame Clytie Vergence and ten thousand from his own account.

"Very good, I told him; I would put through the transac-tion with T. J. Weidler at once. Julian could return in a day or so and we would arrange the final details.

"As soon as Julian left I telephoned Dorcas Fallinch. I asked for the ordinary price on the Fortunatus; he told me that sixty-five thousand sols was about right. And the Fratzengale? He would sell both for seventy thousand sols. On behalf of Sir Denzel Attabus I accepted his offer; the transaction was definite as of the instant.

"Half an hour later a messenger arrived with documents, keys and code-boxes; this morning you found me in the process of transferring seventy thousand sols into the T. J. Weidler account, which will finalize the transaction, which I fear is not affected by Sir Denzel's latest instruction. In short, Sir Denzel's current assets include two space vessels, the original twenty-nine thousand sols and another fifty thousand sols derived from the funds supplied by Julian Bohost."

Glawen asked: "These funds are now frozen into Sir Denzel's account?"

Overman Vambold nodded, smiling his faint smile. "I might mention, on a purely personal note, that, as a Syndic of the Murmelian Institute, I share the views of Sir Denzel, who himself is a Ninth Phase Avatar of the Noble Way. This episode has redeemed my unwise participation in the sale of the Straidor-Ferox gunships to Roby Mavil, when I should properly have applied to Sir Denzel for confirmation. The mistake has weighed heavily upon me; I rejoice that, to some extent, it has been nullified."

Chilke spoke thoughtfully: "Somewhere I've heard it said that among all the human varieties, the most relentless are the pacifists."

Glawen asked: "And Kathcar now controls Sir Denzel's account?"

Overman Vambold referred to the document which Kathcar had tendered him. "Sir Denzel's language is explicit. Rufo Kathcar is granted full freedom of action in regard to the account."

"Which contains most of the LPF assets?"

"Just so."

"Aha!" cried Chilke in exultation. "Can such happy things be real? It seems that Julian's money has disappeared into the crevices of a time-warp."

Overman Vambold's smile became wry. "I must use tact when I explain events to Julian."

"A bald statement of fact should suffice," said Kathcar.

"Julian must learn to accept the vicissitudes of life with a graceful philosophy."

"That is good advice, and I shall transmit it to Julian."

Kathcar nodded thoughtfully. "I too must cope with heavy new responsibilities. Still, I shall do my best, and make no complaint."

Glawen laughed. "We admire your fortitude, but the Conservancy's interests come first."

Kathcar said coldly: "I will make a full analysis and in due course —"

Glawen paid him no heed. "Sir Denzel's account now contains seventy-nine thousand sols, a Fortunatus space-yacht and the Fratzengale; am I right?"

"Quite right," said Overman Vambold.

Glawen turned to Kathcar: "First, the Fortunatus. You may transfer Sir Denzel's interest to Bureau B at Araminta Station, or to me personally. If you choose to make the vessel over to Bureau B, you may be sure that Bodwyn Wook will be highly gratified and will use it as often as he finds convenient."

"That must not be!"

"Then put the title in my name."

"What?" cried Kathcar. "Never! This is all sheer bunkum! I share Sir Denzel's creed, though I have not journeyed so far along the Way. Now I will find some quiet retreat and proceed with my studies, and perhaps I will also maintain a run or two of fine poultry. I intend to employ the funds in Sir Denzel's account to noble purposes, and the betterment of Man!"

Glawen spoke without heat. "Do not struggle, or wrangle, or argue. It will be time wasted. Sir Denzel may be an idealist; he has also financed criminal sedition and his estate no doubt will be confiscated. Your own position is ambiguous, to say the least. If Bodwyn Wook connects you with the gunships, he will take your case to heart."

Kathcar cried out: "I was under dire constraints, as you know! All my life I have battled Destiny! Always my good intentions have been thwarted and turned against me!"

"Not now! Your good intentions are free as birds! So put aside your golden fantasies and start signing papers."

Kathcar said hollowly: "When I first saw you on the *Wanderling*, I told myself: 'There goes bad news.'"

"Let us get this affair over with," said Glawen. "First, the Fortunatus, which Chilke and I will find useful in our work."

Kathcar threw up his arms in a wild gesture and turned to Overman Vambold. "Transfer the Fortunatus and the Fratzengale to Glawen Clattuc, Araminta Station, Cadwal. I must submit to this pitiless martinet."

Overman Vambold shrugged. "As you wish."

"Next," said Glawen, "pay over to Kathcar twenty thousand sols, which he probably does not deserve."

Kathcar gave a poignant cry. "Twenty thousand? I was expecting considerably more!"

"Twenty thousand was the amount you mentioned to Bodwyn Wook."

"That was before I risked my life!"

"Very well, then. Twenty-five thousand sols it is."

Overman Vambold made a note. "And the balance?"

"Pay whatever is left into the Floreste-Clattuc account, here at the Bank of Soumjiana."

Overman Vambold looked to Kathcar: "Are these your instructions?"

"Yes," growled Kathcar. "As always my hopes and plans have been dashed."

"Very well!" Overman Vambold rose to his feet. "If you will return in, let us say, three days —"

Glawen stared in shock. "Three days! We want the business done now, at this instant."

Overman Vambold gave his head a curt shake. "At the Bank of Soumjiana we work at a prudent pace. We cannot risk mistakes, since our apologies are never heeded. Your proposals have darted around the room like frightened birds, which is all very well, since you bear not a puff of responsibility. I, on the other hand, must discharge my duties with caution. I feel impelled to make an orderly evaluation and inquire into your reputation."

"My requests are legal?"

"Of course. I would not consider them otherwise."

"So much for the evaluation. As for my reputation, I refer you to Alvary Irling at the Bank of Mircea, here in Soumjiana."

"Excuse me a moment; I will call in private from my side-chamber." Overman Vambold left the room. Glawen turned to Kathcar and Chilke. "It is most important that we clean out the account before news arrives of Sir Denzel's death; otherwise Julian might be able to recover the LPF account. Hence the haste."

Overman Vambold returned to his desk, his manner subdued and thoughtful. "Alvary Irling has given you a good reputation and suggests that I cooperate with you to my best ability. Therefore, I will do so. Twenty-five thousand sols to Rufo Kathcar; the Fortunatus and the Fratzengale to yourself and the balance, roughly fifty-four thousand sols, into the Floreste-Clattuc account."

"That is correct."

"I will have the funds and the transfer documents brought here. It will only be a moment."

A buzzer called Overman Vambold to the telephone. Looking across the desk Glawen saw the face of Julian Bohost on the screen. "I am here at the bank," came Julian's voice. "Shall I come to your office? I assume that all is in order."

Glawen attracted Overman Vambold's attention. "Tell him to come back in two hours, after lunch."

Overman Vambold nodded. Julian spoke: "Is everything ready for me?"

Overman Vambold used his most colorless voice. "I am sorry, Mr. Bohost, I have been extremely busy, and I have not yet been able to process the papers."

"What! Time is of the essence and I am dangling on tenterhooks!"

"There has been a hitch in the proceedings which I have

not yet been able to resolve and the functionary in charge has gone out for lunch."

"This is outrageous!" stormed Julian. "I resent this inefficiency!"

"Mr. Bohost, if you will meet me here in two hours I will have definite news for you, one way or the other."

"What do you mean by that?" cried Julian. "This is intolerable!"

"In two hours, then," said Overman Vambold. The screen went dead.

Overman Vambold gave his head a shake of distaste. "I do not like being put into a false position."

"You need waste no pity on Julian, who was doing his best to swindle Sir Denzel, who himself was flouting the laws of the Conservancy, and encouraging acts which could only lead to bloodshed. His conduct has not been altogether innocent, Ninth Phase or not."

"Possibly so." Overman Vambold lost interest in the discussion.

Three packets fell into a delivery slot. Overman Vambold gave one to Kathcar. "Twenty-five thousand sols." Another went to Glawen. "Documents, key and codebox for the Fortunatus and the Fratzengale." From the third envelope he withdrew a paper. "Sign here," he told Glawen. "It is the receipt for the transfer of money into your account."

"Confidential, I hope?"

"Completely so. Our business is now concluded, since Sir Denzel's account has run dry."

"One final matter," said Glawen. "Are you acquainted with the name Lewyn Barduys?"

Overman Vambold frowned. "I believe he is a magnate of some kind. Construction, perhaps."

"Does he maintain an office in Soumjiana?"

Overman Vambold spoke into his telephone. A voice said: "L-B Construction is represented in Soumjiana by Kantolith Construction."

"Call Kantolith, if you will, and ask the present where-abouts of Lewyn Barduys."

Overman Vambold made the call and was told that Lewyn Barduys was not on hand, and that no one knew his where-abouts. "The sector office is at Zaster on Yaphet, by Gilbert's Green Star; they will surely have his present location."

The three left the office, Overman Vambold dismissing them with a bow of urbane courtesy.

Departing the bank by the front entrance, they stepped out upon the plaza, now crowded with Soumi moving about their business with that deliberate ponderous gait, almost a strut, head high, shoulders thrown back, which so often caught the attention of visitors.

Kathcar, fretful over lost opportunities, had forgotten the fear which had oppressed him previously. Without demur or reproach he accompanied Glawen and Chilke to an open-air café, where they seated themselves at a table. A buxom waitress brought a platter of grilled sausages, bread and beer.

Glawen told Kathcar: "The time has come for us to part company. I suppose you have definite plans in mind?"

Kathcar gave a rather forlorn shrug. "The episode has been played out, and now I am thrust aside."

Chilke grinned. "You have your money; you've done Julian one in the eye; what more do you want?"

"I still am dissatisfied. I thought I would go to my connections at Foucher on Canopus IX and raise fine poul-try—but the prospect no longer holds appeal."

"Count yourself fortunate," said Glawen drily. "Bodwyn Wook would put you to breaking rocks at Cape Journal."

"Bodwyn Wook is a chancre on the sensitive parts of Progress," muttered Kathcar. "All the same, I would prefer to live on Cadwal, where I could help direct the new order—but I suspect that I would never be safe." Kathcar suddenly remembered his dread of assassination. He raised his head and searched around the plaza, now bright in the pale yellow light of Mazda. Back and forth marched the citizens of Soumji-ana, the men in loose pantaloons gathered under the knee, full jackets over white shirts with loose wide collars. The women wore long-sleeved blouses and full skirts; like the men they carried themselves with prideful rectitude.

"Look!" cried Kathcar. He pointed to a heroic black iron statue at the center of the plaza commemorating Cornelis Pameijer, one of the early explorers. To the side of the pedestal, a Lemurian sausage seller had set up his grill; here stood Julian Bohost, glumly munching bread and sausages.

III.

Glawen, Chilke and Kathcar left the plaza and walked along the Promenade of Strong Women to a cab-rank. Glawen told Kathcar: "Here we will take our leave of you."

Kathcar jerked his head back in surprise. "What? So soon? We have made no plans for the future!"

"True. What sort of plans did you have in mind?"

Kathcar made a gesture, to indicate that the range of topics was almost boundless. "Nothing is settled. So far I have evaded my enemies, but you have forced me into the open, where I am vulnerable."

Glawen smiled. "Be brave, Kathcar! You are no longer in danger."

"Indeed?" rasped Kathcar. "Why do you say so?"

"We left Julian eating a sausage. He looked to be in a bad mood, but he was alone, and not conspiring to kill you, as he might if he knew you were near."

"He might find out at any minute."

"In that case, the sooner you leave the better, and far is better than near."

Chilke said: "At this moment take a cab to the spaceport, board the first packet out to Diogenes Junction on Clarence Attic, at the base of the Wisp. Once you walk across the terminal and mix into the crowds, you'll be lost forever."

Kathcar scowled. "That is a cheerless prospect."

"Still, it is our best advice," said Glawen. "It has been a pleasant association. We all have profited, and even Overman Vambold seemed happy."

Kathcar grunted. "There is nothing to be gained by citing grievances or inveighing against injustice; am I right in this?"

"Quite right, especially since you have fared better than you deserved."

"That is a faulty interpretation of the facts!" declared Kathcar.

"In any case, we will now say good-by."

Kathcar still hesitated. "In all honesty, I am now having second thoughts about the future. It might be to our mutual advantage if I joined you on your quest. As you know, I am both able and astute."

Glawen, glancing aside, noted Chilke's bland expression. He said: "Impossible, I fear. We are not authorized to enlist civilian operatives, no matter how skillful. You would need the standard Bureau B clearance."

Kathcar's face fell. "If I were to return to Araminta Station and offer my services—how would I be received?"

Chilke gave his head a dubious shake. "If you died, you might persuade Bodwyn Wook to dance on your grave."

Glawen said: "If you report what you know about the gunships, I imagine that you will be treated politely, or even rewarded."

Kathcar remained skeptical. "I do not indulge in romantic daydreams, nor do I expect rewards from that niggardly little goblin."

"When you deal with Bodwyn Wook, tact is important," said Chilke. "It is a knack you must learn."

"I treat him as if he were a reasonable man. I expect him to respond to logic."

"Very well," said Glawen. "I will write a letter which you may deliver to Egon Tamm."

Kathcar said grudgingly: "That will be useful. Do not, if you please, mention the twenty-five thousand sols. It is never in good taste to flaunt one's financial status."

CHAPTER 4

I.

The Fortunatus measured sixty-five feet from stem to stern. A large saloon, galley, three double cabins, storeroom and utility room occupied the top deck, with a companionway leading three steps down to the control cupola. Below were engine room, dynamics, crew's quarters, further storage and utility rooms. The exterior skin had been enamelled white, with black delineators and dark red bands around the squat over-size sponsons, which in the upper ranges of the Fortunatus line, were integral with the hull.

The spaceyacht exceeded the most optimistic expectations of both Glawen and Chilke. "I can find no fault with Julian's taste," said Glawen. "I'm afraid that this episode will cause him a great deal of sorrow."

"Especially with Sir Denzel paying all the charges. I like the sensation myself."

"By rights, the title should be half in your name."

"It makes no great difference, one way or the other," said

Chilke. "They'll take it away from us as soon as we get back to the Station."

Glawen heaved a sad sigh. "I expect you are right."

The two sat in the saloon, drinking tea. Astern the yellow sun Mazda shone like a bright golden coin, growing fainter by the hour. Ahead, still lost along the glittering track of the Wisp, was Gilbert's Green Star.

Kathcar had been left at the Soumjiana spaceport, though he had again professed a willingness to join the quest. Again Glawen had declined the offer. "The offices at Zaster will probably have all the information we need."

Kathcar pulled at his long white chin. "But will they release this information?"

"Why not? We carry official credentials."

"Credentials won't help a twitch if it should come to negotiation."

Glawen shrugged. "I hadn't thought that far ahead."

"The time to start thinking is today," said Kathcar. "Tomorrow you might find yourself knee-deep in complications."

Glawen was puzzled. "What sort of complications?"

"Is it not clear? Barduys, though dour and rigid, is rational. You may, however, also be dealing with the inscrutable Flitz. These discussions will be delicate, and here is where I come into my own—where a single glance is worth a dozen contracts."

"We can only do our best," said Glawen.

He took a sheet of paper from his case and began a brief letter to Egon Tamm, in which he described Kathcar as "... a person of intelligence and resource, capable of creative thinking." He wrote on to say, "Kathcar claims to have dissolved all connection with the LPF. He will describe to you our successful confiscation of LPF funds. He has been helpful in this operation. He states that your recent speeches, as well as increasing venality among the LPF have persuaded him to make a clean break with the organization. Both Commander Chilke and I feel that Rufo Kathcar may be useful at Araminta Station in a job suitable to his qualifications."

Kathcar read the letter with raised eyebrows. "It is not precisely fulsome. Still, it is better than nothing, or so I believe."

Glawen now addressed letters to Bodwyn Wook and his father Scharde, describing events at Soumjiana and calling attention to the presence of the Straidor-Ferox gunships somewhere on Throy. He also wrote Wayness a letter, and promised another from Zaster on Yaphet.

Kathcar went off to the ticket counter and secured passage back to Cadwal aboard the *Tristram Tantalux*, which fortuitously would be departing on the morrow. In the interim, he would keep to his room in the terminal hotel.

Glawen and Chilke returned aboard the Fortunatus, set the coordinates of Gilbert's Green Star into the autopilot and departed Soum.

II.

In discussing Gilbert's Green Star, many cosmologists dismissed the unusual green tint as an illusion, stating that the star was actually iridescent white or perhaps ice-blue. They changed their minds only when they saw Gilbert's Star for themselves. The color was most often attributed to heavy-metal ions in the stellar atmosphere: an opinion to which the spectroscope gave equivocal support.

Eleven planets attended Gilbert's Green Star, of which only Yaphet, the eighth, supported human settlement.

Few tourists visited Yaphet, for the best of reasons: there was nothing here to amuse them, except the spectacle of a people intent upon living at their fullest potential.

The landscapes of Yaphet lacked interest; the native flora consisted mainly of marsh-pod, algae and a drab bamboo-like shrub known as 'scruff.' The fauna had been pronounced 'graceless and furtive, insufferably dull' by the great botanist Considerio, who made a virtue of passionless detachment and had found something to celebrate even in the short-tailed lizards of Tex Wyndham's Planet.

Yaphet's climate was temperate; the topography

undramatic and the population clean, careful and moral. Commercial travellers and the occasional tourists were housed in neat hostels, decorated in psychologically correct colors. They dined upon foods which were uniformly nutritious and exactly metered to the needs of the individual diner. Beverages of choice were always offered: barley water, both hot and cold; chilled whey and properly filtered fruit juice.

The city Zaster over the years had become an important industrial and financial node, where all the large concerns maintained representation.

From a directory Glawen and Chilke learned that the L-B Offices were housed in the Excelsis Tower. Exiting onto the street a porter gave them further directions. "Straight yonder, sirs! About two miles along Boulevard Nine, a fine pink and black structure: pink and black signifying zeal and honor, of course, but being off-worlders, you would not be likely to know the scheme."

"Is there public transportation? Or should we take a cab?"

The porter laughed. "Sirs! A cab for two miles? It's only a nice little canter of ten or fifteen minutes!"

"Of course, but as it happens my colleague's leg hurts, so we must ride."

"The gentleman is hurt? A pity! It brings foreboding to all of us! Invalid transfer will be here at once!"

A moment later a white vehicle appeared; the porter and the driver helped Chilke to a seat with great solicitude.

"Take good care of that knee, sir!" the porter admonished Chilke. "Running comes hard to a one-legged man!"

"True enough!" Chilke agreed. "I was a great acrobat, but I fear my career is at an end! Still, I will rest the leg—both legs, in fact—as much as possible."

"That is the answer! And good health to you!"

The invalid wagon took Glawen and Chilke along Boulevard Nine among streams of men and women running to where they planned to take their noon meals.

The invalid wagon drew up in front of the pink and black Excelsis Tower, and Chilke was helped to alight. "The offices are sure to be closed," the driver told them, "but there is a fine restaurant just yonder where you may take your lunch."

Glawen and Chilke crossed to the Old King Tut, where a sign assured them that only extra-nutritious ingredients were used under absolutely hygienic conditions. In the entry they were offered towels damp with antiseptic fluids, and following the example of others, carefully wiped their hands and face, then went into the restaurant proper. They were fed a meal of unfamiliar substances with odd textures and flavors. A sign on the wall read: "Please call our attention to your slightest dissatisfaction, whereupon the Chief Dietician will appear and explain in unforgettable terms the synergistic concepts behind her preparations, and make it clear why every mouthful must be carefully chewed and swallowed."

Glawen and Chilke ingested as much as possible, then departed the restaurant hurriedly before someone should call them back to make them eat their fortified curd and their seaweed with ginger.

L-B Construction Company occupied the tenth floor of the Excelsis Tower. The lift discharged Glawen and Chilke into a reception area, decorated and furnished in spartan style, with a counter along the back wall. The other walls displayed large photographs of construction sites and projects in various stages of completion. Behind the counter stood a brisk young man wearing an immaculate white blouse with blue stripes down the sleeves and trousers striped white and blue. A plaque on the counter read:

TECHNICIAN ON DUTY:
T. JORNE

"Sirs, how may I help you?" asked Jorne.

"We have just arrived from off-world. We have some business with Lewyn Barduys and were told that we might find him here."

"You have missed him by a week," said Jorne. "Mr. Barduys is not on the premises."

"That is a pity! Our business is urgent. Where can we find him?"

Jorne shook his head. "No one has troubled to inform me."

A tall young woman entered the room on buoyant strides. Her shoulders were square; her loins were sheathed with powerful muscles; like Jorne she displayed every aspect of exuberant salubrity. Jorne cried out: "Ah, Obadah! There your are, at last! Where did you lunch?"

"I tried the Old Common, which is four miles out along the Way of the Underwood."

"A bit too far for lunch, perhaps, although I have heard great things of their glutens! However, to business! These gentlemen wish to speak with Mr. Barduys, but I could not help them. Do you know his present place of sojourn?"

"No, but let me find Signatus; he usually keeps all such facts at his fingertips." Obadah ran from the room.

Jorne told Glawen: "Please be patient; she will only be a few moments, though Signatus is never where you expect to find him."

Glawen joined Chilke, who had been studying the photographs which hung along the walls: dams, bridges, structures of various sorts. Chilke stood rapt before the photograph of an enormous crane overhanging a chasm, its magnitude emphasized by the six human figures in the foreground. Glawen asked: "What do you find so enthralling?"

Chilke indicated the photograph. "That appears to be a very deep chasm."

"So it does."

Of the persons depicted, the nearest at hand was a middle-aged man of strong solid physique, close-cropped brown hair, narrow grey eyes, a short straight nose. The face expressed nothing in particular except possibly a hint of obduracy, or—more exactly—a conviction of purpose. Glawen said: "The man with the steel teeth is Lewyn Barduys. I met him at Riverview House about a year ago. As I recall, he did not have much to say."

Along with Barduys, the photograph included a pair of local dignitaries, two engineers and Flitz, standing somewhat to the side. She wore tan trousers, a dark blue pullover and a soft hat of white cloth. Like Barduys, her expression was neutral, but where Barduys' gaze conveyed alertness and even a trace of vigilance, Flitz seemed indifferent.

Chilke said: "I assume that there, in front of my eyes, stands the legendary Flitz?"

"Which one?"

"The female."

"Yes, that is Flitz."

Obadah returned. "I found Signatus. You will never guess where he was lurking!"

"In Tool Research?"

"In Materials Inventory, and you can guess why!"

"Of course, but what did he have to tell you?"

"Signatus knows everything! He informs me that Mr. Barduys has gone to the world Rhea, by Tyr Gog in Pegasus. We have just finished a big job—" "Of course! The Scaime Bridge!" "—and Mr. Barduys wanted to be on hand for the dedication."

Chilke asked, "And Flitz: she is there too?"

"Of course; why not? She is nominally his travelling secretary, but who knows what is what and what is not?"

"Aha!" said Chilke. "So rumors are rife?"

Jorne grinned. "I would not credit mere whispers—but when fact after fact points to the north and a loud noise is heard from this direction, only a lummox runs out into the road and looks south. Am I right?"

"Comprehensively!"

Jorne went on to say, "I myself have noticed her decisiveness. Sometimes it seems as if she were running the company, while Mr. Barduys stands aside and broods. Of course she is intelligent and solves problems at a glance."

"Hm," said Chilke. "She does not look like a mathematician, or an engineer."

"Make no mistake; she is neither moony nor is she frail,

despite her rather slight skeletal structure. Clearly, though, she lacks stamina and I, for one, would not choose her as tandem for the Hundred-mile Dash. You can see for yourself how she lacks power in the haunch. Obadah, step over here a moment!"

"I am not going to show the gentlemen my haunch."

"As you like." Jorne turned back to the photograph. "Regardless of physical deficiency, she and Sir Barduys seem to maintain a good and sensible relationship; after all, they work long hours together. Let us be tolerant; a fine rib cage and dynamic pectorals are not the only things in life!"

"Poor Barduys!" said Chilke. "He leads a hard life, with all those projects and no one to help but the unfortunate Flitz."

Jorne frowned. "I had never thought of it in quite that way!"

"Thank you for your help," said Glawen. "One last question: you remember that Barduys used Yip laborers from Cadwal?"

"I recall something of the sort. That was several years ago."

"By any chance do you keep on file the names of these laborers?"

"It is possible. I can find out in an instant." Jorne worked the controls of an information system. "Yes! The information is here!"

"Be so good as to look for the names 'Catterline' and 'Selious.'"

Jorne entered the names. "Sorry, sir. Those persons are not listed."

III.

The Fortunatus turned away from the Perseus sector and slid off across the Shimwald Gulf. Gilbert's Green Star melted into the Wisp, which in turn disappeared against the luminous background of the Lower Perseid Arm and presently could be seen no more.

Ahead appeared the stars of Pegasus and Cassiopeia, among them the white star Pegasus KE58, commonly known as Tyr Gog, which in due course dominated the sky ahead.

Six of Tyr Gog's nine planets were small worlds of no great consequence. Of the three remaining, one was a gas giant, another a ball of ammoniacal ice; the last, Rhea, exhibited a dozen anomalies, ranging from a canted orbit to a backwards rotation and asymmetric shape. The constituent materials were even more extraordinary. In the end Rhea was adjudged not the usual result of planetary condensation but, rather, a juncture of numerous large pieces including asteroids and fragments of an exploded dead star.

The original locator, David Evans, recognized the strange and wonderful quality of Rhea's minerals, which were like none he had ever seen before. Some of the substances had been created in the stellar interior, in processes which transmuted the standard sub-atomic particles and rearranged their constituents into new patterns, to create theoretically impossible stuffs, so that the eventual yield of Rhea's mines generated an entirely new field of chemistry.

David Evans sold licenses and leases to a syndicate of mining enterprises—the 'Twelve Families'—upon terms which would ultimately make him one of the wealthiest men in the Gaean Reach.

Rhea, small and dense, exhibited a diverse topography and landscapes of dramatic contrasts. The two principal continents Wreke and Myrdal, confronted each other across the equator, with the Straits of Scaime between. The unique minerals of Rhea were most readily accessible on Wreke, which became the site for the industrial complex, and the residential zone for working personnel at the city Tenwy. The softer scenery of Myrdal to the south was reserved for the estates of the 'Twelve Families,' a caste commanding wealth beyond the dreams of avarice.

The continents Wreke and Myrdal approached each other closely; for about a hundred miles the Scaime ran only forty miles wide. The tides and currents joining the two great oceans coursed along the channel sometimes at twenty or thirty knots.

Five years previously the gentry had decided to bridge the Scaime, in order to facilitate transit between Tenwy on Wreke and Myrdal; the contract was let to L-B Construction. Concrete pontoons were floated, towed into place and anchored at quarter-mile intervals. From pontoon to pontoon long flat arches carried the causeway across the Scaime, at a height of two hundred feet above the rushing currents. The bridge was a magnificent engineering feat and the gentry could now ride back and forth between Wreke and Myrdal aboard swift magnetic rail cars in total comfort.

At the north end of the bridge was the city Tenwy and the planet's principal spaceport. The Fortunatus descended and landed; Glawen and Chilke submitted to typical arrival routines, and were passed into the terminal's main lobby. A sign, 'VISITOR'S INFORMATION SERVICE,' hung over a counter; here, on a cushioned stool was perched a plump little woman with a careful coif of brown ringlets, sagging cheeks and a small red mouth. She observed the approach of Glawen and Chilke under languid eyelids. "Yes, gentlemen?"

"We have just arrived," said Glawen. "We need some information, which of course is why we are here."

"That goes without saying," said the woman with a sniff. "Mind you, I am not required to furnish econometric data, nor genealogical information relative to the Twelve Families, and I will inform you before you ask that no guided tours of Myrdal or the Great Residences are offered."

"We will keep this in mind," said Glawen. "May I ask about the bridge?"

The woman pointed to the kiosk of a news agent. "You will find yonder a dozen sources of such information, which you may assimilate at your leisure."

"You do not have such information here?"

"Only if I jump down and grope here and there and waste time. Surely everyone is better served by using a bit of their own initiative, and, after all, Madame Kay at the kiosk deserves to make a living as well."

"We will restrict our questions," said Glawen. "With luck you need not jump down from your stool."

The woman sniffed. "What do you want to know?"

"First, in regard to the dedication ceremonies. Are they in progress now? If not, when do they start?"

"They are over and done with. The bridge has officially been declared operational."

"Too bad," said Glawen. "We must bear with the disappointment. Where are the offices of L-B Construction Company?"

"You will find these offices at 3, Silurian Circus."

"And how should we best go from here to there?"

"You could hire a cab, or you could walk. Personally, I would ride aboard the 'A' street car, which is free. But then, I know where I am going."

Glawen and Chilke, leaving the terminal, found a cab rank and were carried first through a district of foundries, machine shops and supply houses, into an area of office buildings. These were uniform blocks of glass and concrete faced with a black opal veneer which shimmered and swam with a hundred colors. The hills behind were traversed by orderly rows of residences, gray with pink roofs. Some were small, others large, but all conformed to a standard architecture, ordained by someone with a taste for the rococo and capricious, so that arcades, colonnades and bulbous domes were everywhere to be seen, and each house was surrounded by at least two and as many as six tall pencil-cypress trees.

The cab veered toward the Scaime and the wonderful new bridge came into view. Turning into a circular plaza, the cab halted before Number 3. Glawen and Chilke alighted, paid the fare with only a pro forma protest, since the overcharge seemed not excessive. They entered the foyer and went to a receptionist's desk. Here sat a woman, thin and blonde and resolute, with a long thin nose, black eyes, darting and alert.

She wore a severe expression, which hinted that whoever approached her had better conduct himself with propriety since she was in no mood for nonsense.

Glawen spoke in a meek manner: "Excuse me, Miss, I wonder if you can help us."

The response was crisp. "That depends entirely upon what you want."

"We have only just arrived on Rhea—"

"We are no longer hiring; in fact, we are either discharging or transferring crews. If you want further information, apply to the Employment Office at the construction yard."

"That is where we will find Lewyn Barduys?"

The receptionist stared stonily. "What gives you such a foolish idea?"

Glawen grinned. "I assume you know whom I am talking about."

"Naturally: Mr. Lewyn Barduys."

"We want a few words with him. Where might we find him?"

"In this regard, at least, I can offer no assistance."

"Is he still here on Rhea?"

"I have no current information. He was here during the dedication ceremonies; that is all I can tell you."

"Then please refer us to someone who will know the facts."

The receptionist thought a moment, then spoke into a mesh. "Sir, there are two gentlemen here who wish to speak with Mr. Barduys. I am somewhat at a loss as to what to tell them." She listened to her ear clip, then said: "But they are not convinced! They insist upon definite information." She listened, then: "Very well, sir." Turning back to Glawen and Chilke, she indicated a door. "If you will step into the conference room, Mr. Yoder will join you." She added as if by afterthought: "He is Office Manager, his status is Category 3b; no doubt you will recognize this and conduct yourselves with decorum."

Glawen and Chilke, obeying the instructions, entered a

long room panelled in textured white plaster, with a black ceiling and a floor checkered with yellow and brown tiles. The furnishings, a table and a half dozen chairs, were simple if elegant constructions of hand-fitted wood. On one wall hung a large photograph of the bridge, with a group of men and women, evidently high-ranking personnel, standing somberly in the foreground.

A tall gaunt man of early-middle age entered the room, his keen features and corded cheeks at striking odds with his debonair white suit and pale blue cravat. He spoke in a flat metallic voice: "I am Oshman Yoder; may I inquire your identities and your business?"

"I am Commander Glawen Clattuc, and this is Commander Eustace Chilke, of the Cadwal Constabulary. Our status, needless to say, is high."

Yoder seemed unimpressed by the statement. "'Cadwal'? I have never heard of the place."

"It is well known to educated persons, including Lewyn Barduys. We wish to ask him a few questions. You have indicated that he is still on Rhea."

Yoder appraised them coldly. "I recall saying nothing to this effect."

"True, but if he were gone, you would have notified us at once."

Yoder gave a curt nod and had the grace to smile. "Be seated, if you will." He himself settled into a chair beside the conference table. "Lewyn Barduys is a private man. He does not enjoy dealings with the public and he hires persons like myself to conduct these dealings in his behalf. Am I clear on this?"

"Of course," said Glawen. "However, we are not the public, but instruments of the law. Our business is official."

"I wish to examine your credentials."

Glawen and Chilke displayed their documents, which Yoder scanned, then returned. "The situation is not all so easy."

"How so?"

Yoder leaned back in his chair. "I don't know where Mr. Barduys has gone."

Glawen controlled his vexation. "Then why—"

Yoder paid no heed. "We will consult Mr. Nominy. He acts as coordinator between L-B and the Twelve Families. If there is anything which should be known, he knows it, and no doubt much which should not be known, as well." He turned his head. "Didas Nominy!"

A section of the wall slid aside, revealing a large screen which presently displayed the head and shoulders of a round-faced man, cherubically cheerful, or so it seemed. Chestnut curls hung over his forehead and dangling past his ears became mutton-chop whiskers. His nose was a stub, between round pink cheeks; his pale blue eyes were small and narrow, and to some extent diminished his expression of rubicund joviality. "At your service!" called Nominy. "Who is it? Yoder? What is the news?"

Yoder introduced Glawen and Chilke and explained the reason for their presence. "So then: where is Lewyn Barduys?"

"I cannot tell you precisely. He was to inspect three sites, with an eye to further construction, but that was to be done from the air yesterday. Today he had in mind a rather peculiar notion. He wanted to visit a village a hundred miles down the coast."

"Odd," said Yoder. "Which village is this?"

"It's quite primitive; I doubt if it has a name."

From behind him came the voice of a person off-screen. "They call it Yipton."

Glawen and Chilke reacted with surprise. "'Yipton'?"

Nominy spoke on, in a mellow and cultured voice. "From the first we have used teams of workmen with different skills, and some with no skills whatever, from all corners of the Reach. For a period Mr. Barduys experimented with a folk known as 'Yips.' They were strong, with easy dispositions, and quite cooperative, unless they were asked to work: an occupation they found uncongenial. From a gang of three hundred we suffered an attrition rate of about thirty percent a month, until all the Yips were gone and the experiment was pronounced a failure."

Chilke asked: "So what happened to the lazy rascals?"

"They melted away into the hinterlands and nothing more was heard of them until a few months ago. It was discovered that they had drifted a hundred miles down the coast, had taken up with women from the countryside, and now lived in a village of sorts. When Mr. Barduys heard of this village, he in effect delayed his departure a day. The village, so he said, interested him more than the bridge." Yoder looked from Glawen to Chilke. "Odd, don't you think?"

"Most odd," said Glawen. "So where is Barduys now?"

"The time is midday. He is either at this miserable village or in space."

"What is his next destination?"

Nominy shrugged his plump shoulders. "There has been no announcement, and I expected none."

"What sort of ship is Barduys using?"

"It is a Flecanpraun Mark Six, named *Elissoi*. It is a fine ship, and whatever his destination he will make a fast passage. But there may still be time to catch him at the Yip village. You can hire a flitter or, if you like, I will fly you there myself."

"That is very kind of you. Can we leave at once?"

"A good idea. Time is short."

IV.

The flitter flew east beside the Scaime. To the left rose a wild tumble of vitreous crags and polyhedral hulks rearing high into the sky: a repository of exotic minerals which provided the Twelve Families more wealth than they could conveniently spend.

As the flitter flew to the east, the Scaime widened and the continent Myrdal faded over the horizon. Below appeared a meadow. In a multitude of small garden plots women wearing gray smocks and pale blue turbans were at work. From a cliff north of the meadow a waterfall plunged a thousand feet into a pool, then became a stream meandering across the meadow, past a huddle of rude huts.

Nominy landed the flitter close beside the village; the three men jumped to the ground and looked about.

The huts showed a striking variation in quality. Some were little more than piles of reeds and sticks; others had been fashioned with planks cut from punk-wood, and thatched with palm fronds. About a third had been built with care and even skill, on stone foundations with posts and beams of timbers, sheathed with punk-wood planks and roofed with tiles of metamorphosed biotite.

The village was quiet except for pounding and rasping sounds from what appeared to be a communal workshop. Children playing in the dirt paused a few moments to inspect the strangers, then proceeded with their play. A few men and women peered from the doorways, but finding nothing of interest, disappeared back into the dim interiors. The women stalwart, rather squat, with coarse black hair, heavy features and large eyes, lacked the supple beauty of the typical Yip woman, but compensated for the lack through the vigor and efficiency of their work. The fields and garden plots were cultivated by women, though a few, by one means or another, had enlisted the unenthusiastic help of a man, presumably her spouse.

Chilke spoke to Nominy: "I think you mentioned that the women are all local stock?"

"None of them are Yips, at any rate. A few might be from off-world, brought here by bridge personnel. Why do you ask?"

"Because of the children."

Nominy looked them over. "They seem quite ordinary, except for dirt."

"On Cadwal the union of Yip and non-Yip produces no issue*."

---

* A situation ultimately traced to dietary factors: specifically, the presence of black spiderclams in the Yip diet.

"That is not the case here."

"One thing is clear," said Glawen. "There is no sign of Barduys."

"I expected none," said Nominy cheerfully. "But perhaps we shall learn the source of his interest. Such facts are often of utility." He settled his hat and fluffed out his mutton-chop whiskers. "Allow me to conduct the interview; I have had some experience with these chaps and know how to handle them."

Glawen demurred. "Chilke and I are both well acquainted with the Yips. They are more sensitive than you suppose. It will be better if you stay in the background."

"As you wish," said Nominy curtly. "But don't blame me for your mistakes."

The three approached one of the more imposing huts: a structure of two rooms, with walls of stone and a roof tiled with irregular plates of pale grey schist. The shadows of the interior stirred; a man stepped out into the pale light of Tyr Gog. He was tall, with good physique, dark golden hair, golden-bronze skin and well-shaped features.

Glawen spoke. "We are trying to catch up with the ship that landed here this morning."

"You are too late. It is gone."

"Were you here when the ship landed?"

"Yes."

"Were the folk in the ship polite?"

"Yes; suitably so."

"I am glad to hear this, since they are our friends and we are trying to find them. Did they say where they were going?"

"They failed to explain their plans."

"But, as an observant man, you notice many things."

"True. I am constantly amazed by the number of small details which present themselves, to be observed or ignored, as one chooses."

"Can you tell us what you noticed in connection with the folk of the ship?"

"Certainly, if you care to pay me for my trouble."

"That is a reasonable request. Commander Chilke, please pay this gentleman five sols."

"With pleasure, so long as I get it back."

"You may reimburse yourself from the petty cash."

Chilke paid over the money, which the Yip accepted with somber dignity.

"So then," said Glawen. "What happened this morning?"

"The ship landed. Several persons came out. One was the captain; another was a woman of haughty demeanor, or so I interpreted it. In any case, I was unconcerned. The two, captain and woman, came to talk with me. They admired my house, and said that the roof was especially fine. I told them that my woman had become weary of sleeping in the rain and had insisted upon proper shelter. She advised me that stone was a good material, and would save me toil in the end, and I believe she is correct in this, since some of the other huts have already blown down several times in the storm, and now everyone is considering the wisdom of building in stone. One of the ship's crew said something about 'social evolution,' but I do not know what was meant."

Chilke said: "They probably were referring to changes in your style of life."

"Is that any cause for surprise? How could it be otherwise? On Cadwal we lived like fish in a tank. Namour took us away, but he is a great liar, and things were never as he said they would be. Can you believe it? After taking us far from home, and even while sick and lonely, they wanted us to toil."

Nominy said, a trifle scornfully: "If you had done your proper work at Tenwy, you would have paid off your debt and by now you would have been living in one of the fine houses in the compound."

The Yip looked off across the meadow. "When the Yip works, the supervisor laughs to himself. After a time, the Yip thinks of better things and stops working, and the supervisor stops laughing. Here I work for myself. I carry a stone down from the hill and it is mine."

"That is definitely social evolution," said Chilke. "When

you talked to Lewyn Barduys—he is the captain—did he say where he was going?"

"Barduys said nothing."

Chilke thought to sense a nuance in the phrasing of the Yip's response. He asked: "What of the woman?"

The Yip said tonelessly: "Barduys asked if we had seen Namour recently. I said No. The woman told Barduys: 'He will be on Rosalia, and we will find him there.'"

There was nothing more to be learned. As the three turned to leave, Glawen asked the Yip: "Did you know Catterline or Selious?"

"There was an Oomp named Catterline. I never knew Selious, though I have heard the name. He was also an Oomp[*]."

"Do you know where they are now?"

"No."

---

[*]   Oomp: Elite guards in the service of the Oomphaw at Yipton.

CHAPTER 5

I.

A current edition of HANDBOOK TO THE PLANETS informed Glawen as to the physical characteristics of Rosalia, its complicated geography, and much else. Eight large continents, along with a myriad of islands, were caught up in a mesh of seas, bays, channels and, straits, with here and there an area of open water large enough to qualify for the term 'ocean.' In effect, Rosalia, with a diameter of seventy-six hundred miles, aggregated a land-area double that of Earth.

The flora and fauna were diverse, though not, in general, hostile to the Gaean presence. Notable exceptions existed, such as the tree-waifs who lived in high foliage; the water-waifs resident in rivers, swamps and wet barrens of the far north; and the wind-waifs of the deserts. All were notorious for their mysterious habits. Their activities seemed motivated by caprice mingled with a weird logic, so that their antics were a constant source of horrified fascination.

Rosalia was sparsely inhabited. The population of Port Mona, the largest town, varied between twenty and forty thousand, fluctuating with the coming and going of transient workers. At Port Mona was the space terminal, a number of more or less stylish hotels, agencies, shops and the administrative offices of a curious double government[*].

The original locator had been the legendary William Whipsnade, or, more often, 'Wild Willie.' He had blocked off Rosalia's land surface into segments a hundred miles on a side, which he thereupon sold at a grand auction. Fifty years later, when the dust settled, the Factor's Land Management Association was founded, with a membership limited to one hundred and sixty ranchers. By the terms of the Association's First Covenant, the ranchers agreed never to subdivide their acreages—though they might sell parcels to a rancher with lands adjoining their own, so that while some ranches expanded, others dwindled. Boggins' Willow Glen Ranch covered almost a million square miles, The Aigle-Mort and the Stronsi Ranches included almost the same; others· like the Black Lily and the Iron Triangle Ranches measured only a hundred thousand square miles and Flalique barely sixty thousand.

The ranches, in the absence of intensive cultivation, produced little wealth, which in any event was not perceived as their function. To augment income a few of the ranchers took to entertaining tourists at ranch headquarters, bedding them down in bunkhouses, feeding them out of cook-shacks and charging high prices for the privilege. The tourists, in return,

---

[*]   The double government included, first, the Factor's Association which represented the ranchers and arbitrated their differences; and, second, the Board of Civil Regulation, which governed the rest of the population. Neither service recognized the jurisdiction of the other, each claiming paramount authority. Informal liaison personnel managed to keep the two systems working with acceptable efficiency, and for a fact neither wished to take on total responsibility.

were allowed to enjoy the scenery, which included the Wild Honey Plains with its profusion of small flowering plants and moths camouflaged as flowers; the Dinton Forest where featherwoods, pipe trees and brouhas grew seven hundred feet tall, and the tree-waifs were often furiously obnoxious, especially when a tourist wandered alone into the forest; also the Mystic Isles of the Muran Bay and the multi-colored desert known as the Tif, where wind-waifs were wont to produce illusions and awful images formed of smoke in order to terrify the tourists and steal their garments.

Shadow Valley Ranch, with an area of six hundred thousand miles, included within its boundaries the Morczy Mountains, Pavan Lake and a dozen subsidiary ponds, several fine forests and a parkland savannah, where herds of the long-legged yellow bong-bird grazed. Shadow Valley Ranch was owned by Titus Zigonie, a plump little man with a bush of white hair and a pink complexion. One day, at Lipwillow, a town on the Big Muddy River, he chanced to meet an off-worlder named Namour. The event changed Titus Zigonie's life. Namour introduced him to a dynamic lady named Simonetta Clattuc who seemed kindly, soft-spoken and immensely competent—in short, someone whom he could rely upon to handle all the irksome details of life; before he quite realized what was happening, Titus Zigonie had married this fine woman who was always right.

Namour also imported a group of indentured Yips: handsome young men and adorable maidens who would perform the work of the far-flung ranch. The experiment had not proved a success. The Yips never quite understood the process which had transferred them from Yipton, to the strange landscapes of Rosalia. On top of all else, they found that they were required to work amazingly long hours, not just one day, but day after day, without cessation, for no perceptible reason. The circumstances were puzzling, and the goal of paying off the transportation fee (plus a fee for Namour) lacked all appeal.

One day Namour brought out an elderly man from the

world Cadwal, whom he introduced as 'Calyactus, Oomphaw of the Yips.' Madame Zigonie instantly noticed the resemblance between her husband and Calyactus, nor had the resemblance escaped Namour. During a rather strenuous visit to the Garden of Dido, Calyactus—who had not wanted to go in the first place—suffered a tragic accident, and it seemed only sensible that Titus Zigonie should become the new Oomphaw. Who would know? Who would care? Who would protest? No one.

So it was explained to Titus Zigonie. He protested that he had no experience in this line of work, but Smonny said that little work was involved, other than presenting a stern and dignified appearance in public, while in private he need only supervise a retinue of Yip maidens. Titus said, well, he'd give it a try.

With Namour and Smonny, Titus Pompo, the new Oomphaw, journeyed to Yipton, and thereafter was seldom seen at Shadow Valley Ranch.

II.

William (Wild Willie) Whipsnade, the locator who first laid claim to Rosalia, had been notably susceptible to the charms of comely women whom he met in places far and near across the Gaean Reach. To memorialize some of these pleasant episodes, he named his planet 'Rosalia,' its first city 'Port Mona,' and the eight continents Ottilie, Eclin, Koukou, Yellow Nelly, La Mar, Trinky, Hortense and Almyra.

The Fortunatus approached Rosalia and landed at the Port Mona Terminal. Glawen and Chilke dealt with official formalities, then went out into the lobby: a high octagonal chamber, each wall panelled with boards cut from a different local tree: featherwood, coluca, damson, brouha, sporade, native hornbeam, bloodwood, and splendida. Far above, triangular panels of glass, alternately dull orange and ash-blue, joined at a central point, like the cap of an eight-sided crystal. The effect might have been impressive had it not been for a pervasive dinginess.

The lobby was deserted. Glawen and Chilke went to the register which listed spaceship arrivals and departures over the prior six months and a putative schedule for the next six. They found no mention of the *Elyssoi*.

"I see three possibilities," said Chilke. "All pose difficulties. First, Barduys has not arrived yet. Second, he has arrived but landed somewhere other than Port Mona—perhaps at one of the ranches. Third, he changed his mind and is not coming at all."

"If he has not arrived, he will be hard to find," Glawen agreed. The two departed the terminal and stood in the tawny light of the dark-yellow sun. The road was deserted. Beside a nearby dragon's-eye tree stood a Yip, plucking and eating the fruits with no great enthusiasm. The cab-rank was deserted. A mile to the east were the outlying structures of Port Mona.

Chilke called to the Yip: "Where are the cabs?"

"There are no ships, coming or going; why should there be cabs?"

"Just so. Do you want to carry our luggage into town?"

"Naturally not. Do you take me for a fool?"

"For payment, of course."

The Yip looked over the two cases, which were of no great size. "How much payment?"

"Half a sol should be adequate."

The Yip turned back to the dragon's-eye tree. Over his shoulder he said indifferently: "A sol."

"A sol, for both cases, from here to the hotel, now and in our company, not lagging behind or sitting down to rest along the way."

"I should charge you extra, for impudence," said the Yip. He thought for a moment, but found nothing inherently unreasonable in Chilke's proposal. "Give me the money first."

"Ha ha! Now who takes whom for a fool? You shall be paid at the hotel."

"It seems that I must trust your good faith," grumbled the Yip. "It is always thus, and perhaps here is the reason why we are a down-trodden race."

"You are a down-trodden race because you are lazy," said Chilke.

"If I am lazy and you are not, how is it that I am carrying your baggage while you walk light-foot?"

For a moment or two Chilke deigned no explanation of the seeming paradox; then he said: "If you knew anything about the laws of economics, you would not ask such a banal question."

"That is as may be."

The three set off toward Port Mona, across a landscape grand in its desolation, if melancholy, by reason of high skies, far horizons and the beer-colored sunlight. A mile to the north a dozen gigantic thrum-trees stood in a line, lonely and isolated; the intervening waste was grown over with tufts of sedge and a low plant with pulpy pink heart-shaped leaves exuding a tart dry scent. To the south, a cluster of three conical peaks thrust high into the sky.

Glawen asked the Yip: "Where do you live?"

"Our camp is back yonder."

"How long have you been here?"

"I can't tell you, exactly. Years, perhaps."

"You have built good houses for yourselves?"

"Adequately good. If the wind blows away the roof, there is always new grass to be had for the plucking."

The three arrived at Port Mona, passing first through a district of upper-status bungalows, built of local timber to a quaint and angular architecture, then past a miscellaneity of structures: weathered cottages, warehouses and workshops, all somewhat dingy and unprepossessing. The road curved to the south, crossed a dry watercourse and after another fifty yards entered the central square.

The town was so quiet as to seem torpid. No vehicles moved along the streets. The folk who chanced to be abroad walked with no sense of purpose, as if their thoughts were far away.

North of the square the two tourist hotels, the Multiflor and the Darsovie Inn, created an enclave of elegance strik-

ingly at odds with the otherwise sober environs of Port
Mona. Both stood five stories high and were surmounted by
domes of brass mesh and glass; both were surrounded by
lush gardens of ylang-ylang trees, dark cypress, jasmine,
almirantes, stellar flamboyants. The gardens were
illuminated by soft green, blue and white lights and emit-
ted entrancing floral odors.

Elsewhere around the square were shops, agencies,
markets, the concrete structure housing the Factor's Association. At the southern side of the square was a third
hotel: Whipsnade House, a rambling irregular structure
built of dark timber with a rickety two-story gallery along
the front. Glawen also noted an unobtrusive structure of
rock-melt and glass which displayed the blue and white
symbol of the IPCC. He would be expected to pay the
local staff a courtesy call as soon as possible; such was
IPCC protocol, which ordinarily Glawen would have found
unobjectionable. But now the presence of himself and
Chilke would arouse curiosity, which might prove inconve-
nient. On the other hand, if he neglected convention, he
could expect no instant cooperation in the event of emergency. He decided to call at the IPCC offices the first
thing in the morning.

The sun had settled behind a scud of high clouds. The
sky showed the clear pure lavender for which Rosalia was
famous. Chilke indicated the two hotels at the north side of
the square. "They are quite nice, so I have been told, but
the prices are imaginative. At Whipsnade House, the floors
creak and snoring in bed is prohibited, but here is where
ranchers put up when they come to town."

Glawen and Chilke took lodging at the Whipsnade
House, then went out to drink beer on the gallery.

Twilight came to Port Mona. The square was quiet, traversed only by a few shopkeepers trudging homeward.
Glawen looked around the square. "I don't see any cafés, or
public saloons, or restaurants, or music halls."

"That is factor policy. They consider Port Mona a commercial depot, a port of entry for the tourists. Everything else is incidental."

"It's a cheerless place."

Chilke agreed. "The young people leave as soon as they can. There is always a labor shortage."

"Namour had a good idea. The Yips' aversion to toil cost him a lot of money."

"If Namour collected his fee up front, then it was the ranchers who lost their money, not Namour—and of course that was the way it was."

Glawen ruminated upon the circumstances. "If Barduys still feels that he has been swindled, and if he is of a hard and vengeful temperament, then his interest in Namour and the Yips is explained. He wants revenge and he wants his money back."

"On the other hand, if he is of a philosophical nature, he has long ago laughed off the whole silly business," said Chilke. "Now he is concerned with a new project. On Tyr Gog he notices changes in the Yip mentality, and he tells himself that if it can happen on Tyr Gog, why not elsewhere? So he comes to Rosalia to investigate other Yip colonies, and his actions are explained."

"Rosalia is a long way to come just to look at a few Yips."

"Then why did he trouble to visit the village on Rhea?"

"There was something he wanted to find out. Five minutes was enough. He saw that when Yips took up with strong-willed women of the country, they started to work and build good houses. Barduys saw all he wanted to see and set off for Rosalia. He is probably here now."

"I can think of two ways to find him," said Chilke. "We can search here and there at random, or we can solve the problem through the use of pure logic."

"I'd be willing to try the second method if I knew where to start."

"We go back to the village on Rhea. Flitz told Barduys not to worry about Namour, since they would find him on Rosalia. I take this to mean that they were already on their way to Rosalia, but for reasons not connected with Namour. I can't believe that they would come this far just to look at some more Yips. So—what else is on Rosalia? The answer is: 'Shadow Valley Ranch,' also Smonny and Titus Zigonie, perhaps Namour as well. Logic has supplied a clue."

"It is almost too easy," said Glawen. "What could Barduys possibly want at Shadow Valley Ranch?"

"That is why we are here: to ask questions."

"Hmf," said Glawen. "Asking Barduys questions is easy. Finding him is less easy. Forcing him to answer may not be easy at all."

Chilke said thoughtfully. "While you are dealing with Barduys, I will undertake to question Flitz. It is a challenging task, but I think I am up to it."

Glawen asked: "Are you acquainted with the old fable called 'Belling the Cat'?"

Chilke nodded. "My mother was a great one for fables. Why do you ask?"

"If someone wants to question Flitz, first he must arrange that she does not snub him."

In the morning Glawen and Chilke visited the IPCC agency. The senior officer, Adam Wincutz, received them with muted courtesy, carefully devoid of curiosity. Wincutz was thin, all bone and sinew, with a long bony head, sandy hair and opaque blue eyes.

Glawen explained their presence by referring to Namour. The Cadwal Constabulary, so he stated, was dissatisfied with certain phases of Namour's conduct. It was considered likely that he had taken refuge on Rosalia. Glawen wondered if Wincutz had any knowledge of Namour or his activities.

Wincutz seemed only politely interested in the case. "I have heard the name 'Namour' mentioned. He brought in several contingents of laborers from some benighted place at the back of nowhere."

"That place was the Cadwal Conservancy," said Glawen stiffly.

"Ah? In any case, the program came to naught. The Yips decamped from the ranches to which they had been assigned."

"Do you recall which ranches took contingents?"

"There were only three or four. Honeyflower took a gang; Stronsi took a couple gangs. Baramond took a gang and Shadow Valley might have tried as many as three; in fact, there are a few Yips at Shadow Valley to this day. But in general the Yips drifted off like ghosts and the ranchers had no recourse."

"They failed to complain to the IPCC?"

"They had nothing to complain about. Namour guaranteed nothing. He delivered the merchandise; thereafter the Yips were supposed to work."

"And where are the Yips now?"

"The Honeyflower Yips have a settlement near Tooneytown on Ottilie. The Stronsi Yips moved down into the Mystic Islands. The Shadow Valley Yips have a camp near Lipwillow on the Big Muddy River, on La Mar. The Baramond Yips live in grass shanties just past the spaceport, near Faney's Marsh."

"One final matter," said Glawen. "Namour seems to have brought over a thousand Yips to Rosalia. Is there any record as to their identities: a roster of those in each gang, for instance."

"We have no such roster here," said Wincutz. "But I have no doubt that the Factor's Association took such a list from Namour. In what names are you interested?"

"'Catterline' and 'Selious.'"

"One moment," said Wincutz. He turned to his communicator and the face of a woman appeared on the screen. "Wincutz here, at the IPCC. Please check through the entry lists for two names, both Yip: 'Catterline' and 'Selious.'"

"Just a moment." The woman turned away, then reappeared. "No such names are listed."

"Then, definitely, they are not on Rosalia?"

"Not unless they have made an illegal entry, which is unlikely."

"Thank you." Wincutz turned to Glawen. "That is the best information to hand."

"I am much obliged to you," said Glawen.

III.

Glawen and Chilke rented a flitter at the spaceport, on the theory that they would be less conspicuous than if they proceeded about their investigations in the Fortunatus. Upon leaving Port Mona, they flew west by north—above marshes tufted with red and black reeds, small ponds and water-meadows; over a line of rolling hills, then a long lake glittering and winking in the amber sunlight. Trees began to appear: Smoke-trees of amazing stature, standing alone or in disciplined groups; then dense forests of feather-woods, bilbobs, chulastics and thrums which covered the landscape with an intricately detailed carpet of black, brown and tan foliage.

Chilke called attention to a towering tree with masses of small rectangular leaves shimmering in waves of dark red, pale red and vermilion. "That is a pilkardia, but it is usually called an 'oh-my-god tree.'"

"What an odd name!"

Chilke nodded. "You can't see them from here, but the tree is thick with tree-waifs. They mix fiber and gum and some other ingredients to make their famous stink-balls. Sometimes guests at the ranches go wandering through the forests, admiring the stately beauty of the trees. They are warned not to loiter under the pilkardias."

The flitter left Eclin behind and flew out over the Cory-bantic Ocean, with the sun gaining upon them very slowly. At local noon the coast of La Mar smudged the horizon. A few moments later the flitter crossed a long wavering white line, where surf foamed over an outlying reef. A strip of teal-blue lagoon passed below, then a white beach, then an expanse of jungle, which after a hundred miles broke against a tectonic thrust which pushed high an arid plateau.

Over red gulches and yellow gullies, bluffs banded tan,

yellow and rust, flats of bare stone and drifts of mustard-ocher sand slid the flitter. Glawen found the landscape bleak yet disturbingly beautiful. He asked: "Is all this part of somebody's ranch?"

"Probably not," said Chilke. "There is still wilderness for sale, if the Factors find you reliable and suitably sensitive to caste distinctions. You, as a Clattuc, would have no problem on this score. Ten thousand sols would buy you this entire plateau."

"And then: what would I do with it?"

"You could enjoy the solitude, or you might wish to study the wind-waifs.

Glawen looked across the arid expanse. "I don't see any wind-waifs at the moment."

"If you were down there after dark, sitting at a camp-fire, they would come to toss pebbles and make strange sounds. If a tourist is lost they play tricks. I've heard all manner of tales."

"What do they look like?"

"Nobody agrees on this, and cameras won't focus on their images."

"Very odd," said Glawen.

The plateau came to an abrupt end at the brink of a great scarp half a mile high, with rolling plains beyond. Chilke indicated a river meandering lazily westward. "That's the Big Muddy. It's almost like coming home."

The flitter slid across the sky. An hour passed and the town Lipwillow appeared below: a straggle of ramshackle structures along the riverbank, built of rough featherwood timber, weathered to a pleasant grayed tan. The largest structure was a sprawling hotel, with a gallery across its front, like that of Whipsnade House at Port Mona. There were also shops, agencies, a post office and a number of modest dwellings. A long pier, supported by a hundred spindly poles extended into the river, with a deck and a shack at the end; Chilke identified the shack as 'Poolie's Place,' a saloon. Half a mile downstream, a number of huts had been built, using driftwood, plaques of bark and fragments of miscellaneous material scavenged from Lipwillow's rubbish dump.

As the flitter descended upon Lipwillow, Chilke could not restrain his reminiscences of Poolie's Place. It was where he had first met Namour after his departure from Shadow Valley Ranch. Madame Zigonie had paid Chilke none of his wages, and Chilke had arrived at Lipwillow with barely enough money to pay for a pint of beer. Learning of Chilke's plight, Namour had become sympathetic, and had gone so far as to offer Chilke a job at Araminta Station. Chilke had considered Namour a prince among men. Now he was not so sure. "Still," said Chilke, "if we meet Namour in Poolie's, I will buy him a beer, for old times' sake."

"Now you are returning in triumph! It must be a thrill."

Chilke nodded. "Even so, I can't shake an obsessive dread that Madame Zigonie might be waiting down there to give me my old job back. That would be a thrill indeed."

"We shall see," said Glawen. He indicated the clutter of huts beside the alder thickets downstream from town. "That must be the Yip settlement."

Chilke agreed. "It hasn't changed much, so far as I can tell. If Barduys comes to Lipwillow hoping to find a flowering of Yip civilization, he will be disappointed."

The flitter landed in a plot beside the post office. Glawen and Chilke alighted and approached the hotel through the noonday sunlight. On the wooden porch along the front sat three Yips drinking beer. After swift glances, the Yips ignored the newcomers—a Yip mannerism which sensitive folk sometimes considered a subtle form of insolence.[*]

Others blamed the trait upon simple shyness. Chilke long ago had lost all patience with the Yips and their foibles.

---

[*] If the Yip were asked to desist from this sort of conduct, his response was typically puzzled acquiescence and smiling affability. If the expostulations persisted, the Yip, still smiling, would furtively sidle away, hoping to avoid any more of this incomprehensible discord.

He surveyed them now in marvelling disapproval. "Look at those rascals, drinking beer like lords!"

"They seem very relaxed, as if they were tired," said Glawen.

"Are you serious?" demanded Chilke. "To be tired, first you must work. Out at Shadow Valley I implored them to face their responsibilities and pay off their indentures and make something of themselves. They just looked at me mystified, wondering what I meant!"

"Very sad," said Glawen.

As the two stepped upon the porch, one of the Yips rose to his feet. "Gentlemen, would you care to buy a fine souvenir of Rosalia, absolutely authentic?"

Chilke asked: "What kind of souvenir, and how much?"

The Yip displayed a glass bottle containing three balls of matted fiber floating in an oily dark-yellow liquid.

"Stink-balls, three for five sols," said the Yip. "Very cheap and very nice."

"I don't need any just now," said Chilke.

"Your price is outrageous," said Glawen. "Namour told me that you would sell more cheaply if I mentioned his name."

The Yip put on a smile of bafflement. "I know nothing of this arrangement."

"Odd! Namour tells me he saw you quite recently."

"It was not all so recent. We did not discuss stink-balls."

"Oh? What did you discuss? Namour's new project?"

"No. Will you buy the stink-balls?"

"Not until I consult with Namour. Is he here at Lipwillow, or up at Shadow Valley?"

"I will sell six stink-balls for nine sols."

"I must take Namour's advice on this. Do you know where I can find him?"

The Yips looked non-plussed, from one to another, then the vendor resumed his place on the porch. "No matter. We shall deal later. No one will offer you a better price for a like quality of merchandise."

Glawen and Chilke turned into the hotel and took lodging in clean rooms, austerely furnished, fragrant with the odor of dry featherwood.

The time was too late for a visit to Shadow Valley Ranch. At Chilke's suggestion they left the hotel and walked out to Poolie's Place at the end of the pier, where they sat at a table beside an open window, with a view up and down the river. The walls were decorated with a few old posters, oddments and curios. Three local folk shared a table in the corner; another sat hunched over the bar, staring down into a mug of beer as if hypnotized. A pallid big-eyed boy brought Glawen and Chilke a platter of fried river-sprats and took their order for beer. Chilke surveyed the room with care. "Never did I think I would set foot in Poolie's again. A philosopher, whose name eludes me, once declared: 'Life is incredible unless you are alive.' I think I am quoting correctly. In any case, I find the idea reassuring."

"It may get even more so before we are done," said Glawen. "Don't ask what I mean, because I don't know myself."

Chilke looked off downstream toward the Yip huts among the alder thickets. "'Social evolution' still hasn't reached the Lipwillow Yips—but then they are not married to those strong-willed ladies of Rhea who don't like sleeping in the rain."

IV.

In the morning, Glawen and Chilke flew north over a landscape of a thousand contrasts: hills and dales, forests and ponds; flower-fields of many colors, isolated crags thrusting high like black fangs.

Two hundred miles north of Lipwillow they approached the outlying shoulders of the great Kali-kalu mountain range, which rose in abrupt tiers and blocks to a crest twenty thousand feet high. A pair of outlying spurs reached east to shelter the headquarters of the Shadow Valley Ranch. To the north rose a forest of enormous bloodwood and blue mahogany trees; to the south stood individual smoke trees and featherwoods. The ranch-house proper, an informal mansion of stone and timber, obeyed no architectural strictures; over the years it had been rebuilt a dozen times to suit the taste of the current owner. A hundred yards to the north, screened by the foliage of tree-vines, were utility buildings: a bunkhouse, a cookshed, workshop, garage and several storage sheds. Chilke indicated a two-story bungalow painted white, off to the side. "I lived there during the term of my employment, for which—need I repeat?—I was never paid so much as a plugged bung-starter."

"That is an outrage!" declared Glawen.

"Quite so. You are aware, of course, that Madame Zigonie was born a Clattuc of Araminta Station."

Glawen nodded. "She has dishonored the house. But not enough that I feel compelled to settle the debt."

Nowhere could be seen any indication of visitors to Shadow Valley Ranch—most especially, neither Lewyn Barduys' Flecanpraun nor the grandiose Clayhacker spaceyacht owned by Titus Zigonie.

"So much for logic," said Chilke.

The flitter descended upon the ranch complex. Near the bunkhouse a group of Yips sat on the ground, gambling and drinking foxtail beer from tin pots. A dozen naked children played in the dirt.

"It is like old times," said Chilke. "This scene is engraved in my memory."

The flitter landed and the two men jumped down to the ground. Glawen said: "I will go up to the house; you come behind me with your gun ready. If Namour is here, he may be asleep or in a good mood. Make sure he doesn't sneak around from the back and take off in our flitter."

Glawen went up the walk to the front door of the ranch house, with Chilke coming behind. At their approach the door opened. A stout man of middle years, with a ruff of white hair and a pink peevish face stood waiting for them. At their approach he called out: "Sirs? What is your business? I don't recognize you!"

"We are police officials," said Glawen. "You are the superintendent?"

"I am Festus Dibbins; I am indeed the superintendent."

"Are you entertaining visitors? Friends? Guests? Offworlders of any sort?"

Dibbins drew himself up. "That is an extraordinary question!"

"I have a good reason for asking.

"The answer is 'no.' None whatever. What is your concern?"

"May we come in? We will then explain our business."

"Let me see your identification."

Glawen and Chilke produced their warrant cards, which Dibbins examined, then returned. "This way, if you please."

Dibbins conducted the two into a large parlor, with windows overlooking the landscape to the east. Chilke asked: "I take it that Madame Zigonie is not in residence?"

"That is correct."

"And you have no other guests, or visitors?"

"As I have already mentioned: there are none." He pointed to chairs. "Please be seated. Would you care for refreshment?"

"A pot of tea would be most welcome," said Glawen.

Dibbins gave instructions to his wife, who had been peering through the doorway from the dining room. The three men seated themselves: Glawen and Chilke on a massive leather-upholstered couch, Dibbins on a chair.

"Now then," said Dibbins, "perhaps you will explain your presence."

"We will indeed. First of all, let me ask this: you are acquainted with Namour?"

Dibbins instantly became guarded. "I know Namour."

"You have told us that he is not on the premises; am I correct?"

"You are correct. He is not here. Are you looking for him?"

"We would like to ask Namour some questions."

Dibbins laughed humorlessly. "I suspect that if anything mysterious is going on, Namour is the man to ask."

"How well do you know him?"

"Not well. He is a friend of Madam Zigonie. She allows him to come here for his sojourns, and I have nothing to say in the matter."

"Your opinion of Namour is not favorable, then?"

"I work for Madame Zigonie. I am not entitled to opinions. Still, I must deal with Namour's Yips and I cannot avoid dissatisfaction."

"What about Titus Zigonie and Madame: have they visited the ranch recently?"

Dibbins shook his head. "It has been almost a year, and then they were only in and out. But I shall have something to say to them when next they arrive."

"Such as?"

Dibbins waved his hand toward the yard. "I refer to the Yips. They won't work unless you bring out beer to the job; then after an hour or two they become merry and start skylarking and there is still no work done, but the celebration continues until all the beer is gone. Then they lie down and sleep, and nothing will induce them to resume their duties."

"You should give them back to Namour."

"He won't take them. Still, he can't sell any more on Rosalia! Their habits are now well known."

"Are you acquainted with Lewyn Barduys?"

Dibbins frowned toward the ceiling. "The name is familiar."

"He is an important construction magnate. He travels with a young woman whom he describes as his business associate. She is a beautiful creature, highly intelligent, with bright hair and a magnetic figure. Her name is Flitz."

Dibbins' face brightened. "Ah, yes! Now I remember them!"

"What was the occasion?"

"It was several years ago, not long after I first arrived. Madame Zigonie entertained them here at the ranch. They called me in to hear what I had to say about the Yips. I suspect this was at Barduys' suggestion. Namour apparently wanted to supply Barduys two or three gangs of Yips. Barduys mentioned that he had tried Yips before, with no success, but Namour assured him that such problems were in the past, that now they made more careful selection from the available stock, or something of the sort; I remember only that Namour was making assurances to Barduys, and that I was expected to corroborate his assertions. Since I had my job to consider, I made the satisfactory responses, but I doubt if Barduys were deceived. Then I was dismissed and that is all I know."

Chilke asked: "When did you last see Namour?"

For the first time Dibbins hesitated. "It has been quite some time."

"Please be more precise."

Dibbins became surly. "I don't like talking about another man's business. Also, Madame Zigonie might prefer that I keep a discreet tongue in my head. Perhaps I should not say this, but she seems to have made a favorite of Namour, if you grasp my meaning."

Glawen spoke stiffly: "Our authority transcends that of Madame Zigonie. We wish to question Namour in connection with several crimes. Whoever obstructs us becomes an accomplice to these crimes."

"If I must tell you, then I will do so," growled Dibbins. "Namour arrived here something about a month ago. I had the impression that he was waiting for something, because every day at the same time he made a telephone call, I think to Port Mona. Three or four days ago a call came through with the information he had been waiting for, and he left an hour later."

"Where did the call originate?"

"The caller asked for Namour Clattuc. That is all I know."

"After he took the call, was he pleased? Annoyed? Dissatisfied?"

"If anything, he seemed nervous, or under strain."

"Can you think of anything else to tell us?"

"No—because I know nothing."

Glawen and Chilke rose to their feet. "May I use your telephone?"

Dibbins indicated the instrument, on a table to the side of the room. Glawen called the IPCC office in Port Mona; he asked that Namour be apprehended and held in custody if he showed himself. Wincutz gave assurances that appropriate procedures would be initiated at once.

Glawen broke the connection and turned to Dibbins. "You have been cooperative. We appreciate your help."

Dibbins merely grunted and conducted his visitors to the door. Here Glawen issued a last admonition: "Inform no one that we have been here. Am I clear on this?"

"Perfectly clear," growled Dibbins.

V.

Glawen and Chilke returned to Lipwillow on the Big Muddy River. In Poolie's, at the end of the pier, they watched the sun settle into the water, drank beer and discussed what they had learned, which was not inconsiderable. Barduys had not shown himself at Shadow Valley Ranch. This fact indicated much or nothing. Perhaps he had delayed along the route. Shadow Valley Ranch might or might not have been his destination. He might already have landed at one of the other ranches. Perhaps he was indeed interested in the 'social evolution' of the Yips. Why? It was a futile exercise even to frame the question. They already had seen a number of Yips: those of the camp near Port Mona, the Lipwillow Yips and those still resident at Shadow Valley Ranch. There had been no indications of 'social evolution.' There were at least two other such camps: the Honeyflower Yips who had drifted south to Tooneytown, and the Stronsi Yips, now resident on the Mystic Isles of Muran Bay.

In the morning Glawen called the IPCC office in Port Mona, and was informed that Namour could not be found and apparently had not showed himself in the vicinity, but that vigilance would be maintained.

VI.

The flitter departed Lipwillow and set off on a course which took it east by north: back across La Mar, over the Corybantic Ocean to the continent Ottilie. Dawn found the flitter drifting over a vast patchwork quilt of flowers. At noon a line of seven snow-capped volcanic cones thrust above the northern horizon, by which Glawen and Chilke knew that they had entered the territory of the Honeyflower Ranch. Half an hour later they brought the flitter down at the ranch headquarters. The ranch house occupied the crest of a low hill, overlooking a meadow; a mile to the north loomed a typical Rosalia forest: dark, eery, ominous.

The proprietor was Alix Eth, a ruddy-faced man of energy and decision. He answered their questions without hesitation. His assessment of Namour was unfavorable; Eth adjudged him a clever scoundrel who sailed as close to the wind as possible. Eth's experiences with the Yips were typical. When he discovered their inutility, he tried to find Namour, that they might arrive at some sort of adjustment, but Namour was "gone like a wind-waif"—so Eth put it.

As a last resort Eth tried to teach the Yips the basic routines of civilized inter-action. He assembled the entire crew and explained a novel system which would resolve all problems. No longer would he give them orders regarding their work; he would neither curse them nor hector them when they lay down to rest; they were at liberty to perform as they liked. Eth saw by the shine in their eyes and their smiles of happiness that, so far, the program had found favor. "Now then," said Eth, "how shall we regulate the system, to ensure that those who work the hardest receive the most benefits? The system is simplicity itself. The work shall be measured in terms of coupons. When the worker performs a unit of work, he will receive a coupon. These coupons will be valuable tokens. They can be redeemed at the bunkhouse for shelter and at the cookhouse for food. Work equals coupons; coupons equal sustenance. That is all there is to it. Is everything clear?"

The Yips were interested in the system, but puzzled. They examined the sample coupons and asked: "We are to receive these coupons each day and then we turn them in at the compound each night?"

"Just so."

"Very well; it seems needlessly complex but we will try it. Give us the coupons now."

"Not now! You receive the coupons after you perform what we shall call a 'unit of achievement.' That is the novelty of the system."

After a day or so the Yips told Eth that the new system was unsatisfactory; that the different units and their equivalence with coupons was a source of bewilderment. They preferred the old way of doing things which seemed less technical and easier for everyone concerned.

The old way was gone forever, said Eth, and the new way would gradually become less perplexing. The Yips need remember only three words: Work equals coupons.

The Yips grumbled that they did not care to toil all day for little bits of paper, which were worthless except at the cook-house. Eth told them that if they thought they could do better elsewhere, they were welcome to try, and the Yips went away baffled. During the next few weeks the Yips departed the ranch in small groups. They drifted south to Tooneytown, where they settled in a wild area of swamps and thickets near the river Toon.

"They seem quite happy," Eth admitted. "They live off the land and coupons are only a memory."

Chilke asked: "What about the Stronsi Yips?"

"Their condition, so I am told, is similar," said Eth. "They moved to some semi-tropical islands in Muran Bay and live in primordial bliss."

"In other words—why work?"

"I began to wonder, myself," said Eth. "I'll tell you how

I made up my mind. At Tooneytown the Yips live at the back of a thornberry thicket, alongside a swamp, where the fetch-grass grows in tussocks and produces big pods full of seeds. The Yips boil these seeds for their porridge, which tastes like sour mud. They put the porridge in a pot with swamp water, throw in some tamarinds and bitter-root and pretty soon they have a vile beer, which they drink by the gallon. They brought in some low-caste women from Tooneytown to keep them warm at night. I tasted the porridge, I drank some of the beer, I looked at the women, and decided I would rather work."

Glawen and Chilke flew south to Tooneytown. They arrived halfway into the afternoon and took lodging at the Old Divan Hotel: a tall structure of damson planks, posts and pillars, weathered to a somber russet-brown, and built to the tenets of an unusual rococo architecture, which had been the prideful whim of Mrs. Hortense Tooney.

Glawen and Chilke dined in the garden to the light of colored lanterns. They sat long at the table, drinking wine and pondering the progress of their investigation. They decided that 'social evolution' was absent at Tooneytown, and no doubt equally so among the Stronsi Yips. Chilke declared: "I now suspect that whatever Barduys was looking for on Rhea, it was not 'social evolution.'"

"Someday we may learn the truth," said Glawen.

In the morning the two departed Tooneytown. They flew south-by-east and late in the evening arrived at Port Mona. In the morning, after a brief call to Wincutz at the IPCC office, they crossed the square to the Factor's Communications Depot: the joint post office, omnigraph and telephone junction servicing all Rosalia.

A clerk of advanced years, frail, sallow, with dank grey hair and a long lumpy nose, peered at them, then took them into the office of the General Superintendent Theo Callou: a man of great girth, squat and heavy of shoulder with bulging black eyes and a short brush of coarse black hair at the back of a pale receding forehead. Callou's nose was a button, but his jaw and chin were large, harsh blocks of bone. He asked: "Yes? You wish to see me?"

Glawen introduced himself and Chilke. "I believe that Superintendent Wincutz mentioned our business with you."

Callou leaned back in his seat. "So you are the two he mentioned!" The implication seemed to be that Callou had expected persons of a different sort. Glawen said stiffly, "This is Commander Chilke. I am Commander Clattuc. Do you wish to examine our credentials?"

Callou flourished his arm. "No, not at all. Quite unnecessary. There have been telephone calls which interested you; am I correct?"

Glawen nodded. "During the last month a certain Namour Clattuc called from Shadow Valley Ranch to an unknown destination. A few days ago he received a call from Port Mona. We want as much information as possible regarding these calls."

"My dear fellow! To persons of perspicacity all things are possible! Let us look and let us learn!" Callou swung his arm and thumped buttons. Information appeared on a screen. "Ha! See there! Calls from Shadow Valley Ranch to— to where? To Port Mona. Now then, with a will! To where in Port Mona? Ha hah! To the post office, under our very noses! Well then indeed! We push a few buttons and see what we learn!"

"Amazing," said Chilke.

"That is not all!" declared Callou. He turned his head and cried: "Trokke? Where are you?"

The clerk blinked through the doorway. "Sir?"

"Trokke! Explain, if you can, these calls from Shadow Valley Ranch!"

"Oh yes, to be sure! They originate from a gentleman of good quality, a certain Namour Clattuc."

"And their content?"

"Always the same, sir! On each occasion he asked if a message had arrived for him."

"Now then! And what of this call, from Port Mona?"

Trokke blinked, unsure of his ground. "That was my call, sir: notification that his message had indeed arrived."

Callou studied the clerk with intense concentration, eyes bulging, cheeks puffed out. "You were motivated to this deed by your native altruism?"

"There was a small emolument involved. Nothing of an irregular sort."

"Naturally not! Describe the message."

"It came in on the omnigraph: a most cryptic statement. But I read it to Mr. Clattuc and he seemed satisfied."

"And where is the message now?"

"It is filed under 'C' in the Restante cabinet. Mr. Clattuc never called."

"Fetch this message!" roared Callou. "Bring it here on the double-time!"

"Yes sir." Trokke turned away and presently returned with a sheet of paper. "It is a curious document, as you will see, sir. No salute, no signature, not even any substance."

"Never mind; we will perform our own analyses! Hand it over!" Callou took the sheet, squinted down at the characters and read: "'Line-check N.'" He looked up. "Is this all?"

"That is all, sir!" quavered Trokke.

"Most peculiar!"

Glawen took the sheet with the message. "'Line-check N,'" he read. "From where was it sent?"

Callou pointed to a strip of code at the bottom of the page. "This is the date, and the time, and the code for the transmitting office. '97.' Trokke! Who is '97'?"

"That is the Stronsi Ranch, sir."

"Who is in residence at the Stronsi Ranch?"

"That is hard to say. At my last sure knowledge the owner was off-world. Mr. Alhaurin is currently the resident manager."

At the offices of the Factor's Association, the secretary verified Trokke's suppositions. "It's been a strange story up there at Stronsi. After the great disaster, trustees took charge and managed the estate for ten years, I suppose while they were sorting things out. They finally turned the ranch over to the new owner, but no one ever took up residence. Recently there have been rumors of activity and new projects but so far nothing is happening. Meanwhile Mr. Alhaurin has stayed on as ranch manager.

Chilke asked: "What was this great disaster you mentioned?"

The clerk, a round little woman, pink-faced, with blonde corkscrew curls, shook her head in a renewal of shock. "It was quite terrible! It happened at Bainsey Castle; I visited there once as a little girl and it seemed absolutely impregnable!"

"And where is Bainsey Castle?"

"Far to the north, on the edge of the slutes. The family liked to go there for holidays and special times." The clerk rummaged in a file-cabinet and brought out a large photograph, which she placed on the counter. "These are the Stronsis, all twenty-seven of them and all destroyed!"

Glawen and Chilke examined the photograph. At the back stood the elders, with the younger generations on the steps below. They ranged in age from a patriarch of advanced years to four children on the bottom step: a solemn boy of nine, an equally solemn blond girl of seven, two more small boys, aged four and five.

"The old man is Myrdal Stronsi," said the clerk. "This lady is Adelie; she was a wonderful musician, and so was this young man Jeremy. The children were Glent and Felitzia and Donner and Milfred. They were all very fine people!" The clerk sniffed. "I was at school with some of them, and all died on the damnable slues!"

"And what are the slues?"

The clerk lowered her voice, as if verging upon a forbidden subject. "It is a flat waste of black stone, flowing with water from the sea. When the tide is out, there are pools and puddles and the water-waifs skip like black mad things. When the tide turns, sheets of water come swirling and foaming, as far as you can see. When storms blow in off the ocean, waves move across the slues, breaking and reforming to break again.

The Stronsis thought they were safe in Bainsey Castle but it was old and the storms had weakened the walls; still the Stronsi clan went to Bainsey castle for their celebration, and it must have started out in all the best tradition, with roaring fires, plenty to eat and drink and a view across the slues, which was always changing— sometimes blank and wet, sometimes wild and terrible. Sometimes on a calm sunny morning even weirdly beautiful. But it was the season of storms and the view reminded them how secure and cozy they were, and sometimes they could see the water-waifs out in the wastes, dancing and sliding like crazy things. So while the Stronsis celebrated a storm came up and sent black-green waves across the slues and over the castle. The walls creaked and groaned and collapsed. The stones were scattered by the waves and the Stronsi clan was destroyed."

"Then what?"

"Nothing. The trustees took ten years to track down the heir; meanwhile they hired Petar Alhaurin as ranch manager, and the new ownership has kept him on. So far we haven't seen them at Port Mona, but of course they are around the other side of the planet, on the east coast of Almyra."

VII.

Glawen and Chilke had become bored with the cramped cabin of the flitter. The arguments for discreet movement and unobtrusive investigation remained as strong as ever; still, at the terminal they relinquished the flitter and took the Fortunatus aloft. Setting a course to the northeast they flew away from Port Mona: over the continent Eclin, the Saraband Straits and beyond. The sun rolled west and set. The Fortunatus flew on through the night: across the continents Koukou and Almyra, to meet the dawn at the shore of the Maenadic Ocean, near the town Port Twang. Thirty miles north the Stronsi Ranch headquarters occupied the crest of a hill beside the Fesque River: a long low heavy-walled structure with an irregular roof-line, almost indistinguishable from the stony outcrop on which it was built. To the sides and around the back grew a dozen black yew trees; there was no other garden. Glawen and Chilke, approaching at low altitude, discovered no obvious signs of habitancy; neither aircraft nor space vehicle nor surface car were visible.

The Fortunatus landed on a flat near the front of the house. Glawen and Chilke alighted and stood for a moment, taking stock of their surroundings. The time was mid-morning. A fleet of high cirrus clouds moved slowly across the sky, occasionally obscuring the sun. At their backs the ground sloped down to the river. There was nothing to be heard but the whisper of the wind. Glawen said: "If Namour is watching us, he may be tempted to shoot first and ask questions later."

"So I was thinking," said Chilke.

The front door opened and a small servant maid looked out at them. "She's not carrying a gun, and she looks rather frail," said Chilke. "I think it's safe."

The two approached the house across a stone-flagged terrace.

"Good morning," said Glawen. "We want to speak with Mr. Alhaurin."

"Mr. Alhaurin is not here. He's gone off to Port Twang."

"We'll settle for whoever is in charge."

"At the moment that would be the lady."

The servant ushered them into a sitting room. "Who shall I announce?"

"Commander Chilke and Commander Clattuc of the Cadwal Constabulary."

The maid departed. Several minutes passed. The house was silent. A young woman appeared in the doorway. Glawen's jaw dropped. It was Flitz. She looked from one to the other, recognizing neither. Glawen had met her at Riverview House a year or two previously. Had he made so slight an impression? He controlled his pique. Flitz was Flitz; this was well known. She wore tan trousers and a dark blue pullover shirt. She was of medium height, slim with an erect posture. A black ribbon tied her bright hair back from her face.

Glawen decided that he was not as surprised to see Flitz as he might have been. He spoke. "I am Commander Glawen Clattuc, and this is Commander Eustace Chilke. May we speak with Lewyn Barduys?"

Flitz shook her head. "He has gone off to look over a construction site." Her voice was cool but civil.

"When will he be back?"

"Later in the day. This was not a scheduled trip, so I can be sure of nothing."

"What do you mean by that?"

Flitz made a small gesture, which might have been interpreted as a twitch of impatience, though her face and voice remained cool. "He went up to meet our foundations engineer; there was some sort of problem at the site."

"What kind of construction is underway?" asked Chilke.

Flitz surveyed him dispassionately. "Nothing is underway at this time. Several projects are being considered." She turned back to Glawen. "If you care to explain your business, I may be able to help you."

"Perhaps so. Is there an omnigraph on the premises?"

"Yes—in the manager's office."

"May we see it?"

Flitz wordlessly led the way down a long dim hall to a room in the north wing furnished with office equipment. She pointed toward a desk. "There is the omnigraph."

"Have you used it recently?"

"I have not used it at all."

"What about Mr. Barduys?"

"I don't think so. This is Mr. Alhaurin's office."

Glawen went to the machine. He verified that the station identification number was '97.' He activated the automatic recording device, which indicated that the last message had been despatched four days previously, to the Port Mona Post Office. Glawen read the record. "'Line check N.'"

Flitz said: "That is an odd message."

"So it is," said Glawen. "Where is Alhaurin now?"

Flitz showed little interest in the subject. "I think he went into Port Twang."

"You don't know where to find him?"

Flitz merely jerked her shoulders and stared moodily off across the room.

"Are you acquainted with Namour Clattuc?"

"I know who he is: yes."

"This is a message from the manager Alhaurin to Namour. Can you get in touch with Mr. Barduys?"

"I can call his flitter, but if he and Mr. Bagnoli are out on the site, he would not respond."

"It might be a good idea to try."

Flitz went to a telephone, entered a code and waited. There was no response. "He is out on the site," said Flitz. "You will have to wait until he returns." She led the way back to the sitting room. "It will be at least an hour or perhaps two; that is my best guess. Nesta will bring you refreshments." She turned to leave.

"Just a minute. Perhaps you will answer some questions."

Flitz used her cool clear monotone. "Later, perhaps. Not at the moment." She went to the doorway, turned a glance back over her shoulder, as if to make sure that the visitors were not already up to mischief, then left the room.

Glawen gave a grunt of dissatisfaction and went to look out the window. Chilke wandered to the side of the room, where shelves displayed artifacts of virtue and cunning craftsmanship. Glawen turned away from the window and went to sit on the couch. "All taken with all, it has not gone too badly. If nothing else, we have located Barduys and we know why he came to Rosalia."

Chilke joined Glawen on the couch. "You are referring to the construction projects?"

"Correct. Namour is involved—somewhere, somehow. Flitz probably could clarify everything if she were in the mood. But she prefers to snub us, and make sure that we are properly cowed."

"Strange that she is not more curious about us!" mused Chilke. "I suppose it is all part of the inscrutability package."

"More likely it's just what it seems to be: indifference, or some weird sort of hostility, towards the human race."

"Her hormones would seem to be in good running order. I say this on the basis of a casual glance."

Glawen leaned back in the couch. "It's too complicated for me. So far as I'm concerned, the mystery of Flitz must remain just that."

Chilke smilingly shook his head. "There is no real mystery."

Glawen sighed. "Tell me about it."

After a moment's reflection, Chilke said: "Look at it this way. If you were asked to describe that old yew out yonder, your first statement would be: 'It is a tree.' In the same way, when asked to describe Flitz, first you would say: 'This creature is a woman.'"

"Is there more?"

"It is only the starting point. I won't go so far as to say that all women are alike; that is a popular misconception. Still, basic principles never change."

"You have left me behind. How does this apply to Flitz?"

"At first glance she might seem mysterious and inscrutable. Why? Could it be that she is actually shy and demure, and emotionally immature?"

"Marvelous!" declared Glawen. "How do you divine all this, so quickly?"

"I have had experience with these hoity-toity types," said Chilke modestly. "There is a trick for dealing with them."

"Hm," said Glawen. "Can you divulge a few details?"

"Of course! But keep in mind that patience is involved. You sit off by yourself, pretending disinterest, and watching the sky or a bird, as if your mind was fixed on something spiritual, and they can't stand it. Pretty soon they come walking past, twitching just a bit, and finally they ask your advice about something, or wonder if they can buy you a drink. After that, it is simply a matter of docking the boat."

The maid Nesta appeared, bearing a tray of sandwiches, a teapot and cups, which she placed upon a table, then departed. Flitz strolled into the room. She glanced at the tray as she moved to the window and looked around the sky. Then she turned and surveyed her visitors. She nodded toward the tray. "Help yourselves."

"We were waiting for you to pour the tea, since you are the hostess," said Chilke. "In our business we try to be as polite as possible."

"You may pour," said Flitz. "It is not impolite to pour tea."

Chilke poured out three cups of tea, one of which he tendered to Flitz. She shook her head. "Why are you here?"

Glawen hesitated. "It is a complex business."

"Tell me anyway."

"Are you aware of conditions on Cadwal?"

"To some extent."

"Cadwal is now governed by a new Charter, which is much like the old, except that it is stronger and more definite. At Stroma the LPF group is defying the new law. So is Simonetta Zigonie who controls the Yips. Smonny and Titus Zigonie also own Shadow Valley Ranch, as you probably know."

"Yes. I know."

"At Araminta Station we are in trouble. Both the LPF and Smonny intend to move Yips to the mainland of Deucas, and so destroy the Conservancy. These people outnumber us, and in the end they would win. We are fighting for both the Conservancy and our lives. So far, they are deterred by three factors: first, our patrol craft still have an edge in firepower. Second, they need transport to move the Yips ashore. They hope Lewyn Barduys will supply such transport. Third, the LPF and Smonny can't agree on priorities—much less eventualities. If you find this confusing, I won't be surprised."

"I am confused only as to your reasons for coming here."

"We hope to intercede with Mr. Barduys, so that he will not help either Smonny or the LPF."

"You need not concern yourselves. Both Dame Clytie and

Smonny have applied to Mr. Barduys, but he has no intention of helping either."

"That's good news."

Chilke said: "We are also hoping to locate Namour. Apparently you came to Rosalia with the same purpose in mind."

Flitz looked at him with a blank expression. "Why do you say that?"

"We heard something to this effect on Rhea."

Once more Flitz went to the window and looked around the sky. She said, without emphasis: "You were misled—to a large extent, at least."

Glawen asked politely: "Would you care to explain?"

"We had other reasons for coming to Rosalia. Mr. Barduys hoped, in passing, that he might find Namour here."

"Namour was waiting for you," said Glawen. "As soon as you arrived, Alhaurin notified him at Shadow Valley Ranch."

"So it seems. Mr. Barduys will discover what is going on and deal with Alhaurin accordingly."

"Evidently you are not on good terms with Namour?"

Flitz became haughty. "The matter is surely beyond the scope of your authority."

"Not so! Anything concerning Namour concerns me."

Flitz shrugged. "The business is simple enough. Mr. Barduys had supplied Namour an expensive piece of equipment. Namour wanted to alter the terms of payment."

Chilke inquired: "Then L-B Construction has brought you here, and not Namour?"

"That is approximately correct."

"Can you tell us what is being constructed?"

"It is no secret. When we were last on Cadwal, we visited the wilderness lodges. Both Mr. Barduys and I were favorably impressed. He has long been interested in hostelries and country inns, from a philosophical viewpoint. After visiting the Cadwal lodges he decided that he wanted to create something of the same sort."

"And what of you?"

"The lodges are pleasant to visit. I'm not particularly interested otherwise."

Chilke asked: "Why did Mr. Barduys fix upon Rosalia as a site for his constructions?"

Flitz shrugged. "Rosalia has a good climate. The scenery is dramatic. Tourists are fascinated by the waifs and the big trees. He is acquainted with Stronsi Ranch and he has several sites in mind which he considers favorable. So he organized a project team and set the work in motion."

"What of the owner? Does he approve of the scheme?"

Flitz showed the trace of a grim smile. "The owner made no difficulties."

A chime sounded. Flitz went to the telephone. She spoke and was answered by a burst of staccato statements, as if from a release of pent irritation.

Flitz asked a question and was answered. She spoke again, giving instructions, then broke the connection. Slowly she turned back to Glawen and Chilke. She spoke in a flat voice: "That was Bagnoli,"

"The engineer?"

Flitz nodded. "He is still at Port Twang. A message directed him to meet Lewyn at Abel's Store, south of town. He went to this place and waited a long time, then returned to the original rendezvous. Lewyn had come and gone. Bagnoli thinks that Alhaurin was responsible for the false message."

"Alhaurin or Namour."

"So now Lewyn has gone to the site alone, and I am afraid."

"Tell us how to find this site."

"I will take you there."

CHAPTER 6

I.

The Fortunatus flew north over a landscape that became ever more bleak. Below passed a line of stone peaks, naked as shark's teeth; a forest of gnarled witchtrees, a plain where nothing grew but yellow-gray sedge. By degrees the ground sagged and became a morass split by a river of dark stagnant water. "The river is low," said Flitz. "We are just coming into the season of storms." She pointed to heavy black and purple clouds banked above the eastern horizon. "Bad weather is already on the way."

Glawen looked over the landscape ahead, to a line of distant mountains. "How far now to the site?"

"Not far. The slutes are just beyond the mountains, and also the ruins of Bainsey Castle. It is a terrible place—but it is where Lewyn Barduys wants to build the first of his lodges."

The Fortunatus flew on: over a dismal waste marked by patches of black and brown lichen. To the east appeared the leaden glint of open water: the Maenadic Ocean. Hills rose below, then mountains. Across the ridge the land dropped away sharply; and to the north, as far as the eye could reach, spread the slutes: a peneplain of black rock, stark, bare, flat as a table except for shallow basins where water reflected the sky. At the edge of the slutes, near a low crag, were the tumbled ruins of Bainsey Castle. The area seemed deserted; there was no sign either of Barduys or the vehicle in which he might have arrived.

The Fortunatus landed beside the crag, a hundred yards from the ruins. The three jumped to the ground, and immediately felt the force of the fresh wind. The scene, thought Glawen, was both awesome and eerily beautiful, unlike any he had seen or even imagined. Black clouds rolled across the sky: precursors to a storm. Wind propelled waves from the sea upon the slutes; water surged and hissed in sheets over the flat black stone. Out upon the waste water-waifs danced and cavorted like demons. It was an ideal site for a wilderness lodge, a new Bainsey Castle so strong and massive that the impact of green waves could be ignored, where visitors could look out over the unreal panorama in comfort and security.

Glawen turned to Flitz. "He's not here!"

"He must be here! This is where he said he was coming!"

Glawen looked all around the rocky flat. "I don't see his flitter."

"He came up in the Flecanpraun."

Glawen made no comment. Flitz set off down the slope toward the ruins. Glawen and Chilke followed, weapons ready for surprise.

Flitz stopped short and pointed. Glawen and Chilke, looking down toward a tumble of boulders, saw a flitter which had landed on a narrow flat close beside a jut of rock, as if for concealment. Flitz raised her voice to be heard over the rush of the wind. "That is the ranch flitter!"

Chilke scrambled down to the flitter. Almost at once he called back. His words reached Glawen and Flitz blown by the wind. "There is a body down here! It is not Barduys!"

Flitz joined him. "It is Alhaurin." She searched around the area, then finding nothing more she picked her way over the rocks to where she could look across the ruins of Castle Bainsey. "Lewyn!" she called out: "Lewyn! Where are you?"

Her voice was carried away on the wind. The three listened, but heard only the hiss of flowing water and the moaning wind.

The water-waifs had noticed the intruders. Dancing and jerking, they approached by sidling darts and retreats: black figures about man-size, seemingly all arms and legs, so fluid and quick in their movements that the eye was never able to focus upon them, nor determine the exact nature of their being. Flitz paid them no heed. She jumped down into the ruins, calling out and peering into crannies and crevices. Suddenly she gave a cry of startlement and jerked back, so abruptly that she almost fell. From nearby shadows darted four water-waifs brandishing pointed poles. They scurried pell-mell out upon the slutes as if in a hysteria of fear or glee, or whatever might be their emotion; at a distance of fifty yards they halted and skittered about, bounding, sliding, waving their poles.

Flitz looked down into the declivity from which they had issued. Glawen and Chilke joined her. Almost at the bottom, with water from the slutes seething in and out, lay Barduys, half-submerged in a puddle.

Flitz began to climb down the slope. Glawen halted her. "You can't do anything down there! Stay here; cover us with your gun; keep those black things off our backs."

Glawen jumped into the decline, followed by Chilke. The water-waifs disapproved of their actions and came sliding across the rocks. Glawen told Chilke: "Keep me covered." He dropped down the last six feet, and bent over Barduys. He was not dead. At Glawen's touch his eyelids flickered and he whispered: "My legs are broken."

Glawen gripped him from behind, under the armpits, and dragged him from the puddle. Barduys hissed between his teeth, but said nothing. Glawen bent for another effort, and drew Barduys up the slope. He heard Chilke's scream of outrage as water-waifs slid into the pit and flung themselves downward. Never, for so long as he lived, would Glawen forget the feel of that sinewy dank body and its groping limbs. He kicked and fought; something tore at his thigh; something else scratched his face; he was stabbed in the shoulder and chest and leg. Chilke's gun sent explosive slugs into the surging bodies. Glawen tore off the creature which wanted to cling to him and nuzzle his neck with one of its organs. He threw it aside and Chilke shot it.

Water-waifs, coming from the slutes, scurried this way and that, then bounded forward. Keeping them in sight Flitz descended into the pit a short way, adjusted the aperture of her weapon to the third notch and discharged a swath of energy into the swarm. Some became crisps of fiber; the others twittered in horror and tumbled back.

Glawen and Chilke hauled Barduys up from the declivity. He seemed more dead than alive, and his legs dragged as if they were rags. Glawen began to feel dizzy; what was happening to him? He blinked and again saw water-waifs jumping from the ruined walls. Chilke was sent sprawling, down into the puddle. The waifs fell upon him; he seized one and dashed it against the rock; Glawen fired his gun and destroyed the others. Chilke struggled back up the slope. Water-waifs heaved large rocks which struck Chilke and sent him rolling back down into the puddle. Painfully he began once more to crawl upwards; another stone struck him, but he flattened, clung to the ground and saved himself from falling again. A bolt from Glawen's gun destroyed the rock-throwing waif. Chilke continued to crawl, aware of broken bones. He managed, finally, to rejoin Glawen and Flitz.

After an interminable effort, the group reached the Fortunatus. Chilke, limping and stumbling, with Flitz's help carried Barduys into the Fortunatus. Glawen found that he could no longer control his muscles and fell to the ground. Flitz and Chilke, his broken bones grinding, carried him aboard.

Chilke staggered to the controls; the Fortunatus rose into the air and flew south.

At first inspection it was evident that Barduys had suffered a blow to the head; a gun-shot wound in the chest, broken bones, and a number of puncture wounds, already surrounded by yellow discoloration. Glawen had been scratched, beaten and stabbed, his left arm had been broken. Around the puncture marks were puffy rings of purulence. Chilke had escaped with broken ribs, a broken collarbone, a cracked femur, a single poisonous puncture wound; nevertheless he felt light in the head and dizzy.

Flitz called the hospital at Port Mona and asked that emergency medical service be despatched to Stronsi Ranch. She mentioned that members of her group had been attacked by water-waifs and seemed to have been poisoned. The hospital medic prescribed a combination of standard all-purpose antidotes from the shipboard medicine chest. "With any luck it will keep them alive until we can get at them. We'll also send a team from the Port Twang dispensary."

Flitz followed the instructions; Barduys and Glawen desisted from their trembling and relaxed into dazed sleep.

At the moment there was nothing more to be done. Chilke tried to sit but his ribs protested. He hobbled forward to stand by the observation port, holding to a handrail for support. His mental processes were not functioning correctly; they seemed to be impeded by some sort of viscous medium. Perhaps time itself was moving at a decelerated rate. The condition augmented the accuracy of his perceptions. He heard sounds with exact fidelity and when he looked about, all colors and textures were rendered with an amazingly vivid precision. Too bad his mind was confused! "This is the way an insect looks at the world," Chilke told himself. In his ordinary condition, he would have welcomed these new sensitivities.

Gradually order returned to his mind and the unreal awareness began to wane. His thoughts slowly arranged themselves. He considered the awful events at Bainsey Castle.

They had occurred in a shattering rush; death had been close—perhaps too close. Barduys and Glawen lay pale and ominously quiet. Flitz had loosened their clothing and had made them as comfortable as possible. Chilke felt miserably sad. He turned back to the observation port. His mental images were vividly acute. He observed the ambush at Bainsey Castle as if he had been at the scene. Namour had come up behind the unsuspecting Barduys, who could hear nothing because of the wind. He had shot Barduys and pitched him into the pit. For some reason he shot Alhaurin as well, or perhaps Alhaurin was already dead. For a moment Namour stood considering his handiwork, his handsome face without expression. Then he had departed in the Flecanpraun, believing Barduys to be dead.

If Barduys survived, a ghastly surprise awaited Namour.

Chilke took stock of his own condition. It was not good. He ached in every part of his body; his head felt light and loose. Chilke drew a deep breath. He had never felt so oddly before. The effects of the poison? Vertigo? Something worse? He jerked forward and stared at the ground below. He blinked, squinted, moved his head back and forth as if to improve the focus of his eyes.

Flitz became aware of his behavior. She asked: "Mr. Chilke, are you well?"

"I can't be sure," said Chilke. He pointed. "Look down there, if you please."

Flitz examined the landscape. "Well?"

"If you saw a lot of strange colors—lavender, pink, orange, green—then I am sane. If you did not see these colors, I am very sick."

Flitz looked a second time. "We are passing over a swamp. You are looking at large mats of algae, all of different colors."

Chilke heaved a sigh. "That is good news—possibly."

"Is something else wrong?"

"I feel unreal, as if I were floating." He reached for Flitz in order to steady himself, and managed to clasp her with his sound arm. "That is better He looked into her face. "Flitz, you are a fine woman! I am proud of you!"

Flitz disengaged herself. "Come over here and sit down, I think the poison has affected you."

Chilke hobbled to the settee and lowered himself with a grimace.

"I will bring you some medicine. It is a tranquilizer and you will not feel so wild."

"I am better already; I won't need the medicine."

"Relax then and rest. We will soon be back at the ranch."

II.

Glawen and Barduys received emergency treatment from the Port Twang medical practitioner, who took instruction by communicator from senior medical personnel enroute from Port Mona.

For three days Glawen and Barduys lay quiet, less than half-conscious, and for a time Barduys seemed to waver between life and death. The medical team, using self-regulated therapeutic devices, remained in constant attendance, monitoring and controlling vital processes. Chilke, meanwhile, had been splinted, bandaged, treated with bone-mending techniques, and confined to bed.

Time passed. Glawen regained consciousness, but lay flaccid, gaining strength and awareness only slowly. Barduys awoke a day later. He opened his eyes, looked to right and to left, muttered something incomprehensible, then closed his eyes and seemed to doze. The attendants relaxed; the crises were past.

Two days later Barduys was able to speak. Slowly at first, and with frequent pauses to search his recollection, he described what had happened to him. At Port Twang he had received a message purportedly from Bagnoli, stating that plans had been changed and that the two would meet at Bainsey Castle. Barduys, puzzled but unconcerned, had flown north to the slutes. He saw no sign of Bagnoli, nevertheless he landed the Flecanpraun, jumped to the ground, and walked toward the proposed construction site. He passed close by a jut of rock; at this point the world collapsed upon him, and his memory became a set of blurred impressions. There had been a flurry of merciless blows while the sky reeled, then he was thrown into the pit. Down the rocks he tumbled, landing upon a huddle of writhing water-waifs. They cushioned the final shock and perhaps saved his life. Dimly Barduys thought to hear a muffled shot and felt a great blow against his chest. The water-waifs fled shrieking from the pit. There was a time of heavy silence; then the water-waifs were back, bounding and twittering in fury. Barduys painfully found his gun and fired at the waifs until they retreated. As soon as he became dazed, they slyly returned and prodded at him with sharp sticks. His gun held them at bay and finally they left him alone to die.

Flitz told him how he had been rescued. With an effort he looked from face to face. "I will not thank you now."

"You need not thank us at all," said Glawen. "We did what we thought to be our duty."

"So it may be," said Barduys in a colorless voice. "Duty or not, I am grateful. As for my enemy, I know his identity and I know why he tried to destroy me." For a moment Barduys lay quiet. Then he said: "I think that he will regret his failure."

"You are speaking of Namour?"

"Yes, Namour."

"Why should he do such a thing to you?"

"It's a long story."

"You must not tire yourself," Flitz told him.

"I will talk until I am tired and then I will stop."

Flitz gave Glawen and Chilke a disapproving look, then left the room.

Barduys began to speak. "I must go back to the beginning, which would be fifteen years ago. L-B Construction had done some work for the Stronsi family, and they wanted to talk over some new construction. I arrived to find that they had all gone north to Bainsey Castle for a day or two. This was no great inconvenience and I settled myself to wait.

"The whole clan had gone north: twenty-seven of them, many from off-world. The patriarch was Myrdal Stronsi; he and his wife Glaida lived at Stronsi, along with their sons Cesar and Camus, with their children and an aged aunt.

"It was to have been a merry occasion; the Stronsis were happy people, who enjoyed festivities in the old-fashioned manner, and they had gone to Bainsey Castle many times for just such a purpose. But on this occasion, a terrible storm came up, and sent green waves to batter against the castle. They had nowhere to go, and watched in horror as the stone walls collapsed and the green water dashed into the opening, and then it was all over.

"At Stronsi Ranch, when the communicator from Bainsey remained dead, we became worried and flew north to investigate. We found the ruins and the scattered corpses, some of which the water-waifs had dragged out on the slutes. We found no survivors, and, after calling for ambulances, everyone departed. But almost as soon as I was in the air, something began to tug at me. I became uneasy. I tried to reason with myself, but in the end I flew back alone. It was then late afternoon, and very quiet. I remember the scene well." Barduys paused for a moment, then continued. "In the west the sun had found an open space among the clouds and illuminated the slutes with the light that toward evening seems the color of sherry. A million puddles reflected a million spatters of light, and the water-waifs were hard to see for the glitter. I went close to the ruins and stood looking about. I thought I heard a cry, very weak and thin. If the wind had been blowing, I would not have heard it. At first I thought it was a water-waif, but I searched and finally, under a tumble of stones, I caught a glimpse of cloth. It was a little girl, who had been trapped beneath the stones. She had lain there for two nights with the water-waifs prowling about, thrusting sticks, trying to squeeze through the cracks.

"To make a long story short, I finally managed to drag her out, more dead than alive: a little girl about seven years old. I remember seeing her in the family portrait; she was Felixia Stronsi, the only survivor of the entire clan.

"There was no one to care for her. The trustees were far away, off-world and quite disorganized. I did not trust the Factor's Association, which was—and still is—hostile to the Stronsis. In the end I took her in charge, with the intention of finding a suitable foster home for her. But time went by and I made no moves in this direction, and presently I realized that I liked having her around.

"She was a strange little creature. At first she could not talk, and sat watching me with big eyes in a pinched little face. The shock finally wore away, but she had lost most of her memory and knew only that her name was 'Flitz.'"

Barduys paused, summoned the maid Nesta, who brought him the group photograph of the Stronsis, which Glawen and Chilke had already seen. The earnest little blonde girl, sitting cross-legged in the foreground was identified as 'Felitzia Stronsi.'

Barduys went on with his story. He became accustomed to the girl's presence and in the end the trustees of the Stronsi estate appointed him her guardian. He educated her as if she were his son, in the lore of construction, technics and mathematics, music and aesthetic perception, and the crafts of civilization.

Flitz grew through the ordinary phases of life in a more or less normal manner. When she was fourteen Barduys enrolled her at a private school on Old Earth, where she spent two terms. She was still thin and pale, but already conspicuous by reason of her sea-blue eyes, shining hair and delicate features. The staff considered her cooperative, if rather enigmatic.

At the end of the second term Flitz announced that she would not be returning in the fall. Indeed! demanded the head matron, and whyever not? It was simple enough, said Flitz; she wanted to resume her old life, travelling the far places of the Reach with Lewyn Barduys and L-B Construction. Argument was futile; the words 'decorum' and 'propriety' meant nothing. Flitz was sent back to Barduys, who welcomed her without comment.

Flitz eased through adolescence without trauma. Occasionally she took an interest in some stalwart young man, usually a member of the L-B construction personnel. Barduys never interfered; Flitz could do as she liked.

Flitz never liked to do very much. To the general misfortune of her suitors, Flitz could not avoid measuring them against Barduys. Seldom was there any doubt as to who might be the better man. Strangers often assumed that Flitz, was Barduys' mistress. Flitz was aware of the speculation, but cared not a fig. In all her memory he had never been other than gentle and patient; in his company she felt secure.

Flitz' memories of her early life had been muddled by the events at Bainsey Castle. She remembered the patriarch Myrdal Stronsi and her brothers, but her father and mother had vanished into the dark. One day Barduys mentioned that as Felitzia Stronsi, she owned Stronsi Ranch and perhaps it was time to look it over and see what could be done with it.

Flitz lacked enthusiasm for the idea, aware of misgivings which she ascribed to her early experiences. At Stronsi Ranch the ranch manager Alhaurin had taken up residence in the main structure and was not pleased to see them; at the very least they would be sure to dislocate his routines.

Flitz found Stronsi Ranch less menacing than she had feared, and even contrived a few tentative plans for making the massive old pile more cheerful. She found the bedroom once inhabited by the seven-year-old Felitzia, where nothing had been altered since the day of the great tragedy, depressing. Flitz could not bring herself to look through the personal belongings of the ill-fated little girl, and closed the door on the bedroom. One day she would bring in a house-cleaning crew and turn the old house inside out, but not just yet. There was too much to think about; too many plans to make.

Barduys looked through Alhaurin's accounts and was not pleased by what he found. Alhaurin had written invoices for materials which were now invisible. He had issued payment vouchers for work which had never been started, let alone completed.

Alhaurin had a dozen glib explanations ready to hand, but Barduys cut him short. "You need say no more. It is clear that you have been milking the maintenance funds by all four udders. The only answer I need from you is how you plan to make restitution."

"Impossible!" cried Alhaurin, and started a contorted explanation.

Barduys refused to listen and dealt judiciously with the misdeed and its perpetrator. Alhaurin henceforth would live at the manager's bungalow, as in the old days. Further, he must ensure that the supplies he purportedly had ordered and paid for were delivered, and that the works for which he had contracted were put in hand and completed. How Alhaurin would pay for these items was Alhaurin's own business; the money existed; it was noted on the books.

Alhaurin grumbled and complained, but Barduys gave him the choice between restitution and penalties, possibly legal, possibly not, which in either case Alhaurin would be sure to deplore.

Alhaurin threw his arms in the air and accepted his fate, and restitution was set in motion.

About this time Namour brought the first contingent of Yips to Shadow Valley Ranch.

Barduys had became acquainted with Namour, and decided to attempt the use of Yip labor. He contracted with Namour for two gangs of three hundred Yips apiece: one to be brought to Stronsi Ranch, the other to one of his construction sites.

Like all the others, Barduys soon found that the Yips were useless and that he had wasted the indenture fee. He was neither surprised nor annoyed. The Yips were psychologically incapable of functioning as paid laborers; he put the whole affair to the back of his mind and, with Flitz, departed Rosalia to see to a number of other more pressing concerns. When they returned they found that Alhaurin had repaired the worst of his delinquencies, and now seemed to be functioning efficiently. The Yips, so he reported, had all migrated south to the Mystic Islands in Muran Bay, where they lived such sybaritic idylls that Alhaurin wished that he might join them.

Barduys and Flitz found that he had not exaggerated. There were two hundred islands in Muran Bay. Most supported a highly picturesque vegetation, which was not infested with tree-waifs, so that one might explore the islands without fear of malign adventure. White beaches rimmed the calm lagoons, where danger lurked, and the rash swimmer would be pulled down and done to death by the water-waifs.

Yips from Stronsi Ranch had crossed over to several of the near islands. They built huts of palm thatch and lived in blessed indolence, nourished by wild fruit, pods, tubers, molluscs, sphids, and coconuts, from the ubiquitous coconut palm. They sang and danced by firelight to the tinkle of small lutes fabricated from dry red naroko wood.

Barduys and Flitz again left Rosalia, and for a period moved from place to place and world to world, dealing with the affairs of L-B Construction, and other enterprises now under Barduys' control.

During their wanderings they returned to Cadwal. A previous visit had acquainted them with the natural beauty of the landscape, the remarkable flora and fauna, and the unique quality of life at Araminta Station. On this occasion the two visited the wilderness lodges. These were relatively modest hostelries which merged unobtrusively into the most dramatic scenery of Cadwal, where the visitor could experience the sights, sounds and smells of the wilderness and its awesome inhabitants without risking death or—more importantly—disturbing natural processes.

Barduys was impressed by the lodges. The principles which guided their construction coincided with ideas of his own. During his lifetime he had sojourned at hundreds of hostelries and inns, of every sort and quality. On occasion he had noticed the passionate dedication an innkeeper lavished upon his premises: efforts unrelated to profit. Barduys saw that in such cases the inns were regarded as beautiful entities in their own right: 'art-objects,' so to speak. After visiting the wilderness lodges, he began to codify the precepts of this particular aesthetic doctrine.

First, there must be no self-consciousness. The mood of the inn must derive from simplicity and unity with the landscape. The excellent inn was a composite of many excellent factors, all important: site, outlook and their synergistic effect upon the architecture; the interior, which should be simple, free of ornament and overt luxury; the cuisine, neither spare nor elaborate and never stylish; the staff, polite but impersonal; the guests themselves. Additionally, there were indefinables and intangibles, which could not be foreseen and often not controlled. When Barduys remembered Bainsey Castle, he decided that here would be the site for the first of his inns. Next he would build several rustic lodges on the beaches of the Mystic Isles, staffed, perhaps, by handsome Yip men and lovely Yip maidens. The lagoons, at least in part, might be made safe for swimming. Elsewhere the water-waifs added a titillating element of danger to the otherwise idyllic peace of the islands. In small submarines guests could cruise the inter-island channels, exploring coral caverns and jungles of multi-colored sea-plants.

Such were Barduys' schemes. They were not shared by Flitz. She took only a casual interest in the project and refused to join Barduys in his planning.

In the lobby of the hotel at Araminta Station, Barduys was approached by Namour. For a time he chatted airily of this and that, while Barduys listened with grim amusement. Namour spoke of L-B Construction and its achievements. He expressed admiration at the scope of the great bridge on Rhea. "Installing foundations for the piers in those swift currents must have been a masterful feat in itself!" he declared.

"I employ competent engineers," Barduys told him. "They can build anything."

"I understand that you used a submarine during this operation."

"So we did."

"Out of curiosity, where do you use the submarine now?"

"Nowhere. It is still on Rhea, so far as I know. Sooner or later we must dispose of it."

"Interesting," said Namour. "The vessel is sound?"

"So I would imagine."

"What do you suppose its underwater range might be?"

Barduys shrugged. "I don't recall, exactly. It carries a crew of two and a half-dozen passengers. It can move at fifty knots and probably has a range of several thousand miles."

Namour nodded. "It just might be that I could arrange a sale for you, if the price were right."

"Indeed," said Barduys. "What is your offer?"

Namour laughed and made a deprecatory gesture. "Recently I met an eccentric gentleman who was convinced that the ruins of an alien civilization were sunk beneath the waters of the Mocar Sea on the world Tyrhoon. Do you know it?"

"No."

Namour went on. "He mentioned that he needed a small dependable submarine of long-range capability. It occurs to me that I might act as broker for the transaction."

"I will listen to your proposal, certainly."

Namour nodded thoughtfully. "In terms of trade, do you have any particular needs which might serve as a basis for discussion? I might work out some kind of complicated three-way deal."

Barduys smiled a small bitter smile. "You have sold me the labor contracts of six hundred Yips, all worthless, as you well knew. Now you expect me to deal with you again."

Namour chuckled, showing no discomfiture. "Sir, you wrong me. I gave not even the inkling of a warranty—and for a very good reason: I had no control over the working environment. The Yips will work if conditions are right; they have worked at Araminta Station for centuries."

"So what is the secret?"

"It is no secret. The Yip cannot understand a compulsion to work for something intangible, such as the need to pay off a debt. What is past is past. He will function in a system based upon tangible reality. One quantum of work must yield one quantum of payment, both exactly defined. So long as the Yip covets the payment he will do the work. He must never be allowed a surfeit, and never be paid in advance."

"You did not explain this when you delivered the yips."

"If I had done so, it might have been construed as a warranty, which I could not possibly undertake."

"Namour," said Barduys, "I give you credit for plausibility. But in any future transaction, I would insist upon terms carefully defined, from which you could not sidle or slide."

"Mr. Barduys, you wrong me," said Namour, with a pro forma show of indignation, which Barduys ignored.

"I think that I could use another contingent of Yips, of a certain sort. At least, this is my present thinking."

"I see no problem here."

"As I mentioned, the new contract will be defined precisely and its terms must be fulfilled exactly, to the last iota."

Namour pulled at his chin, and looked off across the lobby. "In theory this is desirable. Unfortunately, while I can promise the moon, my principals must approve everything. Still, I believe that the deal has prospects. What, precisely, are your terms?"

"First, I pay over no fees, of any kind. Next, you will transport the Yips in passenger ships, to a place of my designation."

"'Passenger ships'?" Namour's tone was doubtful. "These are Yips, not travelling aristocrats."

"Still, I do not care to have them hauled like cattle. I will charter the ships to you from my own passenger fleet."

"I suppose that is possible, depending upon charter fees."

"Cost, plus ten percent. You cannot do better."

Namour relaxed. "That seems, at the very least, negotiable. How many head do you require? Another six hundred?"

"I will need twenty thousand individuals, the sexes in equal proportion. They must be sound of limb and intellect, under the age of thirty: in other words, young folk in excellent health. These are my conditions. You must meet them exactly."

Namour's jaw dropped. "That is a very large consignment!"

"Wrong!" declared Barduys. "It is not large enough to solve your basic problem, which is the total evacuation of Lutwen Atoll to a hospitable environment off-world."

Namour responded in a subdued voice: "Still, I can't make so large a commitment without consultation."

Barduys turned away indifferently. "As you like."

"One moment," said Namour. "Back to the submarine: what about delivery?"

"That is no great problem. I own a very large transport which could carry the entire submarine as a unit. This I would charter to you on the same terms as those I previously quoted."

Namour nodded. "And what of confidentiality?"

"I don't care to know anything. Pick up the submarine, take it away—to Tyrhoon or Canopus or McDoodle's Planet; or anywhere you like. I will volunteer no information in regard to the transaction. If I am questioned by the IPCC, I shall tell what I know—which is that I sold you a submarine."

Namour grimaced. "I will give you an answer soon."

"It must be soon indeed, since I am leaving Cadwal directly."

Namour returned in a gloomy mood. The news was bad. Titus Pompo the Oomphaw—meaning Smonny—would not allow him a contingent so large. If Barduys wanted twenty thousand Yips, he must be prepared to accept persons of all ages, young to old. Barduys replied that he would accept a few Yips—perhaps as many as two thousand, evenly distributed in ages from thirty to fifty, provided that they were sound and healthy. He would compromise no farther; Namour's principals must accept the deal or forget it.

Namour gave grudging agreement to the terms, and

Barduys in due course implemented his end of the transaction. A large cargo vessel arrived at Rhea, swallowed the submarine and departed, for a destination unknown.

A month passed and Barduys became impatient, but finally the first contingent of Yips, numbering a thousand, was brought to a rendezvous on the world Merakin, before continuing to Rosalia. A team of doctors inspected the group, and instantly saw that Barduys' stipulations had been contemptuously ignored. Half of the thousand ranged in age from thirty-five to seventy-five. Of these, some were rachitic, while others were senile, or spoke in unknown languages. Of the younger group, about half were deformed, diseased, or psychotic. The others were of subnormal intelligence or sexually disoriented. The group could not have contributed in any way to the lyrical sad-sweet mood Barduys hoped to engender on his idyllic islands.

Barduys rejected the contingent out of hand. He sought out Namour, who put on a manner of bemused perplexity, as if at a loss to explain the vagaries of Titus Pompo—meaning Smonny. Barduys came to the point at once. He demanded that the contract be properly fulfilled. Namour agreed that serious misunderstandings had occurred, and that he would do his best to straighten matters out, though, of course, he could guarantee nothing.

Time passed. One day Namour arrived at Stronsi Ranch with discouraging news, to the effect that Titus Pompo had turned obstinate. He was now unwilling to yield so many of his subjects, unless Barduys sweetened the deal, with a few small extra inducements, such as a flight of four Straidor-Ferox gunships.

Barduys gave the proposal short shrift; the original contract must be fulfilled, or coercive action would be taken, into which Namour himself must be drawn.

Namour responded with a sad laugh. The matter, he declared, was out of his hands. Barduys shrugged and mentioned, quite casually, that he could sink the submarine at any time he chose. If it were in use at the time—too bad.

Namour was startled. "How can you do this?"

"'How' doesn't matter; it's what happens afterward that is important."

Namour, now in a subdued mood, suggested no more compromises. He said that he would explain Barduys' position to the other parties at interest, then departed.

"And there you have it," Barduys told Glawen and Chilke. "In the end Namour decided that the problem could best be solved by obliterating its source. He recruited Alhaurin and the two chose Bainsey Castle for their ambush."

Glawen asked: "So now—what next?"

Barduys answered in a soft voice. "I am a practical man, and I lack vanity—so I tell myself. Still ..." His voice trailed off. When he spoke again, the linkage between ideas was not immediately obvious. "The IPCC at Port Mona can find no trace of either Namour or the Flecanpraun. This is surely because both are gone from Rosalia."

"If Namour thinks you are dead, I might guess Cadwal."

Barduys, staring toward the ceiling, spoke, in a voice like metal sliding on metal. "If so, we will meet again quite soon."

Glawen became alert. "You plan to visit Cadwal?"

"As soon as I can step from this bed and walk without falling flat."

Glawen ruminated for a moment. Barduys would not travel so far on the off-chance of a meeting with Namour, gratifying though this occasion might prove. Almost certainly he had other projects in mind. Glawen was reluctant to ask, but he did so anyway. "Why are you going to Cadwal?"

Barduys spoke casually: "A few items of business hang loose in the air. Both Dame Clytie and Smonny have privately asked for my cooperation. At the moment they are bosom allies. Both want me to transport a horde of Yips to Deucas, to smash Araminta Station. Then each plans to harpoon the other."

"I hope that you will not oblige them."

Barduys chuckled. "Small chance of that."

"So what will you do?"

"Nothing."

There was a moment of silence. Then Barduys murmured, as if in afterthought: "That is to say, almost nothing."

"So, what is 'almost nothing'?"

The gaunt face showed a trace of animation. "It is quite simple. I want a word or two with Dame Clytie, to settle her doubts and ease her mind. I intend the same for Smonny; she deserves no less." Barduys paused. When he spoke again, his voice was soft. "Perhaps we will confer all together, and then— who knows what fine things might be the outcome?"

"I hope that Chilke and I will be on hand, if only as observers."

"A good idea." Barduys looked fretfully toward the medic who had come to monitor the therapeutic apparatus. "How long before I am free of these cursed gongs and meters?"

"Have patience! You were ninety-nine percent dead when you arrived. You will be down for at least another two weeks, and after that, consider each breath you take a miracle in itself."

Barduys relaxed. "There is no arguing with these fellows," he grumbled to Glawen. "They hold all the high cards. What of your own condition?"

"I am in relatively good shape, since I had only a fraction of what happened to you."

"And Eustace Chilke? He seems cheerful enough."

"He was soundly thumped. They threw big rocks at him and tried to pull him out upon the slutes with harpoons. But somehow he avoided most of the poison."

"Hmf," growled Barduys. "Chilke was born under a lucky star. That is the reason for his high spirits."

"Chilke is a practical man. He avoids fears, grief and dreary thoughts because they make him miserable."

Barduys considered a moment, then said: "The concept is sensible, but it is a bit surprising because of its simplicity."

"Chilke is often surprising. At the moment he has developed an admiration for Flitz. He suspects that she returns his interest."

Barduys managed a chuckle. "He is an optimist indeed. Such campaigns have been mounted before, with brave advances and hangdog retreats. Flitz may or may not have a soul."

"You do not disapprove?"

"Of course not! How could I? He saved my life—with a little help from you. In any event, Flitz does as she pleases."

III.

Glawen, in a wheelchair and Chilke, limping and hobbling, went out to sit on the terrace. The morning air was cool; the wind no more than a whisper. The balustrade and a pair of ironwood posts, to right and left, framed the view to the south, so that it seemed a landscape executed by a genius artificer in scratchings of black ink and sepia wash.

Glawen and Chilke sat blinking in the sunlight. Glawen told of his conversation with Barduys. "It means that at the very least we can return to Araminta Station and declare our mission a success."

Chilke agreed, with a single reservation. "A purist—such as Bodwyn Wook—might mention the name 'Namour.' We have not apprehended him."

"No matter. That particular case has been taken from our hands and transferred to a new jurisdiction."

"By orders of Barduys?"

Glawen nodded. "Barduys resents the loss of his Flecanpraun, not to mention the attack on his life. It is enough to answer any criticism Bodwyn Wook might make."

"Especially when we relinquish the Fortunatus to Bureau B, for Bodwyn Wook's official journeys."

Glawen winced. "There must be some way to avoid this sacrifice. Try as I might I have thought of nothing legal."

"Nor I."

"Barduys will not be on his feet for two weeks. I should be walking in a week."

"Do not strain yourself on my account," said Chilke. "I too am barely convalescent. Flitz has been taking a personal concern in my case. We are both puzzled as to why the agony in my leg yields only to her massage."

"Some people have the gift of healing," said Glawen.

"That is the case with Flitz. She has many admirable traits, and a bond of mutual esteem is slowly growing between us."

"Interesting! 'Slowly,' you say?"

"Well yes. Quite slowly. These things cannot be rushed. For a fact she is still a bit elusive."

"I think that Flitz senses what you have in mind. She is starting to peek around corners before entering a room."

"Nonsense!" scoffed Chilke. "Women are fascinated by the thrill of danger, even when it is imaginary. It gives them a sense of power and purpose; they are allured like rats to Gorgonzola."

"What is 'Gorgonzola'?"

"It is a cheese found on Old Earth. A rat is a rat."

"Ah! That makes everything clear. You think that Flitz is edging in on the bait?"

Chilke nodded confidently. "I'll have her eating out of my hand in three days, plus or minus four hours."

Glawen gave his head a dubious shake. "I wonder if Flitz has any notion of the danger she is in."

"I hope not," said Chilke. "She is far too fast on her feet already."

Later in the day Chilke found an opportunity to test Flitz' reflexes. He called to her as she was passing through the main hall. "Flitz, this way! Just in time for the poetry reading!"

Flitz halted. She wore a white pullover shirt of dull soft material and pale blue trousers; she had gathered her bright hair away from her face with a black ribbon. Chilke could find no fault with her appearance. She asked: "Who is reading poetry to whom?"

Chilke held up a volume bound in limp leather. "I have here Navarth's *Pullulations*. You can recite one of your favorites, then I'll sing out one of mine. On your way, bring over a jug of Old Sidewinder and two heavy-duty mugs."

Flitz showed a cool smile. "I am not in the mood for poetry just now, Mr. Chilke. But there is no reason why you should not read aloud to yourself, as eloquently as you like. I will close the door and no one will protest."

Chilke put aside the leather-bound book. "That kind of poetry lacks charm. Anyway, it's getting on time for the picnic."

Despite herself, Flitz was brought up short. "What 'picnic' is this?"

"I thought it would be nice if you and I took our lunch and went off somewhere for a picnic."

Flitz showed the faintest of smiles. "With your leg in such painful condition? That would not be wise."

Chilke made a gallant gesture. "There is nothing to fear. The first pang will be a signal for you to apply your magic touch; the pain will go, and we can continue our conversation, or whatever it is we are doing."

"Mr. Chilke, you are deluding yourself."

"Absolutely not, and call me 'Eustace.'"

"As you like. But, for the moment — "

"Now that I think of it, I feel a vicious twinge at this very instant."

"Too bad," said Flitz.

"You wouldn't care to practice this miraculous art, or whatever it is?"

"Not just now." Flitz departed the room, with a final expressionless glance over her shoulder toward Chilke.

At mid-morning on the following day Chilke quietly entered the hall. He settled himself upon a couch and, looking out over the landscape, became absorbed in a reverie.

Flitz presently crossed the far end of the hall. She took note of Chilke, slowed her step, then departed the hall.

An hour later Flitz once again passed through the room. Chilke, engrossed in the flight of a distant bird, seemed not to notice. Flitz halted, looked curiously out the window, inspected Chilke for an instant, then continued on her errand.

A few minutes later Flitz was back. As before, Chilke sat pondering the hazy distances. Flitz slowly approached the couch. Chilke looked up to find her studying him with clinical curiosity. She asked: "Are you well? You've been sitting here in a stupor all morning."

Chilke uttered a hollow laugh. "A stupor? Hardly! I was day-dreaming, thinking beautiful thoughts. At least some of them were beautiful. Some were mystifying."

Flitz turned away. "Dream on, Mr. Chilke. I'm sorry I troubled your rhapsody."

"Not so fast! It can wait!" cried Chilke, suddenly energetic. "Sit down for a moment. I have something to tell you."

Flitz hesitated, then gingerly seated herself at the end of the couch. "What is the problem?"

"There's no problem. It's more like a commentary, or an analysis."

"Of what?"

"In the main: me."

Flitz could not restrain a laugh. "The subject is too vast, Mr. Chilke! We won't have time for it today."

Chilke paid no heed. "When I was a boy I lived at Idola, on Old Earth. My three sisters were popular and brought home their friends, so that I had the misfortune to grow up surrounded by a clutter of pretty girls. They came in all sizes and ratings. Some were tall, some were short, some were built for speed. It was a jungle of pulchritude."

Flitz was interested despite herself. "Why was this a misfortune?"

"For an idealistic youth like myself it was more than I could assimilate: a classic case of too much too soon."

"Too much what?"

Chilke made a vague gesture. "Disillusion? The loss of wonder? At the age of sixteen I was a jaded epicure. Where the ordinary young buck noticed a bit of fluff, adorable and sweet, I saw only a cantankerous little brat."

Chilke straightened himself and his voice became severe. "I am sorry to say that when I first met you, I told myself: 'Aha!

Another pretty face, hiding a personality as insipid as all the others. You probably wondered at my distant manner, for which I now apologize. What do you say to that?"

Flitz gave her head a puzzled shake. "I can't decide whether I should thank you, or quietly leave you to look at some more birds."

"It makes no great difference," said Chilke generously. "I have come to my senses. Despite your superb beauty, I take great pleasure in your company, and I think that I would like to kiss you."

"Here? Now?"

"At your convenience, of course," said Chilke gallantly.

Flitz glanced at him sidelong. What did this odd person have in mind? He was not ill-favored, she thought; his blunt features, wry and crooked, were in fact rather interesting. There was also something about Eustace Chilke which amused her and made her feel alive.

"So: after this appointment, what next?"

"There is a proposal I would like you to consider."

Flitz prompted him. "What kind of proposal?"

"I had rather wait until after the appointment, before going into details."

"You must tell me now. First, I am curious, and, second, our schedules might not allow time for an appointment."

Chilke chose his words carefully. "I have a venture in mind, and I think that you are qualified—let us say, highly qualified—to become an associate in the scheme."

"I am puzzled as to why you rate me so highly."

"Simple enough! I have seen you in action. If we ran into trouble, say, in some rough saloon past the edge of Beyond, I'd know you would be backing me up: kicking, cursing, screaming, busting heads, raising hell with everyone in sight, so that I'd be proud of you."

"Don't be too proud too soon. I might be somewhere else at the time. I try to avoid rough saloons."

Chilke shrugged. "If there is only one saloon in town, you don't have much choice."

"True. But why am I in this place to begin with? Whom am I fighting, and why?"

"As for the fighting, the reasons are unpredictable. I might be sitting quietly, thinking about something, when a lady comes over to talk. You resent the lady's friendly attitude and give her hair a yank, and that is where the party begins."

"Very good," said Flitz. "I now know why you need me for an associate. You might as well explain the rest of it."

Chilke frowned off across the river. "Just as you like. I have to go back a few years, when I was something of a vagabond, wandering here and there and—as I see it now—absorbing an education. I listened to dozens of old locators, explorers, fugitives from deeds no one remembered, not even themselves. They were lonely men and generally talkative, especially over a jug, and I heard many strange tales. After a time I began to take notes. In the end I had a dozen or so accounts of marvelous places and things. Are they true reports, or legends, or drunken fabrications? My guess is: some of each. The authentic cases are out there now, waiting for someone to come find them."

"And whom do you suggest for this investigation?"

"I thought that you and I could glance over the list and settle on a few good prospects. I think Glawen would let me take the Fortunatus; it will do us no good otherwise."

Flitz kept her voice even. "You propose, then, that you and I should fly off into the far regions of space to track down the drunken tales you once heard in a saloon, while probably more than half drunk yourself and, in general, live a feckless irresponsible life."

"Well, yes," said Chilke. "That is the project, in a nutshell."

Flitz heaved a sigh. "Eustace, don't you think I have enough on my mind without having to worry whether or not you are insane?"

"Be assured: I am not insane!"

"That is the worst worry of all!"

"Touch," muttered Chilke.

Flitz rose from the couch. On sudden impulse she leaned over and kissed Chilke's cheek. "Eustace, if nothing else you deserve that much for your valiant efforts."

"One moment," cried Chilke, struggling to his feet. "What about the appointment?"

"Not just now, Eustace."

Flitz left the room. Chilke looked after her with a grin.

IV.

Three days passed. Chilke saw little of Flitz except in the company of others. He made no effort to seek her out, lest she think him importunate, but after a time, doubts began to color his thinking; was it possible that his restraint might be mistaken for complacency?

Chilke became impatient: both with himself and the dilemma. No more pussy-footing! Let the chips fall where they may!

The decision was rendered moot by the arrival of Bagnoli, the architect, and three senior L-B Construction engineers. They would sojourn at Stronsi House, while a residential complex was being erected at Bainsey Castle for the construction crews. Flitz brought in domestic service from Port Twang, but had more responsibilities than ever, or so it seemed to Chilke.

The newcomers conferred daily with Barduys and made frequent expeditions into the countryside. Glawen, who had been present at some of the conferences, kept Chilke informed. "These men are top L-B engineers. Barduys is starting up his Bainsey project; he is wasting no time. I have seen the sketches. They show a low irregular structure at the side of the crag. It is ponderous but impressive, and it seems to be part of the natural landscape. Storms can blast it with green water and the fabric won't so much as quiver. During the evening the guests can look out across the slutes and watch the water-waifs skipping across the puddles. When the storms come and waves roar and foam seethes across the slutes, perhaps the guests will shiver a bit before they go to dine beside the great fireplace."

"The reservation list will be long indeed," said Chilke.

"Undoubtedly. Still, I've noticed something odd. Flitz takes no interest in the project. When Bagnoli or the engineers come into the room, she leaves."

"That may partly be my doing," said Chilke.

Glawen raised his eyebrows. "How so?"

"I decided that she was brooding too much, so I told her some locator's tales; I mentioned Emperor Schulz, who owned the Great Nebula in Andromeda; and Pittacong Pete, who spoke an alien language; I mentioned Farlock, whom I met way out at the edge of the Reach, at a place called Orvil. Farlock had many wild tales to tell, but he could always document them and provide coordinates, unlike most of the things you would hear. I mentioned some of his tales to Flitz and said it might be nice if she and I became vagabonds and went off to investigate them."

"And then what?"

"She said it sounded exciting, but that she'd have to think about it some more."

"Extraordinary!" mused Glawen. "She acts as if you and she were barely acquainted."

"My fault again," said Chilke modestly. "I have backed off, to give her room to make up her mind."

"All is explained," said Glawen.

On the day following, Bagnoli and the engineers moved north to the residential complex erected at the Bainsey site by an L-B task-force.

Two days later, Flitz approached Chilke where he sat on the terrace, writing in a notebook.

Flitz asked curiously: "What are you writing?"

"Oh—just notes and recollections."

"Can you help me with an errand?"

Chilke closed the notebook and rose to his feet. "I am at your service. What do you need?"

"Lewyn wants me to fly some samples north to Bainsey. He would like you to come with me."

"A sound idea. When do we leave?"

"Now."

"Give me five minutes."

The two flew north in the ranch flitter. Flitz wore tan trousers, ankle boots and a dark blue tunic. She seemed somewhat wan, as if she were tired, and had little to say. Chilke made no effort to intrude into her thoughts. After a time she turned to examine him. "Why are you so taciturn? Are you like this all the time?"

Chilke was taken aback. "I thought perhaps you preferred quiet."

"Not total quiet."

"For a fact, there is something I would like to discuss."

"Oh? What is that?"

"You."

Flitz smiled. "I'm not all that interesting."

Chilke waved his hand around the landscape. "Look out there! Miles and miles; rivers and prairies and mountains: all belonging to Felitzia Stronsi. Doesn't that make you feel interesting, and even important?"

"Yes, so it does. I had never thought of it before. But it is true." Flitz pointed. "See that yellow mastic bush down there? If I chose, I could land the flitter, destroy that bush, and no one would be bold enough to question my motives."

"Such power is heady. But before Felitzia destroys the mastic bush, she should do something about her water-waifs. They thumped poor Eustace Chilke and enjoyed every minute of it!"

"Apparently they wanted to teach Chilke a good lesson."

"Perhaps, but it won't always be so easy. When her new hotel is operating and some nice old ladies go out on the slutes to enjoy the view, they will also be thumped."

"First of all, it is not Felitzia, but Lewyn Barduys, who is building the hotel. He can build hotels wherever he likes so long as Felitzia is not involved."

"Then no more need be said. When the ladies come to show you their bruises, refer them to Lewyn Barduys."

The flitter flew north. Flitz indicated clouds at the eastern horizon. "Another storm is on the way. The construction crew will learn something new about the site."

To the east the gray-green ocean converged upon the line of flight and then, ahead, the black expanse of the Slutes became visible.

The flitter landed near a dozen temporary buildings which had been set up: dormitories, a refectory, storage and multi-purpose sheds. Chilke and Flitz alighted, and Chilke brought out the two cases which were to be delivered to Bagnoli. Chilke put his fingers to his mouth and whistled. Thus alerted, one of the workers brought up a carrier and took away the cases. Bagnoli emerged from the refectory, waved his hand to acknowledge the delivery and the mission was accomplished.

Chilke turned back to the flitter. Flitz stood to the side, looking across the site of the old castle, where earth-moving machinery was now at work. Her face seemed pinched; the cool damp wind ruffled her hair. Clouds rolled close overhead and drops of rain were beginning to fall. Flitz' voice seemed to come from far away. "I feel her as if she were still down there, the bedraggled little girl. I hear her wailing, or maybe it is her ghost." Flitz turned away; Chilke found himself with his arms around her, making soothing noises and stroking her hair. "Poor little Flitz! It is different now; I am taking care of you. The hole is just a hole, and a ghost is not reasonable. Why? It is simple. If there is no dead body, there is no ghost. Felitzia was saved; she is now the wonderful clever Flitz who is decidedly alive, I am happy to say. In fact she seems quite warm and snug."

Flitz laughed, making no effort to draw away. She said: "Eustace, for a fact you are habit-forming. Don't ask me what I mean, because I am as puzzled as you are."

Chilke bent his head and kissed her; somewhat to his surprise she reacted without constraint. Chilke repeated the gratifying process. He said: "If nothing else, it settles the nerves."

The rain now fell at a slant. Chilke and Flitz climbed into the flitter and flew south.

V.

At Flitz' instruction Chilke dropped the flitter upon the summit of a barren hill, with a tall forest spreading away to the south.

"I want to talk with you," said Flitz. "Now is as good a time as any. No, Eustace, please do not distract me."

"Speak on," said Chilke.

"Lewyn Barduys has been kind to me, in ways that you can't imagine. He has given me everything—including a quiet affection which has demanded nothing in return. I thought that it would always be this way, and I wanted nothing more.

"Then, something changed. I don't know how or why, but I began to feel restless. I discovered that I was bored with construction. As for the wilderness lodges, which fascinated Lewyn Barduys, I was barely lukewarm. If Lewyn noticed the difference in me, he did nothing to interfere.

"Then Eustace Chilke appeared, with his friend Glawen Clattuc. I barely noticed them at first. One day Eustace made a reckless proposal. He suggested that he and I become vagabonds, and go off to explore romantic places where no one had wandered before. It was a proposal of startling verve, which at first I could not relate to reality.

"Naturally I did not take him seriously, no more than he did himself. Eustace was like a song-bird in a cage, warbling the sweet songs of Never-never Land just to stay in practice. If I had agreed to his foolishness, he would have suffered a heart attack.

"Time went by but the idea would not go away. I began to ask myself: if I wanted to become a vagabond why should I not do so? It might be fun, especially if I traveled in comfort, perhaps with a congenial fellow vagabond. It seemed only fair that Eustace Chilke should be notified that the position of fellow vagabond might well be open."

"And now—I am notified?"

"You are so notified and you can apply at any time."

"In that case, I apply for the position."

"Very good, Eustace," said Flitz. "I'll put your name on the list."

VI.

Glawen and Chilke stood leaning on the balustrade which surrounded the terrace, watching evening settle upon the landscape. The sun was half an hour gone behind a bank of clouds; sunset colors were fading fast, through a mournful gamut of all the browns, from amber through mahogany into the ranges of umber and a few sad streaks of old rose.

Glawen and Chilke discussed events of the day. "Barduys is now in a wheelchair," said Glawen. "He is vibrating with energy; he'll be walking tomorrow, and before the week is out he'll want to be off and away to Cadwal, to take care of what he calls 'unfinished business.'"

"He has not defined this 'business'?"

"Not in so many words. He has mentioned Dame Clytie and Smonny, and he may well have Namour and the Flecanpraun in mind."

"This 'business' sounds interesting."

"More than interesting. When he asked if we cared to be on hand—disguised and incognito—I accepted with pleasure. I hope that I have represented you correctly?"

"Of course. What is the program?"

"Barduys wants to travel aboard the Fortunatus from here to Pasch, on Kars, where Barduys maintains a terminal to house his various space transports. We will leave the Fortunatus, transfer to a larger ship, and continue to Cadwal. First we assist Barduys in his 'business,' then we report to Bodwyn Wook, and accept his commendations, if he is in a good mood."

Chilke stood watching the flow of the slow river, where

the embers of sunset were reflected. Presently, as if musing aloud, he said: "I expect that Kathcar has described the Fortunatus to Bodwyn Wook in exact detail."

Glawen nodded somberly. "Sooner or later we will have to give it up."

"Sooner or later," agreed Chilke.

Glawen's attention was caught by an overtone in Chilke's voice. "What do you mean by that?"

"Nothing substantial."

"And the non-substantial?"

"The ideas are almost as frail." Chilke stirred and straightened, stood with his hands on the balustrade. "One or two possibilities have crossed my mind."

"Such as?"

Chilke laughed and performed a gesture half airy, half diffident. "The ideas are no more than glimmers. Since this is Rosalia, I will say they are as skittish as wind-waifs."

"Hm," said Glawen. "How do you catch hold of them yourself? But don't answer; just start over. What are these remote 'possibilities'?"

"A few days ago I spoke of Flitz. I mentioned my admiration for her many superlative qualities. Do you remember this conversation?"

"Yes, to some extent."

"I told you of a change in Flitz and her attitude toward me."

Glawen nodded. "I noticed it myself. I think she intends ostracism."

Chilke's response was an indulgent smile. "We have decided to put the situation on hold until Lewyn Barduys finishes his business on Cadwal, and after you and I have made our reports to Bodwyn Wook."

Raising his eyebrows, Glawen peered through the dusk toward Chilke. "Then what?"

"Then we have choices to make. Flitz says she will never return to Rosalia, and that Barduys can do what he likes with Stronsi Ranch. She also has had enough of the construction business. She says that one dam is much like another, with water on one side and air on the other."

In a subdued voice Glawen asked: "So what will she do with herself?"

Chilke made another offhand gesture. "I suppose I must take some of the responsibility. I told her of Farlock the locator and she became fascinated, so now nothing will do but what we must go off and explore the Beyond. She wants to find Lake Mar and record the mermaids at their singing; she wants to photograph the Bestiary under the ruins of Agave. I mentioned that the Fortunatus would be useful for such vagabond rambling; she asked: what about Glawen? I told her that you were building a new house and would not need the Fortunatus for a while; I said that the main problem was Bodwyn Wook. She said that he was no great problem, and I let the matter drop."

Glawen stared at Chilke through the twilight. "How do you do it?"

Chilke chuckled. "It's simple enough. A woman likes to be appreciated—sometimes for what she is, sometimes for what she is not but wants to be."

"I wish you would write a book," said Glawen. "I don't want to forget any of this lore."

"Ridiculous," said Chilke. "Wayness appreciates you, so you must be doing everything right."

"You make me feel as if I'm walking a tightrope," said Glawen. He stretched his arms. "Suddenly I'm anxious to get home. It should not be long now. Barduys is starting to walk. As soon as the doctors allow it, he'll leave the Bainsey project to the engineers, and we'll be on our way."

CHAPTER 7

I.

The city Pasch on Kars, Perseus TT-652-IV, served as junction and transfer point for a dozen major trans-galactic carriers. Pasch was also the hub of a hundred feeder routes, circulating into every far corner of the Perseid sector. Two of Lewyn Barduys' transport companies were based at Pasch, and provided a more or less regular connection with worlds in Cassiopeia and Pegasus, and even Beyond. Another line existed mainly to service L-B construction projects, but on occasion moved cargoes of opportunity wherever the prospect of profit directed. All three lines operated from Barduys' private terminal in Ballyloo Township south of Pasch. To this terminal the Fortunatus brought Barduys, Flitz, Glawen and Chilke.

There was a delay of four days, while the *Rondine*, a trim cargo-passenger vessel, was modified to suit Barduys' requirements. Meanwhile, he assembled a crew of fourteen stalwart, if laconic, men with special competencies. Glawen thought them a rather rough lot, though they seemed mature and steady. Each, so he noticed, took pains not to startle any of the others, or come up silently behind them, and none indulged in easy reminiscences of the past.

The *Rondine* departed Pasch and set off across the Great Lonesome Gulf, with Mircea's Wisp to the side and the Purple Rose Cluster ahead. The Fortunatus remained behind in the hangar at Ballyloo.

Barduys finally saw fit to discuss his program. "For a fact, there is nothing definite to tell you. I have a few personal objectives. They include vindictive intentions toward Namour, who threw me into the slutes and flew away in my Flecanpraun. I am also displeased with Smonny. She swindled me in cavalier style, with truly remarkable aplomb. So, as you see, I have grievances which I hope to redress—but on this occasion I suspect that they will become side-issues.

"As you know, both the LPF and Smonny want me to provide them transport, so that they can ferry a horde of Yips to the mainland, but each wants to act independently. That is the context of the present venture. I have arranged a meeting with representatives of the two factions on neutral ground. Ostensibly I am ready for serious negotiations, but I require something more definite than talk. I will ask that differences be compromised and a responsible spokesman appointed. I will suggest that a contract be drawn up and a sum of earnest money be paid over.

"What will happen next? This is an area of uncertainty. Under ideal conditions, all differences would be reconciled; all hurt feelings would be soothed in a surge of joyous bonhomie, and an executive director, perhaps Julian Bohost, would be appointed. He would at once extend me a contract and a hundred thousand sols.

"That is the ideal case. Reality may be different. The format of the meeting will remain the same. After my initial statement, I will have little to say. The others must make their arrangements. What will happen? Who knows? I expect some polite remarks, a disclaimer or two, and finally someone will reluctantly offer to take on the thankless job of executive director. There will be counter-suggestions, then some gentle chiding and urging that the other party yield to reason, in the name of solidarity. Next: expostulation, fanciful rhetoric, and even the exchange of intemperate comments.

"The discussion must be allowed to run its course. Every opinion should be aired, every cherished ambition must be explained, no matter who may or may not be interested. Both parties will gradually become tired; at last they will sit back, perhaps not defeated but disillusioned, exhausted, apathetic.

"Meanwhile, I have committed myself to nothing and, in fact, I have uttered no more than ten words. But at last I speak. I point out that the programs I have heard conflict with established law. However, from sheer altruism, I will resolve the problem in the only way possible. In short, I will transport the Yips to the Mystic Isles of Rosalia, where they will find a congenial environment. I will also transport the LPFers at bargain rates to destinations of their choosing, and even help them adapt to lives of productive work.

"How this proposal will be met I can only speculate."

"And what if they will commit themselves to nothing?"

Barduys shrugged. "Plans are useful when they engage a known problem. We are faced with a hundred variations and planning is a waste of time."

II.

The *Rondine* passed to the side of fat red Sing and its merry little companion, white Lorca, and approached Syrene. Cadwal became a sphere below. The *Rondine* approached from the side opposite Araminta Station. The equatorial continent Ecce appeared below: a long rectangle straddling the equator. Openings through the clouds revealed a blackish-green surface, meshed with wide rivers—a place almost palpably purulent, pulsing with violent life.

The *Rondine* flew west across the ocean, barely skimming

the waves, so that the monitor station above Lutwen Atoll might not be alerted.

A dark smudge showed on the horizon, which presently became Thurben Island, with Lutwen Atoll still two hundred miles to the northwest.

The *Rondine* approached the island and made a slow circuit, discovering a waterless waste, two miles in diameter, with a low crag of rotten red rock at the center. Vegetation was limited to dingy yellow scrub, thorn-bush and a straggle of palms along the beach. A strip of lagoon was protected by an offshore reef, with two passes open to the ocean. Opposite the north pass a broken dock thrust into the lagoon; behind were the ruins of a cabin built of fronds: a place, for Glawen, latent with horrid recollections.

The *Rondine* landed on a flat area of packed sand a few yards inland from the beach, opposite the south pass. "We are a day or so early," Barduys told the others. "This will give us time to make our preparations."

The site was arranged in accordance with Barduys' directions. Three pavilions, of blue- and green-striped fabric were erected and disposed about the area. One was backed up against the ship; the other two faced each other across a hundred feet of intervening ground. At the center of the space so delineated, a square table six feet on a side, was set out, with four chairs, one to a side.

The preparations were now complete; there would be a wait until noon of the following day. Barduys reviewed the instructions he had already issued to Glawen and Chilke. "You will be in deep disguise, of course; no one will recognize you, but still you must stay back, and keep to the shadows. The crew will be wearing uniforms and should have no trouble maintaining order."

The afternoon passed; a melancholy sunset flared in the west and gave way to twilight. The night passed, and morning arrived. The crew donned the black and ocher uniforms which Barduys had supplied, as did Glawen and Chilke, who also disguised themselves with skin-toning, wigs, sideburns, cheek-pads and beards. After pulling the smart short-billed semi-military caps down over their foreheads they could not recognize themselves in the mirror.

Syrene reached the zenith; noon was at hand. Low in the southern sky appeared a flitter: evidently the deputation from Stroma. They were twenty minutes early: an unimportant detail. The flitter circled the area, then settled at the site to which they were directed by signals from members of the *Rondine* crew.

Six persons alighted from the flitter: Dame Clytie, Julian Bohost, Roby Mavil, a gaunt hollow-cheeked woman, a plump pink- cheeked man, and Torq Tump. Four of the *Rondine* crew met them and after an irritable colloquy led the members of the group one at a time through a passage adjacent to their pavilion, where they were deprived of their weapons—articles which all carried save only Dame Clytie. The group entered their pavilion, where Barduys and Flitz met them. Stewards served refreshments and Barduys apologized for the need to sequester the weapons. "I cannot disarm the other side without asking you to undergo the same inconvenience," he told them. "It is of no consequence, after all, since we are engaged in a quest for consensus."

"Wherein, so I hope, justice and reason will prevail," said Dame Clytie weightily. Today she wore a heavy tweed skirt, a tan shirt tied at the neck with a small black cravat, a severe jacket of black twill and sturdy square-toed shoes. She wore no hat; her short straight locks dangled to each side of her weathered brown face.

"Justice is our goal," said Barduys. "Today all avenues must be explored."

"There are not so many of these," said Dame Clytie with a sniff. "Certainly we must opt for the best and most 'democratic'—and here I use the word in its new expanded sense."

"That is an interesting concept," said Barduys. "I will listen intently while you explain it at the conference table."

Julian Bohost turned to Flitz. Today he wore an oyster-white suit, a dull blue sash and a wide-brimmed planter's hat. "Ah there, Flitz! It is a pleasure to see you again!"

Flitz looked at him blankly. "'Again'? Have we met?"

Julian's smile became a trifle less fulsome. "Of course! You were visiting at Riverview House, perhaps a year ago!"

Flitz nodded. "I recall the occasion. There were some folk in from Stroma; you must have been one of them."

"Quite so," said Julian. "But no matter. Then was then and now is now! The wheel of Fate has rolled a full roll, and so we meet again."

"That is as good an explanation as any."

Julian had turned to inspect the surroundings. "What a dismal place for a meeting! Still, it is curiously beautiful in a forlorn sort of way. The lagoon shows a truly halcyon blue."

"Don't attempt to swim. The pipe-fish would streak at you from all directions. In five minutes you would be a skeleton in a white suit, the hat still on your head."

Julian winced. "That is a most macabre thought! Flitz, despite your innocent appearance, you must have a dark side to your nature!"

Flitz responded with an indifferent shrug. "Perhaps."

Julian continued, unheeding. "I am surprised to find you here. It will surely be a dull business, all harangues and stipulations: certainly nothing to interest pretty heads such as yours. But I suppose you must go where duty calls." Julian glanced meaningfully toward Barduys, whose relationship with Flitz he had never been able to fathom. Business associate? Well, maybe. He turned back to Flitz. "So then: what are your views on all this conferencing and parleying?"

"I'm just decoration; I am not supposed to think."

"Come now!" said Julian reproachfully. "You are probably far wiser than anyone suspects. Am I right?"

"Absolutely."

"I thought so! After I have delivered my peroration I shall look to you for applause."

"As you like, but at the moment you should look to Dame Clytie. She seems to be signalling in this direction."

Julian glanced across the flat. "It is nothing urgent; she just wants to comment on the weather, or complain about my sash, which she considers too frivolous for the occasion."

"You are brave to delay."

Julian sighed. "It's all such a bore, and quite unnecessary. Everyone knows how things must go; our scheme has been worked out in detail. Still, if this is what is needed to start the ball rolling, I will make no further complaint."

"Your aunt is still signalling, Mr. Bohost."

"So she is! A formidable creature, don't you think?"

Flitz nodded. "She could swim in the lagoon without fear of the pipe-fish."

"Even so, I will pass on the warning, though I doubt if she is planning to bathe." Julian turned to leave. "Shall we meet again after the conference?"

"It seems unlikely."

Julian gave a rueful laugh. "Time has worked no changes; your moods are as marmoreal as ever!" He doffed his hat, bowed, then marched off to join Dame Clytie. She stood inspecting the table and its four chairs, pointing back and forth in apparent displeasure. Julian nodded, turned to look around the area, but Barduys had retired into his own pavilion. Julian made as if to follow, then halted, as through the pass from the open sea came what seemed to be a fishing boat, somewhat larger than the ordinary craft. It halted ten yards offshore; a dinghy was dropped into the water. Into the dinghy stepped a large woman heavy of chest and bosom, massive of hips and upper legs with disproportionately small ankles and feet. It was Smonny, born Simonetta Clattuc, now Madame Zigonie of Shadow Valley Ranch. She wore a coverall suit belted at the waist, black boots with stylish pointed toes and block heels. Her taffy-colored hair had been twisted into a rope, then wound tightly into an impressive pyramid, under the control of a black net. She was followed into the dinghy by four Oomps. They were handsome men of early middle age, golden-skinned, golden-haired, wearing neat uniforms of white, yellow and blue.

The dinghy grounded in the shallow water ten feet from dry land; heedless of pipe-fish two of the Oomps splashed through the shallows and pulled the dinghy up on the beach. Smonny stepped ashore, followed by the rest of her retinue. She stood a moment looking about the area, then was met by four of Barduys' crew. They apprised her of what must be done and she drew herself up in outrage. At last Barduys joined the group. Smonny snapped: "These demands are demeaning! I see no need for this sort of thing!"

"It must be done," said Barduys. "It is a formality, no more. The group from Stroma also protested, but I explained that everyone must feel at ease. The conference cannot proceed until everyone acquiesces to the rules."

Smonny scowled and submitted to the search, which produced a compact hand-gun from her sash and a dagger from her boot. The Oomps were deprived of their side-arms and directed to the pavilion designated for their use.

Meanwhile, Smonny had gone to the center table, where Dame Clytie and Julian also stood. The two women acknowledged each other's presence with curt nods, but remained silent while adjusting themselves to the atmosphere of the island. Their differences were fundamental. Smonny intended to transfer all the Yips from Lutwen Atoll to the Marmion foreshore, using whatever transport was available—preferably that provided by Barduys. The Yips would then swarm down the coast and overwhelm Araminta Station. Smonny would sit in state and administer dreadful justice upon the folk who had hurt her feelings so badly. After that, the Yips could do as they liked—under her supervision of course.

Originally Dame Clytie and other LPFers had endorsed the basic principle, of moving the Yips to Deucas, and then establishing a true democracy which would give the vote of the lowliest Yip fisherman equal weight to the vote of the arrogant Bodwyn Wook. This had been the basic thesis of the LPF party in the early innocent days, when progressive intellectuals and excited students met to drink tea and debate political morality in the tall drawing rooms of Stroma. The passage of years had brought many changes. Innocence had disappeared. The ideal of pure democracy had been replaced by plans for a more manageable—and useful—system of kindly paternalism, to be administered from a network of fine country estates. When asked how the system differed from manorial feudalism, the LPFer said that the comparison was sophistry of the rankest sort. Serfs were serfs, and Yips were free spirits who would be trained in the arts of folk dancing and choral singing, and who would enjoy many gay festivals, while others would learn to play the guitar.

As for Smonny's chaotic and bloody-handed plan, it must be rejected, smartly and definitely, for a number of reasons. In the first place, the program offered no clear benefits to the LPF and the Yips might well learn bad habits. Smonny's rage must be tempered and diverted into useful channels.

Dame Clytie set herself to the task at hand. With Julian Bohost at her elbow, beaming graciously, she turned to Smonny. "How nice to see you again; it's been quite some time, hasn't it?"

"Yes. I am becoming impatient. Waiting is very hard."

"True! But our time is approaching, and we must carefully mesh our plans."

Smonny gave Dame Clytie a quick indifferent glance, then looked away.

Dame Clytie felt a tingle of annoyance. She spoke on, pitching her voice so as to convey intimacy and assurance, and still give Smonny a hint as to how events must go and who was in charge. "I have been hard at work, and I have prepared a schedule which I hope will guide our operations. Only the first step is sensitive. When the supply ship goes up to the monitor over Lutwen, our men will be aboard, and we will quickly overpower the crew. Thereafter the operation should proceed smoothly."

Smonny listened in contemptuous silence. So far, the plan was as she herself envisaged it. She gave a small curt nod and turned away. Dame Clytie stared at her a moment, then shrugged and became quiet.

The group waited in silence, broken only by muttering among the LPFers.

Barduys came forward and signaled to the occupants of the two pavilions, who filed out into the area and stood in two silent groups.

"This is an important occasion," Barduys told the company. "I am anxious that it succeed. Let me define my position. I am a businessman, not a party to the discussion; my opinions, had I any, would be irrelevant. You may regard me and my staff as neutral observers. However, we will maintain order. The two groups will keep to their pavilions and refrain from unsolicited admonitions, advice, or any interference whatever. The reason for this restriction will be clear to all.

"In passing, I would like to call your attention to my crew. Some of you may recognize their uniforms, which are Scuters, the platoon of heroes who served the fabulous King Sha Kha Shan. My Scuters are not so prone to beard-pulling and ear-lopping as their namesakes; still, it is well to accept their guidance.

"So now, if you will return to your pavilions, we will start our conversations."

Julian, who had been idly chatting with Dame Clytie during Barduys' remarks, turned now and surveyed the table. He started toward one of the chairs, but Flitz, came from the *Rondine* pavilion and seated herself with her back to the lagoon. She carried several books, portfolios and other works of reference which she placed on the table. Julian halted, nonplussed. Dame Clytie and Smonny seated themselves opposite each other; Barduys went to stand by his place at the end of the table.

Julian asked petulantly: "Where am I to sit? There must be a mistake; no chair has been set out for me."

"The seating is purposely limited," said Barduys. "You are entitled to sit in the pavilion with the others of your group."

Julian hesitated, then fretfully turned away, muttering

under his breath. He marched across the area to the pavilion and plumped down beside Roby Mavil, to whom he made a series of disgruntled observations.

"Ladies," said Barduys, "notice these buttons. If you want your group to hear the proceedings, press the red button. To solicit their advice, press the yellow button." He looked from the tight-lipped Dame Clytie to the surly Smonny. "Meetings of this sort often fail because they lose their focus. I hope that we will avoid this pitfall. A plan may already exist; it would be foolish to come here unprepared, even though minor differences remain to be reconciled. Since I am not one of the principles, I can make no substantive suggestions, nor do I wish to do so."

Dame Clytie had become increasingly annoyed with Barduys' manner, which she felt to be disrespectful and even autocratic. She spoke shortly: "You are beating a dead horse. No one is looking to you either for advice or intercession. What we require is transport capacity; no more no less."

"Then we are of the same mind." Barduys seated himself. "Let us get down to cases." He looked from Smonny to Dame Clytie. "Which of you is the spokesman?"

Dame Clytie cleared her throat. "I am in a position to elucidate our program. The operation must proceed with what I shall call 'massive precision.' Our goals are altruistic and philosophically correct: we wish to bring democracy to Cadwal; and here, of course, I use the word 'democracy' in its new, extended sense.

"As good LPFers, we are non-violent and hope to avoid bloodshed. The ruling clique at Araminta Station will be helpless in the face of so much power and must submit to the facts, as gracefully as they are able, and no doubt there will be tasks for all in the new order.

"Now, as to practicalities. We will transport only thirty thousand Yips to Deucas: this number is both adequate and desirable. In its full scope, the plan is elaborate —"

Smonny, speaking in a sharp quick voice, interrupted. "There is no elaborate plan and no need to dance in circles, or otherwise confuse the issue. The single and basic plan is to transport all the Yips to the Marmion Foreshore on Deucas. There are about one hundred thousand people; all must be put ashore as rapidly as possible, in order to paralyze the Station authorities. With this in mind, you may declare how many transports will be needed, and what it will cost."

"Certainly," said Barduys. "I can supply such an estimate in half an hour or less. But certain conditions must be met. First of all, I need a firm commitment. With whom am I dealing?"

Dame Clytie said coldly: "I think that I can explain this bit of confusion. My colleague, as always, has produced an accurate analysis, except in one or two small respects. She still adheres to the tenets of a youthful idealism, in which democracy is equated to nihilism. All of us, of course, have known the bliss of these romantic dreams, but when they exploded around our heads, we were forced to meet the world on its own terms. Now we deal in practicality."

"All very well," said Barduys, "but I can work only with a coherent organization using a single voice."

"Just so," said Dame Clytie. "We must now, each and all of us, unite behind the system which maximizes benefits for the most people. That system exists. It is a program which we call 'structured democracy.' Simonetta, of course, has an important part to play, and her talents will definitely be put to good use, perhaps as —"

From Smonny came harsh laughter. Dame Clytie's eyebrows raised in irritation. "If you please —"

Smonny cut short her mirth. "My dear lady, really! You misread every portent! Events have bypassed no one, and why? Because nothing has changed. Araminta Station is still a citadel of greed and jealous cruelty; everyone scrambles up the golden ladder, pausing only to kick at the faces of those below, while the good and the worthy are cast aside! Those are the realities which we are addressing!"

Dame Clytie spoke ponderously, as if resolved to be

patient despite all incitement to the contrary. "That is, perhaps, a trifle overstated. The Chartists are dour and pompous, but in the end they will see that our way is best. As for the Conservancy, in a modified form — "

"'Conservancy'? What a joke! It conserves privilege and unspeakable selfishness! You are living in a dreamcloud if you expect gratified welcome from the patricians! You will meet only their horrified resistance. They are as stern as iron statues, and must be humiliated and punished!"

Dame Clytie frowned and held up her hand. "I urge that we insulate our personal grievances from aspects of official policy."

Smonny's dog-brown eyes glittered. "The grievances go far beyond my own small tragedies. The Yips have been exploited for centuries; now they will avenge themselves upon this stinking hive of privilege; they will root out the vile Offaws and Wooks, the Lavertys and the Diffins, the Veders and the Clattucs; they will chase their ancient lords south to Cape Journal, over the rocks and into the sea. Why should we interfere? Their way is final and definite."

Dame Clytie closed her eyes, then opened them again. "Once again, I ask for temperate judgments. Too much fervor is not truly helpful, and only makes the official plan of 'Structured Democracy' the more difficult. We have calculated that for the new counties, a population of thirty thousand happy country folk is enough, since we wish to maintain the sylvan charm of this wonderful environment! The remaining Yips will be transported to new homes offworld. These thirty thousand can be kept under strict discipline and will be allowed no looting or pillage, which only destroys property."

Smonny spoke offhand: "The plan is ill-conceived, useless and unacceptable, in all forms and phases. This plan is now defunct. We need not refer to it again."

Dame Clytie forced herself to smile. "My dear lady! You are issuing fiats and manifestos as if we were your subalterns!"

"Well, what of that?"

"It is not appropriate to the occasion. But let it go by. There are crucial developments which compel us to a policy of moderation."

"I know of no crucial developments. I doubt if such exist."

Dame Clytie, ignoring the remark, spoke ponderously. "Recently there has been a large migration of old-time Naturalists from Stroma to Araminta Station. These folk are our own kin; my sister and her two children now live near Riverview House. Every LPFer is in the same position. We cannot endorse the unbridled acts you suggest. They are tantamount to savagery."

Standing in the shadows, Glawen and Chilke observed the interchanges and tried to predict the outcome.

"They are playing by different rules," said Glawen. "Each of them thinks she is winning."

"Both are very tough," said Chilke. "Dame Clytie is probably the more versatile. Listen to her now! She is lathering Smonny up and down with the essence of sweet reason. It soaks into Smonny like water soaking into a rock."

The two stood in sober contemplation of the scene: Dame Clytie, with head lowered, her heavy jaws corded with sinews; Smonny, sitting half-turned away, watching with insulting disinterest.

Conditions were changing in some subtle fashion. Dame Clytie's narrow gray eyes were widening and starting to bulge; a tide of pink crept up Smonny's burly neck. The voices rose and became strident; Dame Clytie's control broke; she rose from her chair and gripped the table with both hands. "I have explained it, and this is how it must be!" She leaned forward and struck the table. "'Structured Democracy' is the way!"

Smonny cried out: "You belching old cow; you shall not roar in my face! Vex me no further!"

Dame Clytie uttered a guttural croak. "Intolerable creature!" She struck out and buffeted Smonny across the face; jerking back, Smonny fell sprawling from her chair. Dame Clytie bellowed: "Hear me and hear me well ..." Before she could continue Smonny heaved herself to her feet and attacked.

The two began a terrible battle on the sands of Thurben Island, spitting, squealing, kicking, tearing out of hair, moaning and groaning in the extremity of their hate. Dame Clytie seized Smonny's proud mass of hair and slung her down across the table, which broke beneath her weight. Snorting like an angry horse Dame Clytie marched forward to inflict further harm, but Smonny scrambled away. She wrested one of the legs from the broken table and heaving herself to her feet, delivered a blow to the side of Dame Clytie's face, then another and another to head and shoulders. Dame Clytie tottered backward; she stumbled and fell flat on her back. Smonny panted forward and sat squashily down on Dame Clytie's face, clamped her legs over Dame Clytie's arms and started to beat on Dame Clytie's abdomen with the table leg.

Julian, face stark with shock, stumbled from the pavilion. "Stop! Stop this insanity! Mr. Barduys —"

The Scuters seized him and pushed him back into the pavilion. "You may not interfere while the discussion is in progress. You heard the orders!"

Dame Clytie, with her torso and arms pinioned, waved her legs in the air. She gave a frantic lurch and managed to dislodge Smonny; red-faced and gasping, she pulled herself to her feet. She faced Smonny. "Before I was only annoyed. Now I am angry! I warn you: beware!" She lurched forward, wrested the table leg from Smonny and cast it aside. "Unspeakable thing with your foul haunches! Now we shall see!"

Dame Clytie was neither so tall nor so heavy as Smonny, but she was constructed of tough substances and her legs were like iron stanchions. Smonny's insensate fury kept her fighting well past her ordinary endurance, but at last she collapsed, and fell to the sand. Dame Clytie, cursing and croaking, kicked at her, until she herself was overtaken by fatigue and reeled backward, and sat upon one of the chairs. Smonny watched through glazed eyes.

Barduys spoke. "Now then! We have cleared the air, and

once again can direct ourselves to the issues. Shall we continue the meeting?"

"Meeting?" moaned Julian. "What is there to meet about?"

"In that —" Barduys began, but no one was listening. Julian and Roby Mavil were escorting Dame Clytie toward their flitter. Smonny, heaving herself to her feet, limped down the beach to her dinghy and was silently rowed to the boat.

The crew of the *Rondine* struck the pavilions, set the pieces of the broken table afire, and cleaned the site of litter. The embers were buried in the damp sand, and no sign remained that folk had come, met and departed.

III.

The *Rondine* lifted into the sky. To the general puzzlement, Barduys set a course to the north, where nothing existed save empty ocean and the arctic icecap.

Glawen finally asked: "Why are we going in this direction"

"What?" Barduys demanded. "Is it not obvious?"

"Not to me. Commander Chilke, is it obvious?"

"If Mr. Barduys says it is obvious, then it must be. But don't look to me for an explanation. Flitz knows, of course."

"No," said Flitz. "Thurben Island has left me limp."

"It was an affecting episode," Barduys agreed. "We were exposed to emotions in the raw. If you recall, I refused to speculate upon what might or might not occur, and quite rightly; an attempt to predict the unpredictable is an epistemological outrage, even in the abstract."

"And so we are flying north?" asked Glawen.

Barduys nodded. "In a general sense, yes. Thurben Island served its purpose, but the meeting ended before we could turn to my own agenda. Smonny made no mention of the submarine nor of her debt, and Namour was conspicuously not on hand. Therefore, we are flying north."

"Everything you say is clear in itself," said Glawen. "But your chain of logic still lacks a link."

Barduys chuckled. "There is no mystery. Smonny needed

a submarine—why? So that she could travel from Yipton off-world without alerting the monitor. The submarine takes her to where she can transfer to the Clayhacker spaceyacht undetected. Where can she locate her depot? Only in the far north are privacy and isolation guaranteed. The submarine needs open ocean; the Clayhacker must rest on something more solid. We find these conditions where ice meets water."

The search began at a point directly north of Lutwen Atoll, at the edge of the icecap. Halfway through the night an infra-red detector noted a glimmer of radiation. The *Rondine* moved aside and stood by until dawn, then approached the area from the north. Glawen and Chilke, with two men from the crew, descended in a flitter and scouted the area. They discovered an artificial cavern under the ice, communicating with the sea by a tongue of water. The landing dock was empty; neither submarine nor any other vessel lay at moorings. Adjacent, on a pair of runways, rested Titus Zigonie's Clayhacker and Lewyn Barduys' Flecanpraun.

Another ten men descended to the ice, and the group unobtrusively made their way into the depot.

Eight Yips comprised the staff of the depot and all were discovered taking their breakfast in the mess hall. They surrendered with rueful resignation. None gained access to the communications office, so that no messages were transmitted to the outside world.

The three space craft flew south. Behind them the depot had been destroyed. The overburden of ice and snow had slumped into the cavity so that nothing remained of the base except a gully in the white landscape.

Barduys flew his Flecanpraun, in company with Flitz; Chilke and three of the crew flew the Clayhacker, while Glawen remained aboard the *Rondine*, with the Yips and the balance of the crew.

Glawen noticed that the Yips all wore the shoulder braid of the Oomp caste. He spoke to the commander. "May I ask your name?"

"Certainly. I am Falo Lamont Coudray."

"How long have you been an Oomp?"

"For twenty years. We are an elite corps, as you know."

"Then it would be limited to a very few persons. How many? A hundred? Two hundred?"

"One hundred ordinaries, twenty captains and six commanders, such as myself."

"There is an Oomp named Catterline. Is he a commander?"

"He is a captain only. He will progress no further, due to a lack of flair." Here the Yip used a term essentially untranslatable, comprising fortitude, grace, and much else, and which was reflected by the mask of smiling tolerance by which the Yip concealed his emotions.

Glawen asked: "And what of Selious? Is he also a captain?"

"So he is. Why do you ask regarding them?"

"When I was young they were stationed at Araminta Station."

"That was long ago."

"So it was."

The Yip hesitated a moment, then asked: "Where are you taking us?"

"To Araminta Station."

"And we are to be killed?"

Glawen laughed. "Only if we can prove that you have committed a capital crime."

The Yip considered. "I doubt if you can prove any such crime."

"Then I doubt if you will be killed."

IV.

Upon leaving Thurben Island, Smonny's boat proceeded west, skimming the swells at high speed. It arrived at Yipton during the middle evening.

Smonny waited not a moment. She knew her most immediate enemy—indeed, the knowledge had been with her for months. She had temporized, hoping that the problem might resolve itself, but this was not to be the case, and she could wait no longer. She went immediately to her desk, sat with a groan, every ache and twinge almost a pleasure, since they foreshadowed what now would and must be.

Smonny touched a button and spoke carefully into a mesh. In response to the request for verification, she repeated her orders, and received acknowledgment.

That was all there need be done. Smonny painfully doffed her garments, bathed, soothed her bruises with analgesics, then sat down to a meal of oyster tart and steamed eel roe in sweet sauce.

Meanwhile a large fishing boat had drifted from the harbor: nothing here to excite the attention either of the crew or the instruments aboard the monitor ship hovering overhead.

The fishing boat moved placidly off to the south until out of range of the monitor; then the deck slid open and a flitter took to the sky. It flew at speed due south, and so passed the night. As Lorca and Sing rose into the sky, bringing a false pink pre-dawn light, the flitter arrived at Cape Faray, at the northernmost tip of the continent Throy.

Below passed the mountains and moors, the crags and crevasses, of the southern land, and presently the flitter, now flying low, arrived at a great gash into the mountains, with a channel of gray-green water at the bottom: Stroma Fjord.

The flitter landed close beside the brink of the cliff. Five Yips alighted, each one carrying a pack, which he slung over his back upon leaving the flitter. Crouching under the weight of their packs, they ran to the elevator terminals. They unslung their packs, arranged reels on the ground and lowered the packs into the shafts, the line paying smoothly from the reels.

The packs grounded at the bottom of the shafts. At a signal the Yips sent impulses down the line. Then they turned and ran to their flitter. A man emerged from a nearby warehouse. He shouted at them and ordered them to halt, but the Yips paid no heed.

From deep within the shafts came the rumble of five explosions, sounding as one. At the top the ground shook and split. A person standing across the fjord would have seen a great slab of rock peel slowly away from the cliff and fall with dreamlike deliberation into the fjord eight hundred feet below. Where the town Stroma had stood, with row after row of tall narrow houses, the first rays of daylight shone on a fresh scar on the side of the cliff.

There was no more Stroma. It was gone as if it had never existed. The population, those who had not removed to Araminta Station, were deep below the waters of the fjord and dead.

On the brink above the warehouseman stared incredulously down to where his home had been, with spouse, three children and furnishings a thousand years old. It was gone. So swiftly? Yes; in the time it might take him to turn his head! He looked to the north, where the flitter was now only a speck. He ran back into the warehouse and spoke into a telephone.

Ten miles south, a camouflaged hangar occupied a clearing in the dense forest. The negotiators, upon departing Thurben Island, had flown to the hangar. The hour was late, Dame Clytie was sore, and the group had decided to delay until morning their return to the town.

The telephone was answered by Julian Bohost. He listened to the frantic voice, then blurted the news to the others.

At first they rejected the information, declaring it a fantasy, or a hallucination. Then climbing into a flitter, they flew to the site of their ancient home, and were dumbfounded, both by the clean simplicity of the disaster and its incomprehensible magnitude.

Julian said huskily: "We would have been as dead as the others, had we not stayed over at the hangar!"

"So she planned it," said Roby Mavil. "Never has there been a deed so evil!"

They returned to the hangar. In a faltering voice Dame Clytie said: "Now we must take counsel, and —"

Kervin Mostick, director of the Action Brigade, cried out: "No more counsel! My home, my family, my little children, my precious things—all gone, in a twinkling! Bring out the gunboats! Let them fly! Let them ram their blaze down that she-demon's throat!"

No one disputed him. The two gunboats took to the air and flew north. Toward middle afternoon they arrived at Lutwen Atoll. The first notice of their presence was the demolition missile fired into Titus Pompo's palace beside the Hotel Arcady. Titus Pompo, born Titus Zigonie died instantly. Another missile destroyed the hotel itself and sent a tongue of fire blazing high. Back and forth flew the gunships, disseminating mindless destruction, leaving in their wake gouts of roaring flame and clouds of vile black smoke, which billowed and wallowed downwind like a viscous fluid.

From the structures of bamboo, cane and palm fronds came screams of terror and despair. The canals became choked with barges and boats, all thrusting toward open water. Some escaped; others were seared by the blaze, until the occupants jumped overboard and tried to swim. At the docks, the fishing boats were swarmed over with terrified men and women. The best of the boats were commandeered by the Oomps, who thrust the previous occupants overboard. The flames roared high; the vile black smoke roiled up, curled and drifted away from the atoll. Boats heavy with survivors moved away from the blazing city; those denied a place on the boats died in the flames, or flung themselves into the sea, hoping to find a trifle of flotsam to which they might cling.

For a dramatic three minutes Yipton burned with a single flame, with rushing winds converging from all sides. Then the fuel began to fail and the fire dwindled and separated into hundreds of separated flames. In an hour nothing was left but steaming black slime littered with charred corpses. The gunships, their mission, complete, returned at best speed to Throy and the hangar in the forest.

The monitor ship above Lutwen Atoll had notified Bureau B of the conflagration. At once all available transport vessels and aircraft, were sent north, including the *Rondine*, the Clayhacker, the Flecanpraun, and a pair of tourist packets currently at the terminal.

The rescue vessels plied back and forth between the waters surrounding Lutwen Atoll and the Marmion Foreshore. The efforts continued three days and nights, until no more survivors were discovered afloat in the waters surrounding the charred crescent of stinking mud. The Yips who had been succored and brought to the Marmion Foreshore numbered twenty-seven thousand persons. Two-thirds of the population had been destroyed either by fire or water.

CHAPTER 8

I.

The Yip survivors were settled in a series of camps on the Marmion Foreshore: beside the sea and along the banks of the Mar River. Titus Pompo had been observed lolling in his palace immediately before the attack; he was certainly dead. Several reports placed Smonny and Namour on the submarine dock under the Arkady Hotel and the probabilities were good that they had escaped in the submarine—though now, with the arctic base destroyed, they had nowhere to go.

As soon as circumstances permitted, Glawen and Chilke made their report to Bodwyn Wook. He extended them a stately, if qualified, commendation. "You have achieved a very fair measure of success: perhaps all that I might have expected, under the circumstances."

Glawen and Chilke said that they were gratified to hear Bodwyn Wook's praise. "We had you in mind at all times, and knew that we must give you no possible cause for complaint," said Glawen.

"Nor any other kind," added Chilke.

Bodwyn Wook grunted, and looked from one to the other. "You both seem quite brisk and well fed, as if you stinted yourselves nothing. I hope that your expense accounts will not reflect this impression."

"We are gentlemen and officers of the Cadwal Constabulary," said Glawen. "We maintained a proper style of life."

"Hmf. Give your accounts to Hilda; she will separate the wheat from the chaff."

"Very well, sir."

Bodwyn Wook leaned back in his chair and gazed toward the ceiling. "It is a pity that you neglected an integral part of your mission—which is to say, the capture of Namour. I gather that while you were resting at the Stronsi ranch, he quietly gave you the slip and attacked Lewyn Barduys. Then, with truly insulting bravado, he escaped in Barduys' Flecanpraun."

"It is true that we met a few setbacks along the way," Glawen admitted. "But even while we lay in a coma, we were subconsciously aware of our duty to you and Bureau B. This urgency hastened our recovery and we are still hoping for success."

"At Bureau B, the word 'hope' is not one of our favorites," said Bodwyn Wook, somewhat sententiously.

"Actually, we have the case well in hand," said Chilke. "Namour and Smonny are in a submarine with no place to go. They are like two flies in a bottle."

"It is not all so jolly and nice," rasped Bodwyn Wook. "They will surface during the night near a beach, come ashore in a dinghy and let the submarine sink. Then they will steal a spaceyacht from the terminal and be away before anyone has time to blink. Have you posted a guard at the spaceport?"

"Not yet, sir."

Bodwyn Wook spoke into a mesh. "It is done now, and

just barely in time, or I do not know Namour. It would be a sorry state of affairs if he bamboozled you again."

"That is true," said Glawen.

Bodwyn Wook leaned forward and ordered the papers on his desk. "Let us revert, if you will, to the Bank of Mircea. I am not at all clear as to the sequence of events—or the events themselves, for that matter."

So far, no one had mentioned Kathcar, but both Glawen and Chilke were assured that, in his attempts at ingratiation, all Kathcar knew had gushed forth like the contents slumping from a split haggis.

Bodwyn Wook spoke on, his voice unusually easy and casual. "According to that rogue Rufo Kathcar, you were lucky enough to deny Sir Denzel's funds to Julian Bohost. Kathcar's version of events is confused; I can't make head nor tail of the transaction, save that certain of the funds found their way into your personal account."

"That is partly correct. I placed these funds into what I call 'the Floreste account'—moneys of which you are aware."

"Hmf. The sum seems to have been significant; am I right?"

"I forget the exact amount; it was probably about fifty thousand sols."

Bodwyn Wook gave another noncommittal grunt. "Whatever the case, it dealt Julian and the LPF a shrewd blow. And what next?"

"We encountered the usual incidents. At Zaster Commander Chilke and I consumed several hygienic meals, but we left the planet before we became truly fit. However, we had taken directions which ultimately led us to Lewyn Barduys on Rosalia. Namour attacked Barduys and we were able to interfere. As a result Barduys will transport the Yips to Rosalia at no cost to us. That is the gist of events."

"Most interesting! And of course there was no other advantage or perquisite gained during this time?"

"Not altogether. Commander Chilke has established a

close friendship with Flitz. More formally, she is Felitzia Stronsi, and she owns Stronsi Ranch. This connection might well be regarded as a 'perquisite' and certainly as an 'advantage.'"

Bodwyn Wook drummed his long fingers on the arms of his chair. "Interesting." He looked at Chilke. "I hope that you confined these activities to off-duty hours?"

"Absolutely!"

"That is good to hear." Bodwyn Wook again ordered the papers on his desk. "And this happy new relationship was the only adjunct or perquisite enjoyed during your mission?"

"Just so, sir," said Chilke.

Glawen added, by way of afterthought: "Except, of course, for the trivial business of the spaceyacht, of which Kathcar has surely informed you."

"He mentioned something of the sort. Where is this luxurious and expensive Fortunatus spaceyacht now?"

"It is stored in a hangar at Ballyloo terminal, near Pasch on the world Kars."

"And why has it been secreted there, when it is the property of the Conservancy?"

"Because we returned to Cadwal in company with Lewyn Barduys, the better to fulfill our mission."

"Hmf," said Bodwyn Wook. "It seems a bit circuitous. But no matter; we shall examine the case from all directions. Conservancy property is sacrosanct." He leaned back in his chair. "That is all for now."

II.

Six days after the two disasters, the Court of High Justice convened in the Moot Hall of the Old Agency building, at the far end of Wansey Way.

The three judges, Dame Melba Veder, Rowan Clattuc and High Justice Hilva Offaw, entered the chamber and took their seats on the dais. The three semicircular tiers were already crowded with spectators. The bailiff struck a gong calling the court to order and the prisoners were brought into the chamber and ushered to seats in the dock. There were eight: Dame Clytie Vergence, Julian Bohost, Roby Mavil, Neuel Bett, Kervin Mostick, Tammas Stirch, Torq Tump and Farganger. All except Tump and Farganger were native-born Naturalists at Stroma and members of the LPF society. All had been present at the hangar when the gunships were sent out against Yipton, and so were considered accomplices to all crimes named in the indictment. Torq Tump gave his place of origin as Smuggler's City on Terence Dowling's World, far off across the Reach. He spoke in a soft voice, without accent, and demonstrated no emotion: neither anger, nor dread nor humility. Farganger, however, had withdrawn into himself and refused to speak, and would not even acknowledge his own name. Unlike Tump, his face was drawn into a mask of contempt for everyone in the chamber.

The spectators found both Torq Tump and Farganger objects of fascination. As for the other defendants, Dame Clytie Vergence, despite the mulish set to her mouth and her generally sullen demeanor, comported herself with dignity. Julian was pale, nervous and disconsolate, and clearly would have rather been a thousand light-years away. Roby Mavil slumped in his chair, his mouth drooping; apparently he had been weeping out of sheer misery and frustration. Bett seemed rueful and glanced here and there with an uncertain grin, as if inviting the spectators to join in his own sardonic amusement for the fix in which he found himself. Stirch sat in a state of morose apathy, while Kervin Mostick glared about in angry defiance.

The bailiff announced that the accused persons sat in readiness to hear and declare themselves in reference to the charges which had been made against them, with defensive counsel at hand. "Now let the prosecutor come forward and state his indictment!"

Elwyn Laverty, a tall thin old man with heavy brows, hollow cheeks and a long keen nose, rose to his feet. "Honorable members of the court, I will dispense with formalities. Six days ago these persons acted or conspired to act in an illicit manner: to wit, they ignited a conflagration at Lutwen Atoll which caused the death of many thousands of men, women and children. The deed is ascribed to them in this fashion. In defiance of Charter law, they imported two Straidor-Ferox gunships and concealed them in a hangar near Stroma, intending to use them against the constituted authority of the Conservancy, as defined by the Charter. If necessary, I can summon witnesses who will attest to this plot, which in itself is a capital offense. These gunships were used to perpetrate the crime of which they are accused. After their attack upon Lutwen Atoll, the gunships returned to Throy. They were followed by patrol craft operated by officers of Bureau B. Upon arrival of reinforcements, an attack upon the hangar resulted in the capture of the defendants. They were discovered in the act of boarding a small spaceship, at one time the property of Sir Denzel Attabus. These persons were taken into custody and brought to Araminta Station and there incarcerated.

"I have given a brief account of the crime, every phase of which can be proved by witness or inference. If the court needs confirmation as to any assertion I have made, I will supply it; otherwise there is no reason for me to prolong my statement."

High Justice Hilva Offaw spoke. "Let us hear from the accused persons. Are you guilty or not guilty, as charged?"

The defense counsel now came forward. "Honorable justices, the persons accused all declare themselves not guilty of the crime imputed to them."

"Indeed! Do they admit to sending the gunships to Lutwen Atoll?"

"They agree that they sent the gunships, but they state that their crime was at worst vandalism; that they intended only to eliminate an eyesore and by this act to improve the natural charm of the environment."

"And the numerous inhabitants burned, drowned, or asphyxiated?"

"There is no proof that such inhabitants existed."

"Interesting! How did they arrive at this conviction?"

"Through the force and solemnity of our own laws, Your Dignity!"

"Even more interesting! Please elaborate and, if you can, cite me the relevant statute."

"It is a matter of reasonable interpretation. For centuries, a firm and fixed doctrine has shaped both our laws and our thinking; this doctrine, indeed, has become the very foundation of our existence as a Conservancy. Both implicitly and explicitly, it has proscribed the habitancy of Lutwen Atoll to any and all persons. The majesty of our institutions and public respect for law makes it necessary to assume that these laws were rigorously enforced, since the idea that we are living in a lawless society is repugnant to everyone.

"Let me reiterate: the thrust of our own statutes denies the existence of habitancy upon Lutwen Atoll. In the absence of such habitancy there was no crime of the sort mentioned in the indictment, which is clearly false, prejudiced, and poorly conceived.

"I declare that the most severe charge which can possibly be placed against the defendants is that of igniting a bonfire without a permit. To this offense the defendants plead guilty. The penalty stipulated for this offense is a fine of not more than twenty-five sols. I therefore petition the justices to fix a reasonable fine, and to allow these worthy folk to settle the matter out of hand and go about their affairs."

Justice Hilva Offaw said to the prosecutor. "Sir, do you care to offer a counter-argument against the compelling statement which we have just heard?"

"No, Your Dignity. It is patently absurd."

"I think not, Prosecutor. There is more to the defense than appears on the surface. In a certain sense, it could be argued that not only the perpetrators of the so-called bonfire, but also every citizen of Araminta Station, living or dead, must share in this guilt."

"Very well, Your Dignity!" said Elwyn Laverty. "Let us

consider counsel's contention that since no person is authorized to take up habitation on Lutwen Atoll, no person has done so. In effect, the defense is pleading that since the laws of gravity forbid rocks to roll up a mountain slope, there are no rocks to be found at the top of the mountain. But no matter! For the sake of argument, let us temporarily accept the position, and agree that the defendants were entitled to expect no human population on Lutwen Atoll as they went about their campaign of beautification, and merely ignited innocent bonfires. Facts however, in the form of charred corpses prove that human beings were indeed present upon the scene of the LPF reclamation program. As to their identities, it is irrelevant. Perhaps they were picnickers from Araminta Station, visiting Lutwen Atoll for a holiday. Now, if counsel will refer to the statute controlling the ignition of bonfires, he will discover that any fire purposely set, without a permit, which results in a fatality may be considered a capital crime, depending upon circumstances. Therefore, even if the charge is merely igniting a bonfire without a permit, the penalty is still severe."

The defense counsel, now somewhat crestfallen, said: "I rest upon my previous statement, which is cogent and should carry the day."

Justice Offaw leaned forward. "You are telling me that the prisoners were motivated by a desire to tidy up the environment when they set fire to Yipton?"

"No one lived there, Your Honor! I have proved this; therefore, what other motive could possibly have influenced them?"

Hilva Offaw said: "Counsel, you have done your best, and your arguments are well reasoned, even though they deal with imaginary situations. This court—and I think that I speak for my colleagues—" he glanced left and right "—reject your theory of the case. The fact that they secretly possessed the gunships and were evidently planning armed rebellion only solidifies the force of the accusation."

The counsel stood silent. Justice Veder asked: "Which of the prisoners piloted the gunships?"

The counsel turned to the prisoners. "Do any of you wish to answer? It cannot affect your case, which is already lost."

Torq Tump said: "I drove one and Farganger the other. We insisted that Julian Bohost ride in one craft and Roby Mavil in the other, since the rest of the group would have been off and away into space, leaving us to face the music. With the two boffins aboard, we knew they would wait until we returned."

Dame Clytie rose to her feet and called out in a loud voice. "I wish to make a statement!"

Hilva Offaw spoke sharply: "I will hear no doctrinal discourses. This court is not a podium for your private opinions. Unless you wish to address the matter of guilt or innocence, you must hold your tongue."

Dame Clytie sullenly returned to her seat. Hilva Offaw said: "There is no mystery as to the court's verdict. The prisoners are guilty of heinous crimes. They are sentenced to death. The executions will occur a week from today."

The prisoners were led away: Dame Clytie marching with chin square, annoyed that she had not been allowed to celebrate the occasion with a burst of oratory; Julian, walking with head bent forward, followed by Roby Mavil on limp legs. Torq Tump and Farganger brought up the rear, muttering together without display of emotion.

The Great Hall emptied. Glawen and Wayness went to the Old Arbor and found a table outside. They were served iced pomegranate juice and sat quietly for a moment. "It is almost over," said Glawen. "I really can't abide these trials; they leave me feeling weak and sick. Perhaps I am not truly suited for a career at Bureau B."

"That's not possible," said Wayness. "You are the youngest commander there has ever been at Bureau B. Everyone says that you will be Superintendent someday."

"No chance of that," grumbled Glawen. "Bodwyn Wook

will never retire. Ah well, no matter. I can't relax yet; Namour and Smonny are still at large, and it is anyone's guess where they are. Perhaps the middle of the ocean."

"They can't land on Ecce. They might survive on Throy, in one of the summer cabins, but only until the supplies ran out. They could land on Deucas, but where would they go? Beasts would destroy them before the week was out."

"Their only hope is the space port here at the station, which is now guarded night and day."

"They'll surely be caught before long." Wayness reached out and took his hands. "And think! In two weeks we'll be married, once and for all, and then you can live a tranquil life."

"That will be nice. I shall enjoy tranquility."

Wayness pursed her lips. "For a time. Then you will become uneasy."

"Perhaps. What of you?"

Wayness considered. "So far life has not been tranquil for either of us."

The two sat quietly, thinking of the events which so far had shaped their lives and what might be still to come.

III.

The refugees from Yipton were fed and sheltered in fourteen camps along the Marmion Foreshore, pending transit to destinations elsewhere.

Tents, lean-tos, huts built of fronds and sticks provided shelter against the warm wind and the occasional rain squall. Bread and protein bars from a synthesizer supplied nutriment, which was supplemented by warehouse stocks and items foraged by the Yips themselves. The Mar River yielded clams, eels, eel roe, and small amphibians; from the countryside came seeds, nuts, pods and legumes. Women and children waded the tide pools for sea snails, despite the presence of poisonous yellow sea toads, spiny coral, and an occasional swarm of pipefish, which were netted and boiled to make soup. Teams from Araminta Station maintained order, provided medical attention, and registered the occupants, by name, age, sex and status.

Scharde Clattuc flew north from Araminta Station to the camp headquarters near the mouth of the Mar River. Here he learned that the Yips were registered at the separate camps, there being no reason to create a master file of the entire population.

Scharde asked: "There is no organization to the camps? By this I mean that the various castes and levels are all mixed together?"

"So I would suppose," said the clerk. "For a fact, I know little of such things; to me a Yip is a Yip."

"That is a good approximation. Still, in the highest caste are the Oomps, and they are especially careful of their status."

"I know that much, at any rate. The Oomps insisted on separate facilities, and we saw no reason not to humor them. They are at Camp Three, a quarter mile up the river."

Scharde walked along the riverbank to Camp Three and went to the supervisor's shack. Here he encountered a middle-aged woman, stout and efficient, an immigrant to the Station from old Stroma. "Yes, sir?"

"I am Commander Scharde Clattuc, Bureau B. How are affairs at Camp Three?"

"I have no complaints. The Yips are courteous and definitely respond to courtesy."

"That has been my own experience, for the most part. I understand that these are all Oomps here at Camp Three?"

The clerk smiled grimly. "At Yipton there were one hundred and eighty-two Oomps. Here at camp they number one hundred and sixty-one. In short, Only twenty-one Oomps died in the fire."

"That is known as 'survivor technique.'"

"Either that or an elbow in the eye."

Scharde looked around the camp. "Where are they now?"

"Here and there; some are picking wild plums from the

grove yonder. All Deucas is open to them if they wanted to escape, but they caught sight of a couple long-necked onniclats on the hillside yonder, and a grasstiger too. The Yips aren't cowards but they aren't fools either."

Scharde laughed. "I believe that you have a record of their names?"

"So I do." The clerk handed him a print-out. Scharde read, then looked up in dissatisfaction. "These are their formal names[*]: 'Hyram Bardolc Fiveny,' 'Gobinder Mosk Tuchinander.'"

"That is true, but those are the names they gave me."

"And you do not list their familiar names?"

"I'm afraid not. I saw no reason to do so."

"No matter. Thank you for your help."

The clerk watched Scharde cross to where an Oomp sat on a fallen log, idly juggling pebbles back and forth between his strong hands. Scharde asked a question; the Oomp reflected a moment, then seemed to shrug and pointed up the river.

Scharde followed the path along the riverbank fifty yards, and came upon a Yip floating face down in the water. From time to time he raised his head for a gasp of air, then resumed his inspection of the bottom. Suddenly he lunged with his right arm, then rolling over, held high a two-foot eel, squirming in the crotch of a forked stick. The Oomp swam to shore and dropped his catch into a basket.

Scharde came forward. The Yip, on his knees disengaging the eel looked up in blank startlement. He was not a young man, possibly as old as Scharde himself, though he looked younger, with his broad shoulders, flat stomach, strong arms and legs. Scharde said: "You are a deft fisherman."

The Yip shrugged. "The eels are easy to catch. They are fat and sluggish."

"Did you catch fish at Yipton?"

---

[*]   See Glossary B

"Not eels. Sometimes I tried for scoons and gyrators, but it is not so easy in the ocean."

"I should think not," said Scharde. "Only a very good swimmer would try at all."

"Yes, that is so."

"I seem to recognize you," said Scharde. "Your name is Selious. Do you know me?"

"I do not think so."

"It has been many years since we met. How long would you say? Fifteen years? Twenty?"

The Yip dropped his eyes to the basket. "I can't be sure."

"Do you know my name?"

The Yip shook his head and rose to his feet. "I will go now. I must skin my eels."

"Let us talk a bit," said Scharde. He moved back a few paces and seated himself on a fallen log. "Put your basket into the water to keep the eels fresh."

Selious hesitated then did as Scharde suggested.

"Sit down," said Scharde. He pointed to a spot on the sand. "Rest yourself."

Selious half-squatted, half-knelt, without pleasure. Scharde asked: "Where is your friend Catterline?"

Selious tilted his head back toward the camp. "He is yonder. We were both lucky to have escaped the fire."

"Yes, that was good luck." Scharde plucked a blade of sawgrass and whisked it back and forth. Selious watched him with a joyless face. Scharde spoke gently: "Do you know something, Selious? I think you lied to me."

Selious cried indignantly: "What is this? Never did I lie to you!"

"Don't you remember? You told me that you could not swim. Catterline said the same. It was for this reason—so you told me—that you could not keep the lady Marya from drowning in Wansey Lagoon."

"After twenty years I remember no such events."

"But you do!" said Scharde, for a sudden instant baring his teeth.

"Never!" Selious cried out with sudden energy. "I told only the truth."

"You told me that you could not swim, and that was why you could not save the lady from drowning. But you and I know better. You swim very well. So did my wife Marya. You and Catterline held her underwater until she was dead."

"No, no! That is not true!"

"Who tipped her out of the boat: you or Catterline? This time I shall find out the truth."

Selious wilted. "It was Catterline! I knew nothing about what he intended!"

"Really. You just swam out with Catterline to keep him company?"

"That is how it was."

"Now then, Selious, we come to the important question, and it will mean much to you. Everyone else at this camp will be leaving for beautiful new homes, but I will take you off and imprison you alone in a little hut, where you will never see the light nor hear voices—unless you tell the truth. Do not rise to your feet, or I will shoot you in the belly, and you will feel great pain. And then, I will take you to the dark hut, and you will be alone forever."

Selious spoke in an anguished voice: "And what if I tell the truth?"

"Punishment less terrible."

Selious bowed his head. "I will tell the truth."

"First, then: who gave you the orders to drown Marya? Quick now! The truth!"

Selious looked to right and left, then said: "It was Namour." Selious suddenly became smilingly virtuous, in a manner typically Yip. "I told him that I did not wish to harm a weak and helpless female. He brushed aside my scruples. The woman, so he declared, was an off-world person, no better than vermin. She was a malicious interloper, with no right to breathe our good air or eat our food or displace qualified persons from posts of honor. It was proper to eliminate such persons from the environment. Catterline felt that there was logic to the concept, and that in any event I must obey Namour's command. I had no choice but to agree, and so the deed was done."

Scharde inspected Selious for a moment or two. Selious began to fidget.

Scharde said: "You are not telling me everything."

Selious protested with vigor: "But I am indeed! What more is there to say?"

"Why did Namour order you to commit such a dreadful deed?"

"I explained this! Namour gave the reasons!"

"Surely you did not find these reasons credible?"

Selious shrugged. "It was not for me to question Namour."

"You truly believed that these were Namour's real reasons for wishing to drown the lady?"

Again Selious shrugged. "Namour's motives meant nothing to me. I was a Yip from Yipton; the Station was a world past my understanding."

"Did someone give Namour orders in this matter?"

Selious looked off across the river. "It happened a long time ago. I can tell you no more."

"Did Smonny give Namour the orders?"

"Smonny was gone."

"Then who gave the orders?"

"If ever I knew, I cannot remember now."

Scharde rose to his feet. "You have been cooperative, apparently so far as you were able."

"Yes, that is absolutely true! Be assured: you may rely upon my veracity! Now that all is in order, I will return to my eels."

"Not just yet. You robbed Marya of her life."

"Well, yes: twenty years ago. So then, consider: she has been dead twenty years; she will remain dead forever. What is this twenty years when compared to the infinity still to come? It is almost trivial. After, let us say, a hundred thousand years, this twenty years will seem no more than a wisp."

Scharde heaved a sad sigh. "You are a philosopher, Selious. I am not so gifted, and now I must take you and Catterline to Araminta Station."

"But why? I can tell you no more!

"As to that, we shall see."

IV.

Scharde took Selious and Catterline to Araminta Station. They were isolated and questioned separately. Catterline's recollections matched those of Selious, in all significant areas, though they were less explicit.

Selious was taken to an old Bureau B consultation chamber, seldom used by reason of its gloom and archaic fittings. Selious was escorted into the chamber and seated upon the cushions of a massive old chair facing the dais and the magistrate's lectern. Here he was left alone for half an hour, that he might brood upon the grim circumstances to which his association with Namour had brought him. The room, panelled in dark brown fanique burl, was illuminated by three small panes high in the back wall, which seemed to augment rather than dispel the gloom. Selious sat quietly at first, then began to fidget, drumming his fingers on the arms of the chair, in time to the erratic rhythms of Yip music.

Bodwyn Wook, wearing an unusual costume of baggy black breeches, a dull red tunic, black boots, a white cravat, and a soft judicial cap of black velvet, entered the chamber, mounted to the dais and seated himself behind the lectern. Only then did he examine Selious. "You are a murderer."

Selious stared in fascination. Finally he managed to say: "Whatever happened was long ago."

"Time means nothing," intoned Bodwyn Wook. "Look at your hands! They pushed a woman down deep, and deeper still, while she struggled to breathe and died at last, to her own great distress. Do you have anything to say?"

Selious cried out in a reedy voice: "It was not explained to me thus. I was told I was doing a great deed, and who can say that I was not? This was a creature brought from an alien world and given the best, while in Yipton we were not considered human."

Bodwyn Wook raised his eyes to the ceiling. "That sort of argument is now moot; you must speak to the point."

"What can I say? Everything is known to you!'

"Not everything! You are withholding facts—even though you do not realize this yourself."

Selious blinked. "I will cite these facts if you tell me what they are."

"The question is this, and it is of the highest importance. Namour ordered you to drown the lady—but who gave Namour his orders?"

"That is unknown to me, sir."

"Perhaps yes, perhaps no. I will explain this seeming sophistry. Your brain is like a great warehouse, containing a million parcels of memory, or more. Each parcel is catalogued, and arranged according to the rules established by your individual retrieval system. We shall call this system your 'clerk.' When you need to recall a fact, the clerk glances into an index and instantly knows where the fact is filed and fetches it up for your attention. The clerk's efficiency is marvelous. Still, each day new parcels enter the warehouse, to be indexed and cross-indexed. Inevitably the brain becomes cluttered or crowded. Sometimes the clerk discards old parcels, or even tears out whole pages in the index. More often it simply pushes the old parcels back into the cobwebs. As time goes by the clerk reorganizes the index. Sometimes the clerk becomes lazy or fastidious and pretends that these dirty old parcels are better left ignored, and gives back a false report. And at last heaps of trash pile up at the back of your brain. Is all this clear?"

"You speak with authority! I must accept your concepts."

"Just so. Now: to the point! I will ask a question. You

must send your clerk out hot-foot to find the answer. Are you ready?"

"Yes, sir."

"My question is this: who ordered you to drown the lady Marya?"

"It was Namour."

"Ha ha! The clerk has done its job smartly and well. Now, another question: who gave Namour his orders in this regard?"

"I do not know!"

Bodwyn Wook scowled. "The clerk has scamped his duty. Send it out again with fresh instructions. Tell it to check its index with special care."

Selious threw his hands to the side. "I can tell you nothing. Now, if you please, I will go."

"Not just yet; in fact, we have only started."

"Ay caray! What next?"

"It is no great matter. We have discovered a way to help the clerk. First we search the index thoroughly; we must look here and there, prodding in odd places, startling up all sorts of lost memories. Your brain in effect is like a wilderness of lost regions and secret landscapes, which we must explore, venturing into the most inaccessible regions. Perhaps sooner, perhaps later, we will find the parcel we are looking for, but it is a tedious job. We learn more about you than we want to know."

Selious spoke in a subdued voice: "It seems a pointless task, especially when the parcel you seek may be utterly lost."

"That is a chance we must take," said Bodwyn Wook. "We will start the search at once; there is no reason to delay."

In the Bureau B laboratory a pair of specialists anaesthetized Selious, then fitted instruments of exquisite delicacy to his neural apparatus. The analytical process was set in motion. In the end the episode under investigation was brought into focus and explored.

The facts were as Selious had stated, with a filigree of detail. They revealed a chilling lack of emotion incident to the drowning.

Among the details was a wry joke made by Namour, coupled to a name and a glance over his shoulder.

The allusion was clear; the name was definite.

There was now nothing more required of Selious and he was restored to consciousness. A pair of Bureau B constables took him to the old jail across the River Wan, where he was housed in a cell with Catterline, pending a final adjudication.

Scharde and Bodwyn Wook conferred in the superintendent's office. Hilda served tea and biscuits. "Finally," said Bodwyn Wook, "we come to a resolution of the case."

"It has weighed on me for twenty years."

"And now what will you do? The decision is yours to make."

"I will resolve the case as it must be resolved. There is no other way."

Bodwyn Wook heaved a deep sigh. "That is my viewpoint. What of Glawen?"

"He must know that his mother was drowned. Call him here now, and we will put the facts before him."

"As you say." Bodwyn Wook spoke into the communicator mesh. Ten minutes passed, while dusk came to Araminta Station. Glawen appeared in the doorway. He looked from one man to the other, then came forward and at Bodwyn Wook's gesture seated himself.

Bodwyn Wook in dry terse phrases acquainted him with the information gleaned from Selious and Catterline.

Bodwyn Wook finished the recital and leaned back in his chair. Glawen looked at his father. "So what do we do now?"

"We will pursue the investigation in the morning."

V.

At dawn a rain squall blew in from the sea, then fleeted away over the hills to the west. Two hours later the sun broke through the clouds and Araminta Station seemed to glisten.

Six persons approached Clattuc House. They entered the foyer, and Scharde Clattuc spoke to the doorman. He heard what he wished to hear, then the six climbed the stairs to the second floor: Scharde, Glawen, Bodwyn Wook, a pair of Bureau B underlings and a matron. They trooped down the hall and stopped before the door giving upon Spanchetta's apartments. Scharde pressed the bell button. There was a long pause, during which Spanchetta presumably inspected them on her guardian screen.

The door remained closed; Spanchetta had decided to receive no visitors on this particular morning. Polite convention now required that the rebuffed visitors depart, interpreting Spanchetta's coolness in any way they chose. Scharde, however, pushed the button again, and then again.

At last Spanchetta's voice sounded peevishly through the annunciator. "I am not receiving this morning. You must call at another time, but not today, nor tomorrow."

Scharde spoke into the mesh. "Open the door, Spanchetta. This is not a social call."

"What do you want?"

"We must consult with you on an important matter."

"I am not in the mood for consultations; indeed, I find myself indisposed. You must come back some other time."

"That is not convenient; we must see you now. Open the door, or we will send for the master key."

Another minute passed, then the door was snatched open, revealing Spanchetta's imposing person, dressed in a sweeping gown of cerise velvet, with a black embroidered vest and incongruously small pointed dancer's slippers. Her lustrous dark hair as always was twisted into coils and piled into a pyramid of unlikely proportions above her broad white brow. Her bosom was magnificent; her hips were grand; as always, she seemed charged with a coarse heavy-blooded vitality. She stepped back angrily as Scharde pushed the door open wide, and entered the sumptuous marble reception chamber.

Spanchetta cried out in a poignant contralto: "What boorish behavior! But then, you have never acted otherwise! You shame the House of Clattuc!"

The remaining five members of the group entered the room; Spanchetta inspected them with revulsion. "What is this all about? Tell me and leave; I will attend to it later. At the moment I lack the patience to deal with you."

Bodwyn Wook said: "Spanchetta, you may now cease your sputtering. We are about to perform the usual routine." He spoke to the matron. "Search her well, in every fold and crevice; she is a sly one."

"Just a moment!" bawled Spanchetta. "Did I hear you correctly? Are you bereft of your senses? What is the charge?"

"Don't you know?" asked Scharde. "Your crime is murder."

Spanchetta became very still. "Murder? Of whom?"

"Marya."

Spanchetta threw back her head and laughed—in relief?—and the monumental pillar of dark curls swayed dangerously. "Surely you joke? Where are your indications? In fact, how can there be evidence for a non-existent crime?"

"You will find out in due course. Matron, search the prisoner. Hold quiet, Spanchetta, if you value your dignity."

"This is an abominable persecution! I shall take all legal action against you!"

"That is at your option."

The matron made a perfunctory search, finding nothing.

"Very well, then," said Bodwyn Wook. "We will take you to my offices, where you will be formally arraigned. Do you care to change your garments or put on a cloak?"

"This is detestable nonsense!" stormed Spanchetta. "I believe that you are insane, and I will not go with you!"

Bodwyn Wook said: "You may walk, Spanchetta, or you will be trussed hand and foot and ride in a barrow. Still, you must come. The matron will help you into serviceable garments."

"Bah! What an inconvenience," muttered Spanchetta. "I

will put on my cloak." She started from the room. At a sign
from Bodwyn Wook, the matron and the two sergeants followed. Spanchetta halted, and made an irascible gesture. "I
shall get my own cloak! Stay where you are!"

"That would be irregular," explained Bodwyn Wook.
"It would not be proper procedure. You may not go unat-
tended."

"I will do as I choose!" Spanchetta thrust the matron
aside. "You must wait here!" She turned toward the hall.

"I am obliged to obey orders," said the matron. "I will
accompany you."

"You may not do so! It is unreasonable and I will not
have it!"

Scharde and Bodwyn Wook looked at each other, puzzled
and suddenly alert. Spanchetta's conduct had become false
and unnatural.

"Just a moment," said Bodwyn Wook. "You are distrait. Sit
in this chair and regain your composure. We will procure your
cloak."

Spanchetta would not listen and tried to run from the
room. The sergeants conducted her to a chair and forced
her to sit. She was handcuffed to the chair and left in the
charge of the matron. The others cautiously explored the
apartment. In Arles' old bedroom they found Smonny,
drowsing on the bed. In the adjoining study Namour sat
reading a book. He looked up with no surprise. "Gentlemen? What is it this time?"

"It is the end of the line," said Bodwyn Wook.

Namour nodded thoughtfully and closed the book. He
reached to place the book on a nearby table; Glawen jumped
forward and seized his wrist, and pulled it away from a small
weapon which would have dazed them with an explosion of
light, enabling Namour to kill them. Scharde folded Namour's
arms together and constrained them with tape. He searched
Namour, found and removed a gun, a dagger and a dart
ejector. "Namour is a walking arsenal," said Bodwyn Wook.
"Have you truly made him meek?"

"I hope so," said Scharde. "With Namour nothing is certain. He might have a poison squirt under his tongue, so don't peer too directly into his face."

Namour gave a weary laugh. "I am not the maniacal warrior you take me for."

Scharde showed a thin smile. "One way or another, the corpses accumulate behind you."

Bodwyn Wook asked Namour with clinical interest: "Have you ever kept count?"

"No sir." Namour seemed bored by the question. He asked Scharde: "So now, which is it to be: Bureau B or Schedule D?"

"Schedule D, of course," said Scharde. "Otherwise we must expend our efforts and give up our time at three separate trials. Schedule D is indicated."

VI.

The prisoners were quietly removed from Clattuc House by a back entrance, and taken to where Chilke waited in a tourist air omnibus. They were loaded aboard and shackled to their seats, despite strong objections from both Smonny and Spanchetta. Namour had nothing to say.

Chilke took the omnibus into the sky and set the autopilot; the craft flew to the west, with Scharde, Bodwyn Wook and Glawen aboard, along with the three prisoners. Bodwyn Wook told them: "Make yourselves comfortable; we have far to go."

Smonny demanded: "Where are you taking us?"

"You will see. It is a place you know well."

Spanchetta cried out: "This is a farrago and a scandal, quite illegal!"

Bodwyn Wook spoke in a kindly voice: "So it might be, if we were acting on behalf of Bureau B. That is not the case. We are wearing our IPCC hats, and the rules are different."

"It is a farce! You are a strutting little weasel! I fail to understand."

Bodwyn Wook's voice was somewhat less tolerant. "In

essence, the doctrine is simple. The IPCC Mode Manual describes four levels of reactive conduct appropriate to four levels of venality. Schedule D is the most drastic. When an offense transcends the ordinary, such as the destruction of Stroma, Schedule D is the approved response."

Spanchetta cried out: "I had nothing to do with Stroma! Still you are dragging me out in this dirty car!"

"In the case of Stroma, you are an accessory after the fact."

Scharde said somberly: "Additionally, you are twenty years a murderess. You induced Namour to drown Marya, which he did, using Catterline and Selious as his instruments. They have confessed; the crime is certain, and you both must pay the penalty."

Spanchetta turned to Namour. "Tell them that it is not so, that I never gave you any such orders! You must do so; there is no reason for me to be dragged away!"

Namour said: "Spanchetta, I am tired. An inexorable current is carrying us to remote places, and I have no will to resist it. The truth is as we have heard. I will not deny it, and you too must drift on the current."

Spanchetta gave an inarticulate cry and turned to look out across the wonderful landscapes which she would never see again.

The omnibus flew through the night, over the Great Western Ocean, and at dawn arrived at the equatorial continent Ecce. Over black slime and carpets of rotting jungle flew the omnibus. Halfway into the morning the gray cone of the dead volcano Shattorak lifted above the horizon: an island in an ocean of festering swamp. The summit of Shattorak was now deserted; at one time it had served Smonny as a jail for the detention and torment of her enemies, which had included both Chilke and Scharde Clattuc.

The omnibus landed; the prisoners reluctantly alighted, and stood looking around the area. The old structures had now decayed, except for a small concrete box which had served as a communication cubicle.

"So here you are, and here you will spend your days," said

Bodwyn Wook. "Expect no visitors nor succor nor tidings of any kind. In short, you must take care of yourselves."

"You may or may not wish advice," said Glawen. "I will give it to you anyway. You will notice that a stockade surrounds the summit. It is broken in spots and your first concern should be to repair the holes; otherwise you will be attacked by visitors from the jungle. We are leaving a dozen cases of provisions; there may be more in the old cook shed."

In a woeful voice Spanchetta cried out: "And when these are gone, we shall surely starve!"

"Not if you work," said Scharde. "Smonny knows the routine. Outside the prisoners raised crops; you should have no difficulty doing the same, and we are leaving you gardening tools and seeds. There are also nuts, pods, berries and tubers in the jungle, but it is a dangerous place. Still, you will soon learn the tricks of survival. Smonny's prisoners built nests in the trees, with ladders which they raised at night. Perhaps some of these will still be useful. All in all, you will find life at Shattorak an interesting challenge."

"It is a dreadful prospect!" cried Spanchetta. "Is it right that I, Spanchetta Clattuc, must now climb trees that I may sleep in security?"

"It is a unique prison," said Scharde. "You can escape any time you like. The gates to the stockade are always unlocked, so you need make no furtive plots. If and when the mood comes on you to escape, simply step through the stockade, walk down the slope and make for the coast."

"Your advice is inspiring," said Namour. "We shall start making plans at once."

Chilke spoke to Smonny: "It is really too bad, Madame Zigonie, that this is how it had to end. We have had good times and bad times together; you once bought me a fine dinner, but on the other hand you put me into that doghole yonder. We can go to look at it now, if you like. I still wake up screaming from the nightmares. Also, you never paid me my six-months salary. I don't suppose you are in a position to settle up?"

Smonny merely glared.

"No matter," said Chilke. "I hold no grudges, despite my time in the doghole."

Chilke climbed into the omnibus; the others followed. The three prisoners stood in a group, watching as the omnibus lifted into the sky, dwindled away to the east and was gone.

CHAPTER 9

I.

The Yips were gone from the Marmion Foreshore; the fourteen camps were as if they had never existed. To the east the ocean lay blue and tranquil save for a few low swells. Surf slid up the beach, gurgling and foaming, to slide back without haste. Wind blew through the palm trees, though now there was no one to listen. The Yips had come and the Yips had gone, leaving not so much as a charred ember to mark their stay. One and all, they had been transported to the Mystic Isles of Muran Bay, on the world Rosalia.

II.

Glawen and Wayness were wed at Riverview House. Cora Tamm had yearned for a traditional ceremony, complete with candles, music and the ancient rite of the golden hoops, and so it had been. Now, in a temporary cabin on their grant of land at the foot of the Bolo Hills, Glawen and Wayness planned their new home. They would build on a low slope beside a quiet river, using walls of rammed earth and timber posts. At the back of the site stood two gnarled flame-apple trees, with a pair of sylvanic elms to either side. While they waited for the equipment which would dig their foundations and form their walls, they planted vines on the hillside and an orchard of fruit trees on a nearby meadow.

III.

Lewyn Barduys revisited the wilderness lodges operated by the Conservancy and was relieved to find that his old enthusiasms were not misplaced. On this occasion his mood was analytical and he took careful notes. The charm of the inns, so he discovered, derived not from mysticism or the expectations of the visitors, but from practical and consistent techniques.

The first thesis governing every inn was definite: it must be an integral part of the landscape, with no interference from elsewhere in the form of color contrasts, discordant shape, music or other entertainment. Comfort, quiet and good food were essential, since the visitors would be distracted in their absence. Similarly, the staff should wear an unobtrusive uniform and be trained to conduct themselves in a formal and impersonal manner, devoid of familiarity and over-affability.

Barduys visited each of the inns in turn, spending two and sometimes three days at each. On this occasion he travelled alone; Flitz' interests were now directed elsewhere.

Barduys presently returned from his inspection of the wilderness lodges. His business at Araminta Station was complete. He had secured for the Mystic Isles a population which precisely fitted his purposes. These ex-Yips were easy, pliable, of great physical charm, with an aptitude for the environment of music, flowers and festivals he intended to encourage. There would also be schools and ample opportunity for social mobility, should anyone choose to wrench himself or herself away from the Mystic Isles. Further, Namour and Smonny had disappeared from human ken. Barduys, despite his previous emotion, now could not contemplate their joint fates without a shudder. He put them from his mind and resolved never to think of them again.

The time had come for his departure. A good deal of L-B Construction business awaited him at Zaster, on Yaphet by Gilbert's Green Star. He must undertake a comprehensive overview of his far-flung enterprises. There would be consultations, feasibility studies of new projects, and a flurry of executive decisions. Then, unless emergency called him elsewhere, he would continue across space to Rosalia and the work which had become his preoccupation.

Egon and Cora Tamm had arranged a farewell party for Lewyn Barduys at Riverview House. After lunch the guests went to sit on the terrace. Autumn had come to Araminta Station; the air carried a faint reek of wood smoke and old leaves. Spatters of sunlight sifted through the trees; the river flowed placidly to the side, almost directly under the terrace. A mood of gentle melancholy pervaded sky, air and all the landscape.

On the terrace conversation was languid and voices were muted. Among the company were folk originally from Stroma: ex-Warden Algin Ballinder, his wife Etrune and his daughter Sunje; another ex-warden, Wilder Fergus and his spouse Dame Larica; several of Wayness' old friends: Tancred Sahuz and Alyx-Marie Swarn. Also on hand were Dame Lamy Offaw and her son Uther, the one-time Bold Lion, Scharde Clattuc, Claude Laverty and his spouse Walda. Bodwyn Wook sat somewhat apart, a loose-crowned black cap pulled low over his forehead. Glawen thought that he seemed out of sorts; certainly none of his jaunty mannerisms were on display.

For a time the company discussed the unprecedented amount of home construction now in progress across the Araminta enclave, which made for many delays. Dame Lamy declared that blunders, obfuscation and inefficiency at Bureau D was responsible for the inconveniences. She suggested that Lewyn Barduys call in L-B Construction and put an end to the muddle. Barduys was inclined to agree with her assessment of Bureau D, but he politely rejected the proposal. Now then, if Dame Lamy had asked him to build a dozen more wilderness lodges, he would be only too happy to oblige. There were sites on Throy which cried out for quiet little inns: for instance, on Throop's Heath, where the andorils played their odd version of bowls; also, among the rocks above Cape Wale, where the great southerly storms dashed waves against the cliffs.

The proposals were interesting, said Dame Lamy tartly, but if Lewyn Barduys had his way, there would be hostelries at two-mile intervals everywhere across Deucas and Throy, and why forget Ecce? Were the tourists not interested in horrid monsters?

Barduys conceded that, without a doubt, Dame Lamy knew best, and that he would be guided by her views.

For a time the group sat quietly, lulled by the tranquility of the afternoon. Egon Tamm sighed and roused himself. "The bad times are gone; there is nothing left to smite and destroy save Bureau D."

"Bower Diffin does not deserve execution," said Glawen, referring to the Bureau D supervisor, "even though it will be two months before we can have our excavations."

"True," sniffed Larica Fergus. "But a good horse-whipping would smarten him up a bit."

Uther Offaw, who was in training as an academician in the field of historical philosophy, said grandly: "The present is now! The past is gone and already seems unreal! We have entered an age of blandness; it is safe to become outraged over small nuisances."

Larica Fergus said tartly: "I have known enough sensation; I am happy with blandness."

Uther Offaw frowned up at the sky. "And when does blandness become lethargy; when does lethargy lapse into sloth? Where then are the higher virtues? Where is romance? Achievement? Adventure? Glory? Heroism?"

"I am too old for such exploits," said Dame Larica. "I fell down yesterday and hurt my knee."

"It is all beside the boards," snapped Dame Lamy Offaw. "We have had a surfeit of tragedy. Even the mention of your sore leg is in poor taste."

Ex-Warden Ballinder pulled thoughtfully at his black pirate's beard. "Recent events have been awesome, but perhaps they may serve as a salutary catharsis, especially if our descendants learn from our travail."

Sunje Ballinder told her father: "I am your descendant. What is it again that I am supposed to learn?"

"Remain honest, steadfast and true! Adopt no weird philosophies. Avoid exotic cults and intellectual miasma."

"You should have told me sooner," said Sunje. "The hay is in the barn."

Algin Ballinder gave his head a sad shake. "I wonder what you will tell your own children."

"Sunje is rather secretive," said Alyx-Marie. "She may well hide their shoes to keep them home of nights and out of mischief."

Sunje stretched her long legs languorously. "I am not at all secretive; quite the reverse. No one asks my opinion because I make such embarrassing disclosures. At the moment I can't help but feel that the world is a less amusing place with Dame Clytie gone. I mourn for the old she-buffalo."

Dame Lamy Offaw showed a prim smile. "There is still Bodwyn Wook and his picturesque antics. Enjoy them while he is still with us; once he goes you will not soon find his like again."

Bodwyn Wook jerked himself forward and struck the table with his fist. "Your words are a catalyst! As of this instant, I resign my position as Superintendent of Bureau B! The decision is irrevocable! When now you insult me you insult a liberated man, so beware!"

The statement stimulated a spate of excited outcries. "Impossible! Bureau B will be a hollow shell; who will chide the criminals? Who will scold the Bureau B constables?"

Wayness called out: "We will need a new Superintendent. I nominate Rufo Kathcar!"

Cora Tamm said gently: "Bodwyn Wook is just joking. He wants to dissolve our ennui."

"I distrust the old rascal," grumbled Dame Lamy Offaw, an ancient adversary of Bodwyn Wook at Garden Society meetings. "He is a master at getting everyone's hopes up."

Bodwyn Wook roared: "I am doing one thing only. I am trying to slip quietly away into oblivion, and even this causes an uproar!"

Egon Tamm asked Barduys: "Where is Flitz, by the way? She was invited, and so was Eustace Chilke; neither are on hand."

Barduys smiled. "Flitz and Eustace Chilke, like Bodwyn Wook, have resigned their positions. Chilke now commands a Fortunatus spaceyacht. He made this fact known to Flitz; they conferred at length and in the end decided to become vagabonds and wander among the planets."

Sunje was startled. "Chilke? Flitz?"

"Yes. They have more in common than one might think. I expect that one of these days they will drop by Araminta Station and bring you news of distant places."

Later, when most of the guests had departed, Barduys joined Glawen and Wayness at the side of the terrace. "Chilke holds title to the Fortunatus we left at Ballyloo. Neither Egon Tamm nor Bodwyn Wook will protest, in view of certain concessions I have made to them, including the Clayhacker space yacht. I also advised them in regard to the holdings of Titus and Simonetta Zigonie. The Conservator is entitled to sue the pair for damages, which the two caused to be inflicted on Stroma and the surrounding cliff. This is real property owned by the Conservancy. After securing a judgment, the Conservator could sell Shadow Valley Ranch for a large sum, which could be added to the 'Floreste' fund. I indicated that L-B Construction would build the New Orpheum on favorable terms. For these reasons Bodwyn Wook failed to so much as whimper when I suggested turning over the Fortunatus to Chilke and Flitz."

"That is very generous of you," said Wayness.

Barduys merely waved his hand. "Now then: to another detail, namely my wedding present to the two of you. It is another Fortunatus, identical to the first. It is waiting for you at the space terminal, here at the Station. I wish you the enjoyment of it, and of all your years together. The keys and codebox are at the dispatcher's office."

Glawen stammered: "This is a most wonderful gift! I don't know what to say."

Barduys, not ordinarily demonstrative, touched Glawen's shoulder. "I have a great deal of money, but few friends. I count you, and now Wayness, among them. And I need not mention the deep cold hole at Bainsey Castle which we shared." After a pause he continued. "I must go, before I become sentimental. One last word: please come to Rosalia in your Fortunatus and visit me at the Bainsey Castle Lodge, when it opens for business. Flitz and Chilke have promised to be on hand."

"Then we will be there too."

A few minutes later Egon Tamm took Bodwyn Wook aside. "I cannot believe that you have definitely resigned your position. What will you do with yourself? You will be like a fish out of water."

Bodwyn Wook made an expansive gesture. "This talk of vagabonds and wandering here and there has made me nervous. I have never been anywhere save a week's excursion to Soum, which took me to ten breweries and four temples. Everyone has something to say of Old Earth; some praise it mightily: others tell me that they put out their shoes to be cleaned, only to have them stolen. I must see for myself. When I come home, I will be chairman for the New Orpheum project. Floreste will have his great dream after all."

Cora Tamm brought out a fresh pot of tea, and sitting on the terrace the group watched the sun settle into the hills beyond the river.

GLOSSARY

The Gnosis is a philosophical quasi-religious system devoid of both formal organization and a hierarchy of priests. The thrifty Soumi reasoned that a credo purporting to provide enlightenment must be readily comprehensible; if expensive specialists were needed for interpretation, the doctrine must be considered unsuitable and impractical. One of the elders deputed to select an optimum doctrine was blunt, averring that 'only fools would foist a religion upon themselves which cost them their hard-earned money.'

Gnosis itself was not without interest, and embodied a number of novel concepts. The Cosmos, or ALL, as it was known, included the whole of its own equipment and required no further assistance in the form of a deity or 'prime mover,' thus obviating the need for an expensive class of intermediaries, priests or other interpreters of the divine will.

ALL existed in the shape of a four-dimensional torus

rotating at a stately rate, so that beginnings and endings constantly merged with each other, and each human being lived over and over again in the same body, either perfecting itself through careful practice of the Ameliorations, and eventually moving upward or failing, whereupon it must attempt the same life again, over and over until satisfactory adjustments had been made, so that it might enter a new 'Xoma,' which once again must be lived in exact accord with propriety. In general, Gnosis was considered a cheerful and optimistic doxology, since the worst that could happen to a transgressor was that he or she might backslide a Xoma or two.

The Ameliorations were taught children along with other schoolwork, so that at an early age they were trained to gentility, cleanliness, industry, thrift, and respect for their elders.

From time to time an individual might show strange or unusual personality traits, so that he became known as a 'wild jay,' and prompted his family and friends to a good deal of rueful head-shaking. Often these 'wild jays' would go to live in a special quarter of Soumjiana, known as 'Lemuria.' In the streets and plazas of Soumjiana hundreds of vendors grilled sausages on braziers and sold them to passers-by; most of the city's sausage vendors, musicians and street artists were 'Lemurians.'

In his private life, the Soumian was generally prim and fastidious, his most notable vice being, perhaps, over-indulgence at the table. His sexual habits were somewhat mysterious; overt sexual misconduct, however, incurred his disapproval, and also aroused a great spate of gossip. The offending parties quickly became notorious, and slunk about their daily routines trying to pretend nothing had happened.

To the off-world observer wealthy folk were hard to distinguish from persons of ordinary income, since everyone made a great point of owning only 'the best,' meaning goods of durability, excellence of finish and practical func-

tion. The affluent could be picked out only by the most
subtle of indications, and great skill was used in demon-
strating one's position in life while carefully avoiding
'bouschterness'*. All Soumi, no matter what their caste,
reckoned themselves ladies and gentlemen. A paradox of
Soumi behaviour is their emphatic dedication to egalitarianism, while simultaneously supporting a society of rigid
stratification into as many as twenty levels of status. These
status levels are not formally recognized, nor are they char-
acterized by a nomenclature; nevertheless their reality
impinges upon everyone and he or she is continually gaug-
ing his or her personal status against that of everyone in
sight. Soumi are insistent upon asserting superiority of
caste over their inferiors, while caustic and envious of those
who assert superiority over themselves. Such tensions create a dynamic quality of striving and maintenance of gen-
teel standards; scandals are always enjoyed if for no other
reason than the diminished status of the persons involved,
which, by a sort of transcendental osmosis, augments the
status of other folk.

The workings of this mysterious system are fascinating. If
a dozen strangers are placed in a room, within minutes the
hierarchy of caste will have been established. How? No one
knows, save the Soumi themselves.

Despite the absence of titles or precise nomenclature,
the level of a person's caste is denoted exactly by a subtle
use of linguistic tonality, or phrasing of a sentence, or the
choice of appropriate terminology: nuances which the
Soumi ear instantly recognizes. Still, the overt basis of
Soumi society is expressed in an almost aggressive doctrine, a slogan taught in the schoolroom: "Each person the

---

* 'bouschterness,' untranslatable, is roughly equivalent to 'conspicuous vulgarity,' or 'obviously absurd and unsuitable display,'
such as wearing an expensive garment at an inappropriate occasion,
or flaunting extravagant ornaments.

equal of all! Each person a full-fledged Ameliorative! Each person of full gentility!"

GLOSSARY B:
YIP NOMENCLATURE.

Each Yip adult is denominated by six names, except in the case of special circumstances. The Yip, when asked to identify himself, responds with his formal name, for instance: Idris Nadelbac Myrvo. 'Idris' is his birth name, chosen for symbolic attributes. 'Idris,' for example, indicates a personality daring but unassuming. 'Nadelbac' is the lineage name derived from the father; 'Myrvo' denotes the mother's lineage. Additionally, there is the familiar name, to be used by non-Yips or persons friendly but not intimate. For instance, Idris Nadelbac Myrvo might use the common or 'open' name 'Carlo.' There would be two further names: both secret and self-applied. The first designated a quality to which the person aspired, such as 'the Lucky' or 'the Harmonious.' The second, most secret of all was the sixth name: 'the Ruha.' It was also the most important of all the names, and, in effect, was the man himself.

The 'Ruha' figured in a peculiar Yip custom. At the center of old Yipton there had been a cavernous hall, the Caglioro. The dimensions of the Caglioro astounded tourists, when guides led them along a rickety balcony forty feet above the floor, with the ceiling still another forty feet overhead. From this vantage the tourists could overlook an area of amazing extent, crowded with Yips, squatting around small flickering lamps. The tourists always complained of the terrible stench, and spoke of 'the Big Chife.' Nevertheless they never failed to be awed by the carpet of human flesh below, only darkly to be seen by the twinkling little lamps; indeed it was a scene surpassing their imaginations. Inevitably they asked their guide: "What brings these folk here? Why do they crouch in the darkness?"

"They have nothing better to do," was the usual bland response.

"But they are doing something! They seem to be moving or stirring about; we can see this by the shine of the little lamps."

"They come to meet their friends, and trade fish, and they also come to gamble. It is their obsession."

If the guide were in a good mood, or if he hoped for a large gratuity, he might describe the gambling. "It is not always a light-hearted game. The play often becomes intense. The stakes might be coins or tools or fish: anything of value. When an unlucky or unskillful gambler loses all he owns, what then does he use for his desperate wager? He puts up a fragment of his Ruha: in effect, himself. If he wins, he is once more whole. If he loses (and being unskillful or unlucky, this is often the case) he parts with a one-fortieth portion of himself, such being the recognized fractions into which a Ruha may be divided.

"This deficiency is noted by fixing a white cord to the hair at the back of the head. Often he continues to lose, and pieces of him may be scattered all over Yipton, and ever more white strands dangle down his back. If and when he loses all forty parts of his Ruha, he has lost all of himself and is no longer allowed to gamble. Instead he is called 'No-name' and made to stand at the side of the Caglioro, staring blankly over the scene. His Ruha is gone; he is no longer a person. His first four names are meaningless, while his wonderful fifth name has become a horrid joke.

"Out on the the floor of the Caglioro, another process starts—the negotiations between those who owned parts of the Ruha, in order that the entire property may be brought under a single ownership. The bargaining is sometimes hard, sometimes easy; sometimes the parts are used as gambling stakes. But in the end the Ruha is brought under the ownership of a single individual, who thereby augments his status. The 'No-name' is now a slave, though he owes neither service nor duty to his master; he obeys no orders and runs no errands. It is worse; he is no longer a whole man; his ruha has been taken into the soul of his master. He is nothing: before he is dead he has become a ghost.

"There is a single mode of escape. The man's father and mother, or his grandfather and grandmother, may give up their ruhas to the creditor, so that the first ruha is returned to its original owner. He is once more a whole man, free to gamble as he chooses out on the floor of the Caglioro."

THE BEST IN
SCIENCE FICTION

☐	51083-6	ACHILLES' CHOICE *Larry Niven & Steven Barnes*	$4.99 Canada $5.99
☐	50270-1	THE BOAT OF A MILLION YEARS *Poul Anderson*	$4.95 Canada $5.95
☐	51528-5	A FIRE UPON THE DEEP *Vernor Vinge*	$5.99 Canada $6.99
☐	52225-7	A KNIGHT OF GHOSTS AND SHADOWS *Poul Anderson*	$4.99 Canada $5.99
☐	53259-7	THE MEMORY OF EARTH *Orson Scott Card*	$5.99 Canada $6.99
☐	51001-1	N-SPACE *Larry Niven*	$5.99 Canada $6.99
☐	52024-6	THE PHOENIX IN FLIGHT *Sherwood Smith & Dave Trowbridge*	$4.99 Canada $5.99
☐	51704-0	THE PRICE OF THE STARS *Debra Doyle & James D. Macdonald*	$4.50 Canada $5.50
☐	50890-4	RED ORC'S RAGE *Philip Jose Farmer*	$4.99 Canada $5.99
☐	50925-0	XENOCIDE *Orson Scott Card*	$5.99 Canada $6.99
☐	50947-1	YOUNG BLEYS *Gordon R. Dickson*	$5.99 Canada $6.99

Buy them at your local bookstore or use this handy coupon:
Clip and mail this page with your order.

Publishers Book and Audio Mailing Service
P.O. Box 120159, Staten Island, NY 10312-0004

Please send me the book(s) I have checked above. I am enclosing $ _____
(Please add $1.25 for the first book, and $.25 for each additional book to cover postage and handling.
Send check or money order only—no CODs.)

Name _____
Address _____
City _____ State/Zip _____
Please allow six weeks for delivery. Prices subject to change without notice.